T0193622

SCOTT FREE IN
CHINATOWN

DIANE DRYDEN

WESTBOW
PRESS®
A DIVISION OF THOMAS NELSON
& ZONDERVAN

WestBow Press books may be ordered through booksellers or by contacting:

WestBow Press
A Division of Thomas Nelson & Zondervan
1663 Liberty Drive
Bloomington, IN 47403
www.westbowpress.com
1 (866) 928-1240

ISBN: 978-1-9736-1769-3 (sc)
ISBN: 978-1-9736-1771-6 (hc)
ISBN: 978-1-9736-1770-9 (e)

Library of Congress Control Number: 2018901376

Print information available on the last page.

WestBow Press rev. date: 04/03/2018

This book is dedicated to the four people with whom it all began
Matt, Daisy, Ben and of course, Terry

AKNOWLEDGEMENTS

I would like to thank my proof readers, Carol Waltz and Jean Bolt for tireless efforts on my behalf as well as Elaine Brown for helping me through some rough spots.

I would also like to thank the Editor of the Washburn County Register, my boss for ten years, Gary King, for believing in me.

Thank you all so much.

CHAPTER 1

"I think they call him the Cowboy," said Clay as he added a generous spoonful of sugar to his coffee while he sat in the homeless shelter's dining room on Chicago's northwest side.

"Cowboy? No. I think they call him the tamale man and," asked the Duffer horrified to see what Clay was doing, "how can you drink that coffee with so much sugar in it? No wonder you're buzzed for the day." Duff considered himself an expert in all areas of life, his or anyone else's and felt free to give his opinion whether it was asked for or not.

"Are you kidding? Working around here, shoveling all that snow, I need a good buzz in the morning," Clay retorted, going on the defensive. "I, for one, will be glad to see spring come," he added while reaching for the sugar again out of sheer defiance.

"Hey Duff, what's for lunch today?" Johnny asked as he wandered through the dining room into the massive kitchen, opening the refrigerator and staring inside.

"It's Saturday, remember, it's left-over day."

"Oh great, just what I was looking forward to, your famous left-over buffet."

"Hey Mr. Founding Father, some of my most creative meals come on a left-over day."

"Right, creative," said Johnny as he closed the fridge and looked around for anything he could grab to eat. "Think I'll run down to the deli and eat there. I've got a lot on my mind, and I need to have some time to myself to think."

"Ooooh," said Clay his voice in full teasing mode, "it must have something to do with Sandy." He patted the chair next to his invitingly and added, "Have a seat and tell us your problems my son and we can give you a sure-fire solution based on our own vast experience."

"That's all I'd need, advise from you two."

As Johnny stormed out of the dining room, the Duffer whispered to Clay, "It's Sandy all right. Nothing else ticks him off as she does and now that there's that big mess with her mother and her new-found twin sister, things are more complicated than he can handle."

"I can't say as I blame him," answered Duff as he slowly pulled the sugar bowl closer to him, hoping Clay wouldn't notice. "It's hard enough to have a regular girlfriend, but one who has just had a few startling surprises in her life like Sandy had, well, he must be overwhelmed.

"Hey," said Clay "wasn't he finally going to propose on Valentine's Day? Somebody said that our other Founding Father, you know, the current Chicago big shot restaurateur, was even going to give them a free meal at Annetties, his la-de-da restaurant."

"Ha, Tony would probably give him a table by the kitchen door, you know, the loser spot."

"And how would you know there was a table by the kitchen door?" Queried Clay. "If you remember it was me who helped out at Annetties during the holidays for several private parties, not you, and I don't think that you've ever been to any fancy restaurant in your life."

When the Duffer didn't answer, Clay kept up the barrage. "So, exactly when was it you had a meal there? Huh? At what point in your past could you have afforded anything so grand?"

"First of all, my funny Irish friend, you're grammar is still appalling. You said it was me who helped out. I think the proper sentence should be it was I."

"I, me, who cares, you're deliberately getting off the subject. Just answer the question, have you or have you not been to Annetties?"

"Actually, no I haven't. But every restaurant has at least one crummy table. It's their overflow one that they use only for cheap customers or for people not bright enough to make a reservation."

"And just how would you know that?" asked Clay as he reached across the table for the sugar bowl so he could stir even more sugar into his cup. "Just because you were a cook in the Navy, it doesn't make you an expert when it comes to restaurants."

"Don't worry, little guy; I haven't always been a Navy cook. There is a world of information about me you don't know, and I don't ever plan to tell. Besides, I've watched my share of old movies and know all about the loser table."

Clay was about to respond with an acerbic comment about old movies when Johnny came back into the room pulling on his coat. "Either of you two nut-cases heard from Leon lately?"

Both men stared absently at him and silently shook their heads simultaneously as though a common string connected them. A beat later, as though he just heard the question, Clay answered, "Nope, no sign of him."

"Just what do you two do all day, anyway?" Johnny asked as he stood looking around the room.

"Hey buddy," said Clay, "check out the sidewalks, nice and clean without a flake of snow, that's what I do. And you will notice that the entryway is also mopped and almost dry. It isn't easy keeping up with this wet weather you know. And if you would like to step into the laundry area you will see that dryer number two is now functioning normally." Now it was Clay who was on the defense and itching for a confrontation.

"Want to talk about it Johnny?" asked the Duffer with surprising sensitivity thereby diffusing the potentially volatile situation between the two men.

Johnny seemed to deflate in front of their eyes. "It's Sandy," he said sitting down heavily.

Both the Duffer and Clay glanced at each other sideways with a knowing look passing between them.

"I had everything set for Christmas Eve and then her absentee mother breezes into town from Brazil of all places and monopolizes her for the entire holiday. Then I planned something in January that fell through and I even had plans for Valentine's Day, and she couldn't make it. I mean," he said, practically whining, "Tony was willing to foot the bill for an expensive dinner and 'she just couldn't make it,' "he said adding a sarcastic sing-song feminine lilt in his voice.

"What woman would turn down dinner at Annetties on Valentine's Day?" prompted Duff.

"Sandy, I guess. Sometimes I wonder if she wants to marry me, or marry anybody for that matter." After the words were out, he realized that these two guys were probably not the ones he should confide in or spill his guts to either. "So, did you say Leon was stopping today or not?"

The Duffer pulled the sugar bowl away from Clay again and smiled, "Here's a thought, why don't you call him yourself and find out? You do know how to use a phone don't you; there's even one in the hall if you remember, just put in your dime and dial his number."

With that comment, Johnny turned on his heal and walked out; sorry he ever stopped to talk to the two craziest guys he'd ever met. One was enough, but when you put the two of them together, neither one made much sense. But, he decided as he opened the front door and walked out into the cold, they did a reasonably good job of running the place. After all, they were the only official employees of the homeless shelter now that Tony had his restaurant and barely even showed up for the staff meetings and the other man who helped start the Five, Steve, had joined the Air Force and not only moved on with his life, but was stationed far away. That just left him as one of the "founding fathers," and he was finishing his last year of college and then probably joining his fathers' firm, making it Sinclair and Sinclair. The board would have to start looking for someone to take over the running the privately funded shelter soon.

The Duffer and Clay were only the second-string guys who had each come to the shelter almost a year ago, both finding employment and staying at the Five. They freely offered a free one-year plan for any resident who was willing to stay and work towards a better future. The Five had linked with the YMCA to take advantage of their night classes in the basics of reading, writing, and arithmetic. They also joined hands with an employment agency to help the residents find jobs and they might as well of be coupled with the Brocks Candy Company just down because many of their residents were working there.

The original idea of the shelter was to give people a leg up so they could move on, wiser, healthier and more qualified for employment and life. So far, none of the residents had stayed the full year. Many had even left within the first few months because after living with entirely no responsibilities in their lives, they found the Five required more than they cared to give. They knew when they left they were giving up the five necessary things that were important to getting ahead; food, shelter, warmth, privacy and an address. They were all fully aware that without an address they couldn't apply for a job, get any mail or even make a request for government aid. They knew it all, but still chose to leave the only place that cared about them in order to spend the remainder of their days back on the streets of Chicago where cops woke them in the streets and parks by hitting them on the bottoms of their feet with their nightsticks and telling them to "Move it on down now fella," and that the Pacific Garden Mission on the south side of the city was the only place they could be assured of a hot meal and warm bed after listening to a gospel message.

Because Johnny was responsible for keeping the books straight and the place running smoothly, he was the only one of the original three guys that lived in one of the eight by twelve-foot rooms that joined cheek to jowl in two long rows along with the other residents, the sixteen men and four women.

Johnny had been one of the first to move into the shelter even though his family, who lived way north of the city in a distinctly rich community, would have loved for him to come back home to live while he finished his final year in college. Well, at least his mother would want that, his father probably wouldn't even notice that he was back. And to be honest, both his parents, although they said otherwise to his face, were truly embarrassed that he chose to live where he did and to live with whom he chose to live. But Johnny didn't mind his fellow tenants who had also spent time living on the streets of Chicago and he preferred someplace closer to his school and closer to Sandy.

But anymore, there was little time to get close to Sandy, either physically or emotionally.

A street-smart girl at fifteen, she had turned into a different person after meeting Leon McKee, a homeless man that had secretly slept on a pile of draperies where she worked at the Band Box Laundry and Cleaners over on Clark Street while pretending he was doing the job as a night watchman. He eventually worked into a genuine employee, even marrying the boss who, he found out after he proposed, practically owned the entire city block where the cleaners were.

Sandy had been a disgruntled teenager and nearly kicked out of high school for missing too many days of school. She didn't want to tell anyone that her mom wasn't providing for either one of them, drinking up her meager paycheck she earned as part of a cleaning crew that worked nights making some of the tall building clean and shiny when the employees returned the following morning. It was also in those buildings that she found her erstwhile lovers that she entertained on her nights off right in the apartment.

Sandy had to work so she could provide her own cash for food, clothes and school supplies. If she ever told any authority how she lived, she'd be in a foster home before she could finish the sentence. So she ended up working more hours than she went to school. During her last visit to the principal's office, a new guidance counselor told her of an equally new program called the DE program, DE standing for Diversified Education. The program offered students who were on the verge of dropping out some reason to stay in school; reduced class time. It was the only option she had left, so on the urgings of the school counselor, she enrolled. Now she was only required to attend classes in the morning, then after lunch she and twenty-six other students were dismissed to go to their jobs.

Sandy worked at the cleaners from one o'clock until six each weekday afternoon and seven to five on Saturdays. It was just as well she worked the hours she did because it coincided with the hours her mother entertained her 'callers,' having worked all night and sleeping in until at least noon. By working these hours, she also avoided some of the smarmy advances from a few of her mother's loser boyfriends.

Sandy found herself staying longer and longer at the cleaners after work because once Leon arrived as 'night watchman', the atmosphere of the place took on a decided change. Vivian, the manager since forever eventually softened to both Sandy and Leon and by the time Leon and Vivian got married two years later, Sandy's life had changed too. The McKee's became her substitute parents, and she decided to put a real effort into graduating with her class to make the two people, whose opinion she valued most, proud of her.

But somehow as her life went into overdrive with the entrance to a prestigious Chicago design school, her boyfriend Johnny's seemed to have bogged down in discouraging regularity. He always complained that his life was a toss-up as to which decision was the dullest, years of business school or the prospect of working in his father's stuffy firm as a flunky. But he had to admit that for the first time in a very long time, he and his father seemed to be closer to being in agreement. Something had changed in his father's attitude towards him. It was as though he now had worth and value, which was confusing to Scott seeing his father had seldom approved of him even though he only saw him a few hours each day. Most days Scott was ignored by the man who was engrossed in being a captain of industry instead of a father. But the last time he was home, his father shook his hand when he left saying, "You're turning out to be quite a young man." He almost added the word, son.

Whatever changed, Johnny was glad it did. But he still really wasn't sure if he was truly looking forward to getting his business degree and becoming like his father; tied to the businesses; no more like married to the business.

A call to Sandy profited him nothing, even though she was now living at Sophie's rooming house over on Foster Avenue. She and her newly found twin sister were always together, usually doing wedding shopping for their landlady's wedding, not to mention the upcoming plans for her sister Sarah's wedding, even though it was still a full year away.

Carol, the twin's mother, finally made a clean break of the past when she finally told the girls that it was because of her alcoholic husband that she had only kept Sandy but gave Sarah to the up-scale Jewish family for whom she not only cleaned for but lived. He was not happy about one child; it would have been disastrous if she brought home two. As it was, he only stayed a month after Carol brought Sandy home before leaving, never to return. A lawyer from Alabama contacted her about their divorce and served the papers, much to her relief.

All of this cataclysmic information came as a shock for everyone, especially the two girls who had both been living in the same Foster Avenue rooming house, never realizing they were sisters.

Sarah, he thought to himself, Sandy's sister wasn't interested in the guy she was now engaged to until he cooled things down between them and even pretended to be involved in one of his employees. Hmm, that seemed to work pretty well for her guy Pete, and Sandy and Sarah are sisters. A thought began to form, if it worked for one sister, it just might work for the other one.

Using what he decided was his new found wisdom; Valentine's Day came and went without his extending an invitation to Sandy for a romantic Valentine's dinner. She didn't seem to notice. In hindsight, he wondered about his decision to ignore her because it robbed him of a fantastic meal at the famous Annetties' Italian restaurant that would have been entirely free of charge. The place was known all over the city for their authentic minestrone served with that crusty bread and their melt-in-your-mouth veal medallions that were a luxury from the first to the last bite. And the desserts, they were to die for, especially when served with that dark Italian coffee that came with the lemon wedge for rubbing around the rim of the cup.

But he was resolved to ignore the woman he desperately loved, as hard as it was, so even Easter came and went without her. He struggled through May, dancing only the most perfunctory attendance to the girl who once was wholly his and who was now drifting farther and farther away. He was beginning to think that ignoring her was the most stupid thing he had ever done. "Love, who needs it?" he asked the sidewalk as he kicked a rock into the street while he waited for his bus to come.

Unknown to Johnny, Sandy was having trouble putting her life and the life of her sister in perspective without being angry. Here she was, stuck with a mother that had seldom been present in her life and when she was there, it wasn't pretty. Sandy had pretty much raised herself in their apartment on Chicago's west side, making her breakfast and packing her lunch, being careful not to disturb her mother, who hadn't gotten home until the wee hours of the morning, sometimes with a visitor and occasionally alone. Meanwhile, her lucky twin sister was raised in the lap of luxury by adoptive parents who loved her very much. The fact they were also wealthy didn't hurt. It was hard to think about, so it became another part of her life that she worked hard to ignore every time the thoughts of gross inequity came to her. Why couldn't her mother have given her away to the same family?

Each time she began to sink into a personal pity party she had to remind herself that it was the luck of the draw that Sarah was the chosen one and not she. No, she told herself, there was no luck involved. Thanks to Vivian, I've given my life to God, and I have to continue to believe that He's always had a plan for my life, Sandy told herself as she buttoned her coat, even before I was born He knew me. As she skipped down the stairs she mused, For some unknown reason, this has been His plan for my life from the very beginning. Maybe someday I'll understand it, perhaps not. Either way, I chose to trust that He knows me best and He loves me most. She brightened visibly when she remembered that He had given her Johnny, hadn't He, her unofficial fiancé?

Johnny, she thought as she crossed the street to stand in front of the diner to wait for a bus downtown. He's unusually patient for a guy. He's even giving me time to spend with my new-found sister to sort things through while we work on the two weddings and me with all the pressures of design school. She started to hum to herself while smiling and thinking of her man and checking her watch. But it was a little odd when she gave honest thought to the past few months, questions and doubts starting to creep into her heart like small dust balls gently moving around under a bed when a gentle breeze blew in through an open window. Now that I think about it, it's been a long time since he's called. He must be busy with school and the Five and learning the ins and outs of his father's business. I was hoping by now we'd be planning our wedding.

She shivered from a sudden chill as the bus pulled up.

Clay and Duff were back at it. "They do not call him the tamale man, they call him the cowboy," said Clay as he filled the salt and pepper shakers on each table getting ready for the next meal.

"What are you talking about? Duff asked. "What cowboy?"

"Remember a while back we were talking about the guy with the funny tube-shaped thing attached to his backpack. You know, the one he tied on vertically so when you saw him from the front it looked like someone was standing directly behind him? I said they called him the Cowboy because he had a cowboy way of talking."

Duff rolled his eyes as he lifted the wooden spoon to his lips to taste the soup. "And just what is a cowboy way of talking and why in the world are we back on this subject?"

"I don't know," Clay stopped his cleaning and looked around the large dining room trying to gather his thoughts. "I was just thinking about the guy, and maybe it wasn't an accent, perhaps it was more how he phrased his words, you know, 'mind if I set a spell?'"

"So you've talked to him?"

"Several times, I'll have you know, and that's why I know everyone calls him the Cowboy or at least most of the bums that slept in the same alley with him. Each time he entered an alley just before dark he'd always say something like 'howdy'."

"Howdy? He said that?" Asked the Duffer as he added more seasoning to his latest creation and eyeing a box of macaroni.

"Well, something like that."

"Oh yes, then what did he say, I've been out all day rounding up them-there doggies?" Duff asked as he shook out a few handfuls of pasta into the large pot in front of him.

"I'm surprised that you never met him, he was all over the city. Wherever you went, he eventually showed up there. But each time he came into a group he was always well-mannered and talkative, two traits you don't often find in your common, ordinary transient."

Duff looked like he was ignoring him as he continued to scan the spice shelf with interest, but Clay continued. "I think what he was doing was checking out the clientele of the alley. You know, checking out the drunks, the loonies, and the druggies before deciding if it was safe to stay. No one ever wants to get near a druggie, I don't care what they say, marijuana was terrible enough, but this LSD stuff is beyond scary. I saw a guy try to cut his arm off one because he thought it was a snake burrowing into his body -creepy I tell you, just scary.

"Anyway, this cowboy fella always approached a group very cautiously, you know, getting the lay of the land, if you know what I mean. No pun intended," he added to see if his fellow employee was listening.

The Duffer grunted his response as he momentarily questioned the addition of some old tarragon leaves.

Clay continued not discouraged. "After he said howdy, or something similar, he'd add something like, looks like it's gonna be a nice night or hope it doesn't rain, as he looked skyward. I think that if he got the right responses and thought he'd be relatively safe, he'd walk over to a wall and settle in."

Even though Clay knew by this point the Duffer had utterly lost interest in what he was saying, he continued. "The interesting thing about this guy was his bedroll."

"You mean his tamale," Duff answered surprising Clay that he was listening. Duff lifted the spoon to his lips smiling at the results of his creativity.

"I do not mean tamale; I mean bedroll." Clay had seated himself at the now clean table and put his feet up on a chair he had pulled out and continued. "He'd carefully pull off his backpack and cautiously undid his bedroll." No response. "In fact, the whole procedure was something to see." Once again Duff didn't rise to the bait seeing his head was now deep into the restaurant size refrigerator looking for more leftovers and eyeing a wilting head of lettuce.

Clay started again and this time didn't stop until he finished his step by step oration of the cowboy's precision and the layers of his bedroll.

"I distinctly remember, "Clay said with the voice of authority. "It was clear, heavy plastic on the outside, a layer of multi-colored splotches on a gray background carpet pad and then a blanket on top of the other two layers. All three layers were sewn together somehow with rough string, and when the guy rolled himself into it, he had perfect protection from the weather, no matter what came."

"Oh yea," Duff commented as he put down the lettuce and a few old carrots on the counter that he had found in the back of the fridge.

"That tamale he carried on his back was long, but you didn't say it was taller than he was, did you? I'll bet it wasn't long enough to cover all of him when he climbed in, was it? What did he do about his shoes and head if it rained, smart guy?"

Clay seemed to glow with his response. "I suppose if you weren't there, you wouldn't know, but since I was there, I'll do you a favor and tell you."

Ignoring the sarcastic look on the Duffer's face Clay started out again sweetly.

"In case it looked like rain, he took off his boots, changed his socks to clean ones, pulled a plastic bag over each foot and then put his boots and dirty socks in his backpack; one boot on each side of the backpack and then used it as his pillow."

"How about his head? You never said anything about his head."

"I didn't want to degrade the conversation," Clay said as he looked at his fingernails as if to check an expensive manicure which didn't exist. "He had a plastic bag that he put around his head and tied it beneath."

"Tied it like a little girl?"

"I suppose you could say that, but he didn't seem to care. Once he was ready for sleep, he rolled up his bedroll around himself and went to sleep; he wasn't long on conversation.

"The funny thing was," Clay continued, "he was never there in the morning, and no one ever saw him leave."

"Like the Lone Ranger, I suppose?

"Okay, maybe. I never thought of that."

"Of course not, small Irish person with small brains to match. Now if you're interested, I also saw him once, and the people I was with called him the tamale man because of the colors in his bedroll, it looked like a tamale with all the toppings."

"I suppose to someone who thinks they're a cook but isn't, it would never have occurred to you that it's a taco that has toppings, not a tamale. Either way, those of us who slept in the same places as the guy and listened to him talk the way he did; it was just natural to refer to him as a person, the Cowboy, and not a piece of food."

"How did we ever get back to this conversation anyway? I think we started this months' ago and here we are still at it." Duff sat down opposite Clay and asked softly so no one else would hear if they were in the hall, "Any word on lover boy?"

"If you mean Johnny, nope, not a word. He spends so much time between summer school, and time at his father's prestigious office downtown, he's seldom here. Comes in late and leaves early, you know."

"Ah, yes," quoted Duff from some unknown author, "true love never doth run smooth."

"Doth?"

"Never mind," said the Duffer as he returned to the kitchen to check his soup. "Hey Clay," he said while stirring the pot. "Better erase the word soup on the menu and write in casserole. Who knew that a little macaroni could thicken soup this much?"

She walked into the dining room tentatively and cautiously looked around the room. She reminded Clay of the way a cat slowly and warily enters a place to check if it's safe to cross the threshold.

Claire was tall, almost six feet Clay imagined, and she walked into the dining room with the grace of a dancer.

"Help ya?" Clay asked as he wiped yet another table from its lunch mess.

"Um…um is this where I mean, do people live here?"

"Most generally," he answered knowing he was no help at all, if it were up to him this would be only a man's world; no females allowed. And if she was looking for some ner-do-well boyfriend or husband she wasn't going to get help from him to find the bum.

"Oh, never mind, maybe this wasn't a good idea after all."

As she turned to go Duffer came out of the kitchen and was just in time to see her leaving.

"What did she want?" He asked Clay.

"I don't think she knew," he said dismissively taking up his table-wiping task again and cleaning an already spotless surface.

Duff was suspicious, and instead of trying to get a decent answer out of Clay he hurried out to the hall just as she opened the door to leave.

"Hey, wait," he said, his long legs quickly filling the gap between them. "Pay no attention to that guy; I'm probably the one you wanted to see anyway. See, I'm kind of in charge here." He said as he pulled in his stomach wishing he would have taken off his dirty apron. She was a good looking blond and just his height- what luck. He hoped that she was looking to connect with the Five in some way so he could connect with her on some level.

"I, um," she started to falter again.

"Take your time," he told her sounding more like a counselor instead of head cook. "This place can be overwhelming your first time here. Now," he looked directly into her eyes that he noted were delightfully at the same height as his, "what questions can I answer for you? What do you want to know, I mean, are you looking for someone in particular?" He intoned, sounding somewhat like an undertaker during a funeral.

"Actually," she advanced a few steps and was now standing fully in the main lobby, and she started again. "I was just wondering if this was the place where people stayed until they got on their feet." She was about to add something else but thought better of it and didn't.

"You've come to the right place if you're looking to stay; you are looking to stay aren't you?"

"Um, maybe, I need more information first."

He steered her to the office mainly to avoid Clay's eavesdropping and sat her on the badly cracked imitation leather chair opposite his with the large thrift store table in between them that still had a wad of napkins under one leg to make it stable. He hoped the distance between them provided by the table would make her feel safer. "Now, how can I help you?"

Johnny usually didn't return to the Five until late afternoon, if at all, but today he was back early and saw the Duffer talking to an attractive young woman in the office. "Hey, what gives with the babe in the office?" He asked Clay as he walked past losing his tie on his way to his room.

"Not a clue. She wanted some information, so he whisked her in there, and then he shuts the door so no one can hear their conversation. Not that anyone cares what they're talking about, mind."

Wondering if it was some official business, Johnny walked back to the office and opened the door. The look on Duff's face registered both irritation and embarrassment at the same time. "Uh, Claire here, I mean I was just giving this young lady some information about this place. She might want to join us."

As soon as the words were out of his mouth, he realized that his help was no longer needed and he got up to give Johnny the official man-in-charge chair. Smiling weakly to one of the most attractive women he had ever seen, he quietly left the room, closing the door behind him.

"At least you could have left it open a wee bit so we could hear what's going on," was Clay's acerbic comment.

A short time later both Johnny and Claire left the office and headed for the front door. Duffer and Clay wandered quickly out into the central area pretending to check the bulletin board to make sure tomorrow's menu was in place. The only thing they heard as they tried to look busy was "Okay then, let us know."

When Johnny turned and saw the two men waiting for some answers he shook his head as he walked by them. In passing, he did casually mention to no one in particular, "Now she's got an interesting story if I ever heard one," and kept right on walking while hiding a smile.

"How could he do that to us?" asked Clay dumfounded. "Here's a guy that's seldom around, he can't even figure out his relationship problems, and now he's clamming up too us. Honestly," added Clay. "I'm so unappreciated here that there are days that I'd just like to walk out and never return."

"And where exactly, Mr. 'back to sleeping on the streets man,' would you go?"

After only a short pause Clay conceded, "Okay, you've won that round, but I bet I'll find something out about that woman before you do."

"You think so, well I don't, so you're on my friend," challenged Duff.

"Oh great," said Johnny as he walked back through to retrieve his jacket in the office just as they were shaking hands. "Whatever it is," he said looking directly at them, "I don't want to know."

I know I'll have to deal with it. Eventually, he told himself as he continued into his room, but I've had enough to deal with today already.

"Well," said Clay, "he might know more about that woman than we do, but we know more about that guy Scott, from the other day, than he does. You think he'll ever come back?"

"Who? Johnny?"

"No, you wingnut, Scott."

"Which one was Scott?"

"Oy vey," answered Clay as he hit his forehead with his hand.

"And what exactly does oy vey mean? I thought you were Irish?"

CHAPTER 2

The young man stood with one foot propped behind him for balance as he raised his face to the sun. Every afternoon for the past month he could be found leaning against the large salmon-colored two-story building that housed the Three Happiness Restaurant on the busiest corner in Chicago's Chinatown, twenty-two blocks south of downtown.

Now that Scott had graduated from high school, this twenty-something near north-side guy preferred to spend his time on the south side, an area that was removed from anything related to his old life which included a neighborhood awash in thriving poverty in both the buildings and the people. A place where the Blue Line L train regularly rumbled past their second floor flat, missing their structure by a few yards and exposing their kitchen and living room to the daily commuters as it traveled on it's twenty four hour loop in and out of the city.

Once, out of sheer boredom, he and his next oldest sister staged what looked like a hanging to shock the rush hour trains. They attached a rope to the ceiling beam above the kitchen table, and then they put it around Scott's neck. He stood on a low stool behind the table, and it honestly looked like he was dangling and dead. His sister's part was to stand with her hand over her mouth staring at him in horror. Eventually, she got bored with her silent role and added the flailing her arms and looking like she was screaming. By train number five or six she carried her acting career to the heights by silently screaming and then fainting.

It took the cops only twenty minutes to locate them, pound up their stairs and threaten them with all sorts of charges if they ever pulled such a dumb stunt again. Luckily neither of their parents was home at the time, and the cops never carried through with their threat to call them.

Occasionally their father would stand in his undershirt and shorts, unshaven for days and be holding a bottle of beer while yelling at the endlessly passing faces, "Ya wanna see Chicago at its finest folks, just cast your eyes over here to our palatial abode. Go ahead and look, take it all in, then go home and be grateful for the place you've got."

His father was one of those hardened drinkers who worked nights in a metal factory and held fast to his unfailing attitude of poor me. He said he drank to forget, but Scott often wondered, forget what? If anyone had the right to such an attitude, it was Scott's gentle mother, Ellen. From what his Aunt Della said, her sister had once been a vivacious young woman who had been happily working for a local printing firm when she met her future husband when he came in to place an order for brochures for his car rental company. Unfortunately, he swept her off her feet with his dynamic personality and charm, so she married him a brief six months later against her family's wishes. She then spent a lifetime regretting her hasty decision.

"Hey, need help with that?" Scott asked taking his foot off of the wall ready to help a middle-aged white guy who was struggling with a large piece of signboard.

"Naw, I've got it," he all but growled.

This cranky older man had been passing by Scott several days in a row, always struggling with strange objects that looked like bits and pieces of construction materials. Chinatown was located right next to an industrialized section full of factories and slow freight trains that inched their way in and out of town on tracks high above the street. Because of the city noise ordinance, the trains were only allowed to sound their horns softly as they passed over the traffic below. Scott always thought the horns sounded like the distant fog horns he had heard when his mom and two sisters were treated to a trip to the east coast when he was very young, thanks to the generosity of his Aunt Della who had a summer home near the ocean.

This south-side manufacturing section housed the second South Water Street Market, a unique group of individual food warehouses that sat cheek to jowl and crammed into several city blocks. Even though he had never seen the market personally, he had done an extra credit report on its history for school and knew they were originally started back in the 1800's on the north side of the city but moved south as Chicago's downtown began to grow. It fascinated him that each market stall specialized in only one or two wholesale items like melons, apples, butter, nuts, eggs, peaches, poultry or vegetables. These foodstuffs came from the adjoining states, shipped in by train or arriving by boat and distributed through a series of the 200 individual long and narrow warehouses to businesses, restaurants, and hospitals throughout the metropolis.

He was tired of standing against the building so he joined a crowd crossing the busy street and headed for the dim sum restaurant before it got busy. As he passed endless stores, he thought about the once famous Water Market shops again.

He would never forget the sad fact that still fascinated him when he thought of it, that the wild success of the first market was also the cause of its demise. Evidently, the number of horses and wagons lining the street while loading their wares created an almost impassable barrier along the entire riverfront and burgeoning downtown area. Once the motorized trucks joined the fray, they only exacerbated the problem, making it impossible for pedestrians to walk on the crowded downtown sidewalks. Somewhere in the dim recesses of his mind he also remembered that in its heyday, the market was responsible for over 200 million dollars in commerce annually. That was a lot of money, even by today's standards, he thought. Wentworth Avenue was crowded enough for him this morning; he couldn't imagine what it must have been like being even more crowded adding horses and squeezing in even more shops.

Scott had been in Chinatown many times due to his mom being an enthusiastic Chicago resident. But he never remembered a trip to the Water Market nor the Stock Yards; his mother did have her standards after all.

She would scour the papers each Friday to see what was going on in the city and then they all traveled the city by L or bus and sometimes by taxi to every corner and every ethnic neighborhood's celebration.

"My kids aren't growing up ignorant of the city and the people in it," she told a complete stranger as her little family stood watching the populace of Greek Town barbecue whole goats and sheep on long metal spits over beds of coals. They served the resultant meat on soft, flatbread covered with onions, cucumbers and the most delicious yogurt dressing.

As he reached the restaurant, he also dimly recalled something his mother said about Daniel Burnham, the man who was the Architect of Chicago and whose name was plastered all over the city. Everyone in the city knew he was responsible for the famous Rookery building on LaSalle and the World Columbian Exposition but not everyone knew that in his Plan of Chicago, he subtitled it, Chicago, Paris on the Prairie. Thanks to his mom his head was full of useless information. He even knew that it was part of the Plan to move the famous market to south 28th Street, still on the Chicago River, but considerably more south and not far from Chinatown. The move kept the market near the main highways and still accessible to the trains and the Chicago River but it was the invention of the refrigerated trucks that dealt the death-blow to the market.

The tiny Asian hostess dressed in the required black pants and white shirt pointed him to a small table wedged between the bathrooms and the hall to the kitchen, and by the time his tea came, he was thinking of the final blow that all but closed the market. It wasn't long before the larger accounts began buying their own produce directly from the grower and shipping it right to their own outlets, thanks to the new trucks and better roads.

As the restaurant filled with people, all talking and laughing in several languages, his thoughts turned to how the first market must have sounded when the chaos of the day began.

Because most of the buyers and sellers were either immigrants or first-generation Americans, he could imagine the Italians, Greeks, Jews and the Irish and Germans bartering products at the top of their voices and the horses whinnying and pawing the ground anxious to get started down the narrow street to their destinations. Carts full of farm-grown food from Wisconsin, Indiana, and Michigan, much arriving by train or through the waters of Lake Michigan before reaching the quiet of the Chicago River.

When his waitress accidentally nudged him with her cart, he was startled out of his reverie.

She opened one of the bamboo steamers and put her head to one side as if to ask, "Would you like this?"

He looked into the round box with its four little steamed pasty things and once again saw food he didn't recognize. He took a chance and asked what it was.

"Pork," she said, adding no further information about the dish and emphasizing the o in pork. He nodded no and she opened another bamboo steamer as he looked in and she once again said 'pok' even though this dish looked nothing like the last one. No matter what it looked like she said it was pork so he finally just chose one and she placed it on the table in front of him.

The ritual continued with the steamers on the second shelf of her cart and when it came to the third shelf, he just pointed to one, not knowing what he would be eating. Within five minutes she was back with a different cart and they began their ritual again with a completely different variety of foods.

As he ate the remarkably delicious foods, he observed the other people work their way through the carts and his mind turned back to the beginning of the century and all the things his mother taught him about the era. She had mentioned more than once the "milk trains" that traveled south each day from Wisconsin farms and how a farmer could send not only his milk, but a butchered calf or cow on the morning's train to the Chicago hotels and receive his money the next day on the return train. She had also read to him about the American Indians up north who would fund their livelihood by picking and sending cases and cases of sweet wild blueberries to the city. These trains were often dubbed the blueberry trains and later the cranberry trains or even the ice trains when valuable ice was shipped from the crystal clear waters of the Shell Lake 400 miles north of Chicago and was off-loaded in towns all along the route so fresh food could be preserved. In desperate times, ice was shipped to service both the live and dead bodies when sickness was rampant in some of the countless little towns along the milk train route that wound its way daily to the big city. Scott began to understand his mother's wisdom and was finally starting to get a small glimpse into how much she had influenced his life without him knowing it.

Lunch finished and lost in thought he almost missed the homeless guy carrying his 'find' of the day that afternoon.

He guessed the guy must have some connection with someone on the other side of the tracks somewhere, but, Scott wondered, where was he taking all the oddball stuff and what was he doing with it? Just about every day the old guy would drag his latest treasure down to the stop light on the corner, then under the Red Line L platform and across an abandoned lot that was littered with debris and then disappears into the neighborhood of ancient and dilapidated houses beyond. Scott offered his regular, "Hey, how ya doing?" to the man and received the usual grunt in response.

Scott, willingly homeless for the most part, usually stood in front of the Three Happiness in the afternoon to catch the short-lived mid-day heat. Even though it was July, it was discouragingly chilly. "Coldest July in weather history" commented the perfectly quaffed weatherman on the TV in the aging electronic repair shop window several blocks away.

Scott preferred to sit somewhere instead of always standing, but due to the robust Chinatown Chamber of Commerce and the local family associations, there were no benches anywhere, and there were strict rules about loitering in their little section of the world. They preferred people in their shops buying things or sitting in their restaurants eating things.

Occasionally a tired tourist would make the mistake of sitting on the only cement stairs that led to the always busy hardware store which was always overcrowded. Their shop was the only one with an entire wall of woks and wok accessories, and they also carried skimmers and teapots and kitchen tools and paper lanterns and tea thermoses and intricate cookie cutters or were they for something else and everything anyone would ever need to make their life complete.

But the stair sitters were soon chased away with a torrent of either Cantonese or Mandarin and the flapping of hands from one of the ancient brothers that ran the shop while the other brother kept a practiced eye out for shoplifters who would take advantage of the distraction to stuff a few items under their shirts doing the common Chicago five-finger discount.

Knowing this, Scott not only stayed upright during the day, but he took a nightly risk by sleeping under a truck behind the Three Happiness. Every evening after dark he cautiously returned to his makeshift bed of cardboard and happily found it still there as he slipped underneath the vehicle. He knew his days, or instead, his nights, were numbered even though the big white truck sat parked in a tiny private parking lot, it was very public as it sat at the beginning of a well-used narrow and twisting alley. During the day there was activity continuly in the driveway as merchant's filled and unloaded stock from their storage garages across the alley from the back of their buildings.

He had no illusions that this truck, which provided him shelter from the storm, might be moved any day, so he packed lightly; an unfolded cardboard box for a base that separated him from the dirt, a sleeping bag and a small backpack that contained only his few possessions and a change of clothes that he used as a pillow at night. He had never really planned to stay in this part of the city for longer than a month so this was more like a camping trip than a permanent residence.

The private lot was enclosed by chain link fencing on three sides with a large yellow sign at the front corner indicating it was not open to the public. It insinuated that 'they' could park across the street in the pay for parking area along with the daily L riders and the endless tourists. Since the truck never seemed to move, Scott took the risk that the old truck was more of a parked sign than a suitable vehicle because the side that faced the street was being used as advertising. Best yet, there were significant chunks of old plywood embedded in a giant pile of dirt near the side of the vehicle that provided an effective means of blocking his presence from the street. Scott knew the coast was pretty clear if he rose early and waited until near dark before slipping back under his temporary home. Most business owners left their businesses well before they closed and drove out to the suburbs where they lived, never using the lot at night. But getting up early and going to bed late at night left him with many hours of nothing to do.

He'd visited the library, the post office, the cultural center and even the Asian church. He'd completely scoured the rest of the small neighborhood always impressed by the number of impeccably kept gardens and the women who faithfully tended them, bringing out their dishpans after each meal to pour the water on their organic gardens. It must be some holdout from the old country, Scott thought. Nothing was ever wasted.

Maybe if that old coot that passed him every day would let him help carry some of the stuff he was lugging, it would break up his day; but so far, no good. He'd made few personal contacts during the month he'd been in Chinatown, but had met some interesting people when he traveled north of the city to a place called simply the Five.

"So," asked Clay as Scott made himself comfortable in the dining room. "Just what brings you to our part of the world again? You did say you grew up on the north side and were living in Chinatown now, didn't you? That's quite a ways to come for a visit."

"Seeing I am unemployed at the moment, it helps fill my day coming up here."

"You here just for our pleasant company or do you have some other reason to be up in our neck of the woods?"

Scott didn't care if Clay was asking personal questions because when Clay asked it was more like friendly banter than honest inquirers bordering on nosiness.

"Like I said the first time I came, I heard about you at the mission and thought I'd check you out."

"Again?"

"Okay, part of the reason for my return visit is that you speak English and I miss hearing it. Don't get me wrong, I like where I live now, but English is hardly ever spoken, even by the tourists, half the time I don't know what language they're speaking either. I always thought I wanted to live abroad in some exotic country, but I know now that I'd miss so much of being here and I'd never know what people were saying."

"So, what's keeping you there?" Clay had gotten up to go into the kitchen and yelled, "coffee?"

"Sure. It beats green tea."

Sugar bowl in hand Clay emerged from the kitchen balancing two coffees, the creamer and a bunch of individually wrapped pastries. "Just think, if you moved in here you could eat like this every day and drink coffee whenever you wanted it."

"Believe me; it's tempting. I like knowing I'd have a permanent place to live and an opportunity to take some classes, but at this point, I still don't know what I want to do in life. I'll need a job soon, and I need to find a quieter place to sleep."

"Redline keeping you awake?"

"Hardly, I grew up with the Blue Line inches from our apartment but only two doors down from where I sleep is a fire department, and they seem to be busiest at night. No sooner do you get into a deep sleep and the fire alarm rings and within minutes the trucks pull out blasting their horns loud enough to wake the dead. The worst part is you know that just as you get back to sleep, they will be back and then you get to hear the noise of the huge doors opening as they back each truck in."

"Can't say as I've ever lived near a fire station," said Clay looking at the ceiling as though trying to remember. "When I was little we did live near a gas station for a while. It's funny, now that I think about it; everyone else in the family complained about the bell, but I slept right through it."

"Your gas station had a little bell?"

"Yeah, you know, it's in that hose thing you run over. It rings the little bell, and that's what brings the attendant out. You know, ding, ding."

"Yeah, I know what you mean."

"Anyway," Clay continued, "we've only got a few rooms open here now and who knows what it will be later, so I would suggest you make up your mind soon and let us know as soon as you do."

"Got it, say, Duffer isn't in today, is he?"

"Unfortunately he's here every day like I am because we live here. But he's out on his food run now. I don't know how he does it, but he's made some great contacts, and we have some mighty fine products coming in, for free no less. The sad part," he continued hanging his head "is what he does with the stuff he gets. Navy cook or not, that boy needs some instruction. Once a woman was living here named Jane and she was the reason that he started this buffet thing on Saturdays and when…"

Scott had already been an unwilling audience to one of Clay's long rambling one-sided conversations, so he quickly said, "Wow, I almost forgot, I've got to get back before rush hour begins." As he walked toward the door, he turned briefly and added, "Hey, thanks for the coffee and pastry, I'll be back, you can count on it."

CHAPTER 3

Scott was slowing working into a daily routine, and each morning he joined at least forty other men who crowded in for morning tea and indistinguishable breakfasts at the local bakery. There were no menus on the tables or meals listed inside the dining area, but each morning in Feida's shabby bakery on the main drag, the men-only clientele were devotedly devouring their disgusting looking breakfasts along with their pots of green tea. Scott liked eating with these guys because he was not required to be either social or polite or vocal.

The dining area behind the bakery at Feida's was a large room furnished with three round tables down the middle that sat twelve each and then five square tables that were tightly lined up on one side and a counter that filled the other side where the tea was made and dispensed. None of the chairs or tables matched and no one seemed to care. The linoleum floor was cracked, and the massive mirrors that filled the entire upper wall on one side of the room, no doubt to make the place look bigger, were streaked with dirt to the point of being opaque. But business was brisk, and no one seemed to care that the bakery looked like; it was making money and that's all that mattered to the owners.

He grimaced each time he visited the bathroom with its filth and inadequate plumbing.

What brought him back day after day was the fact he could just sit and listen to their conversations and watch the television in the corner that was on some channel that only played in Chinese or Cantonese or something he couldn't understand. It always seemed to be some sort of soap opera and some he guessed were traditional Asian plays due to their period costumes that usually ended up tragically, but no one seemed to care because few men were actually watching. They did look up every time the old battered aluminum doors opened in the back of the dining room that led to the back bakery where the ovens were full with all kinds of delicious looking items. Large trays of freshly baked products would disgorge each time the door opened, some placed on one of the large round tables in the corner directly under the TV to cool, and some trays were taken straight into the bakery at the front of the shop, wedged into the already loaded shelves. Feida's bakery always did a brisk morning business as well as the other three bakeries in town, each one filled with men eating the strange looking see-through foods that reminded Scott of giant, slimy garden slugs.

The cranky old guy passed by Scott again later that day and this time Scott remained silent.

"Sure," the man grumbled as he passed. "When I had tiny loads you'd ask to help me, but now that I have something large, you don't say a word. Thanks a lot bub."

Struck by the oddity of the statement, it took Scott a few moments to understand that this must be this crazy man's way of finally asking for help. He immediately grabbed an end of the wood that was as large as a full piece of plywood that looked like it was part of a much larger sign, maybe a billboard. The man didn't say anything but headed to the stop light with Scott struggling to keep up and then continued on his route to somewhere in the surrounding neighborhood. When they got about four blocks down, the man told Scott to put his part down and that he could take it from here. "Thanks, bub," was the only thing he said as he dragged the oversized piece of board into an alley.

"No problem, man."

There was a sign in the window of the Tai Wah shop. It was a hand-lettered Help Wanted sign, and it was propped up in front of the barbequed ducks hanging in the corner window. The grocery/gift store was noted for their delicious duck, but the display was repulsive. The ducks were hung in a row by their feet with their heads still attached, hanging upside down above nests of their barbequed entrails and nestled into these were the barbequed baby ducks. Tourists were always snapping pictures of the nauseous display.

Scott wasn't sure how long the sign had been in the window because he passed by the shop several times a day, but thinking about it as he continued his walk, he suddenly realized why it seemed so unusual to him; it was written in English and not in the usual foreign script. That was odd; yes, it was decidedly odd. Nothing here being geared to anyone but members of their race and Scott's recollection, he hadn't seen a white employee-ever.

"Do you speak English?" He asked the woman behind a counter s filled to overflowing with the brick-a-brack that tourists' loved; fans, postcards, fancy chopsticks, candies whose wrappers written in Chinese plus an all-time favorite treat, the rice candy in its customary red box. Inside the box were 8 squares of soft red candy individually wrapped in rice paper and then in cellophane. The reason this was everyone's favorite was that not only were they cheap, but to eat them you just removed the outer plastic wrap and then popped the candy, along with the rice paper that was still attached to each piece, into the mouth, waiting for the sensation of the rice paper melting.

The woman at the front counter listened to what he was asking and then answered in her language. He stepped to the window to hold up the sign for her to read and she suddenly began to screech in a high Asian voice. Afraid she thought he meant her harm, Scott slowly backed up to the door but before he could make his escape, a young Chinese man he had seen once or twice before driving a hot little red car with yellow dragons painted on both sides walked hurriedly to the front and spoke to the woman. She immediately went back to her cash register. "Sorry," he said not looking sorry at all. "These people bring their old habits with them when they come from the old country, and she was just yelling at me in the back to get my attention. I've already told her several times not to do that."

"Oh," was the only word Scott could think of at first and then he added, "so, may I ask what this sign means?"

"It means we're looking for help."

"I understand that part, I mean, it's written in English, and I thought that rather odd. Are you looking for just any help or English-speaking help?"

The tall, thin Asian couldn't have been much older than Scott, he was probably somewhere in his mid-twenties and immaculately dressed giving him the appearance of a professional model in a men's magazine. His shiny and very thick black hair was combed straight back and it was apparently full of some hair product to keep it that way; he also reeked of heavy aftershave that smelled a lot like the new and wildly popular Jade East. His suit was obviously tailor-made and even his dark shoes gleamed with polish.

"My name is Henry," he said in perfect English but did not offer his hand, "and I was the one that put the sign in the window. I'm looking for someone to hire who is not Asian. Are you interested in the job?"

When he replied, "I could be," Henry took him by the elbow and accompanied him to the back of the shop and propped him up in front of a counter filled with seafood riding on waves of ice and surrounded by other products, some recognizable, some not. To his right, there was a refrigerated case with jars of strange looking items inside them all covered with liquid. To Scott, they looked a lot like human organs.

"Wait here," Henry said as he disappeared into the back of the shop. The small Asian man behind the counter continued to chop fish as though he was still alone.

Now might be a good time to leave, he thought. Just slip out the back door and disappear. While he was scanning the rear wall looking for an exit, he realized there was no back door, at least not in this part of the building. Then he remembered that in this neighborhood and on this side of the street, there wasn't the traditional alley running behind the shops. That was why the traffic in front of the business moved so slowly. The delivery trucks would pull up to the storefront and unload as quickly as possible while nearly every employee rushed out to help unload the truck. It usually meant the driver had to double parking on the wrong side of the busy street for a quick delivery and then he had to try to get back in the right lane, blocking even more traffic trying to get out in order to make another delivery further down the block.

Because Scott, due to a combination of boredom and curiosity, had thoroughly checked out the neighborhood for blocks on every side and knew the area behind these stores did not have an alley. There was only a significant space bordered on three sides by the backs of houses, businesses, and apartments creating a horseshoe shape of buildings with a block-long open area that faced the next street. Cluttering this space was a large patch of weeds and junk. The first time he saw it he remembered how his mother longed for a yard of any sort. She loved flowers, and she was continually dragging her children anywhere they could go by public transportation to see gardens.

Expensive as it was, they never missed the Chicago Flower Show at McCormick Place on Lake Michigan or any of the small gardens tucked here and there in the city. On one city ramble, they even found a beautiful garden hidden in a church courtyard right on busy north Michigan Avenue and between expensive stores. Once, Scott remembered, she even took them up to Glencoe to visit the Chicago Botanic Garden. One of her sisters, who also lived in Chicago and married a pretty wealthy guy, had invited her and the kids to a day out. They spent most of it at the garden entranced with the thousands of spring bulbs that blanketed the area. There were daffodils, crocus, snowdrops and tiny blue flowers called squill everywhere. It was a chilly day, but they still took the little cart ride around the garden amazed at its size. They huddled tightly together for the tour and were grateful when they returned to the main building where auntie treated them to a hot lunch. Scott's sister, who was an unofficial authority on everything, told him the aunties who had no children needed someone to spend their money on and that day their auntie was focusing on her nearly destitute sister and her equally poor children.

They attended a boring lecture after lunch as well as one workshop and they watched a few floral demonstrations, but they preferred the gift shop and of all the things they did, it was the cafeteria where they ate large bowls of chili and mounds of garlic bread and drank Cokes that remained their happiest memory. The day ended too soon for all of them, but it instilled in a life-long love of the earth and what it could become.

As he stood by the vast amount of dead grass in the empty lots, he imagined what it would look like if each owner took an interest and tended to their spots behind their apartments. They could create a place of wonder with a series of magnificent gardens, maybe with a central spot that had a fountain or a free-standing pergola surrounded by formal beds and maybe some benches. But there it was, an ugly patch of ground behind buildings whose backs hadn't been painted or repaired for years. Evidently, the prevailing attitude of the owners was if the spot couldn't make money, why bother to fix it up?"

Lost in thought Scott was startled when Henry came back and said, "Come with me."

Henry wove Scott through the tightly packed store to the farthest corner. Even though Scott had been in all the shops, he noticed for the first time that this was three stores put together. The first section was the grocery part with rows of unidentifiable food, and the next two sections, or former shops, were filled with decorative flower pots, bamboo rice steamers of all sizes, stacking side tables and glass counters full of incense. There were woks of all sizes and blankets, knives that ranged in size to blades small enough to fit in a boot to the swash-buckling swords complete with tassels on their hilts. There were dishes, decorative jade pieces of all colors and large jars full of peacock feathers. While looking to the left and right, Scott almost missed seeing Henry take a sharp turn and slip through an open door that led to the messiest office he had ever seen.

Two large desks faced each other and every spot that could have papers piled on it did. The walls contained photos, political posters, Chinese red and gold good luck banners, years of greeting cards and a few scraggly plants in the window starving for light. They didn't linger long in the office and the only woman, who was awash in book work, didn't even look up as they hurriedly walked past her on their way to the stairway in the back next to a door.

Ah, here's the back door, he noted to himself as he hurried by it. I knew there had to be one here somewhere.

When they arrived on the second floor, they walked all the way down the long shabby hallway whose old wallpaper was curling badly, to the very last door. Henry stopped and motioned for Scott to take a seat in one of the elaborately ornamental gold chairs against the wall. Suddenly Henry looked more like a child entering the headmasters' office instead of the cool dude look he usually projected. He removed his shoes and placed them vigilantly on the intricately detailed rug outside the door, knocked softly, waited for a reply, and entered the room.

This door was unlike any other in the hallway Scott noted. Highly lacquered in black with a dramatic gold dragon skillfully painted as though it was crouching to one side of the door, it appeared to be waiting to pounce on unworthy entrants. Seconds after the door closed Scott got a whiff of powerful incense which made him wonder all the more what he was getting himself into. He distracted himself by looking out of the dirty window close to where he was sitting that oversaw the second-floor restaurant across the street. This upscale eatery was known for its fresh seafood which swam in the back of the restaurant in an extensive collection of immaculately clean tanks. When you passed by the tanks on your way to the bathrooms, you could see the fish and the crabs living as though life was as good as it got for them. He had eaten there once when he was still flush with graduation money, and everything impressed him from the young and immaculate wait staff to the impressive bank of floor to ceiling immaculately clean windows. If a diner was lucky enough to get a seat near the windows that overlooked the street below, they could watch an endless parade of people wandering the street and discussing among themselves where they wanted to go next and trying to read menus short on English or any other language that hung outside various restaurants.

Lost in reverie as he stared at the people in the street below, it seemed like only seconds later when Henry was back out in the hall motioning to Scott that he should follow him, first looking down at Scott's shoes indicating that he needed to take them off and place them meticulously next to his.

Scott tried to hide the hole in the toe of his sock.

Henry opened the door and thankfully entered first. Scott drew in a quiet breath at the majesty of the room. He had never seen, much less been in, a room that was so overwhelmingly opulent. This could be a room in a palace in China, he thought. Its beauty was phenomenal.

Henry had already reached the large desk which had been set dramatically in front of windows which looked down on the main drag, Wentworth Avenue. Scott lagged behind Henry attempting to take in the amazement of the rest of the room and the softness of the thick pile carpeting.

"There was an aura in the room that took your breath away," he later told his mom on the phone. "There were massive palm plants in equally large vases on either side of the windows, and the room seemed to be done entirely in silk fabric. It was on the walls and on the furniture and there was one full wall that looked like the wood had been intricately carved by hand creating magnificent ships and birds and plants and buildings. There was a stick of incense burning in a beautiful jade bowl on her desk, and it wafted its exotic aroma into the conversation.

"This, Auntie Chung, is the fellow I was telling you about, his name is Scott," he turned around and asked, "Scott what?"

"Uh, West, Scott West," he stammered. So, this woman is his aunt. Now things are beginning to make sense, he thought to himself.

"Yes," Henry began again quite condescendingly. "Scott West has applied for the job."

"Does he know what the job entails?" asked Madam Chang, a tiny Asian woman whose age was questionable due to her dyed hair and heavy makeup. She was also using an unanticipated superior tone.

"Not yet, Auntie, I wanted to pass him by you first to get your approval."

Scott stood mutely by as though he was a small school child and his teacher had taken him to the principal's office, and together they were about to mete out an appropriate punishment.

"Yes, that's right," Scott interrupted, "I don't know what the job is because all I did was inquire about your help wanted sign in the window and…"

She cut him off with a look. "Are you looking for employment?"

"Well, yes, but…"

"Very well, are you strong?"

"Strong?"

"Yes strong," she answered as though talking to an imbecile. "Can you lift things?"

Scott almost asked how heavy the things were but decided not to prolong the conversation and just said, "Yes."

"If my nephew decides to hire you," she said almost dismissively, "I will agree to it. You will receive a fair wage in cash each week, and my nephew will be your boss, and he maintains the right to relieve you of your duties at a moment's notice. You will have no further contact with me, and you will run all your queries through Henry. That is all; you may go." She returned to her papers as they backed out of the room.

Scott's mother had taken the L south to Chinatown, and as they sat in their favorite dim sum restaurant ordering more pork and other unrecognizable dishes, Scott continued his original narrative he had started on the phone only that morning.

"I mean, it's hard to believe it even still." He paused for only a second and continued, "You know I've always been drawn to Chinatown because it's like a city inside a city, I mean it might be Chicago everywhere else, but for a few blocks in each direction it's a different world. A world where no one speaks anything but Asian dialects, the smell of incense is everywhere, and the food and the souvenirs and everything else is so authentic that it's like really being in a different country, but I'm telling you that this woman's office was…"

"Unbelievable?" His mother asked amused by his all-out fascination with Madam Chang.

"Well that and astonishing and astounding and beyond belief," Scott added.

"Gracious!" Is what she said aloud, but she wondered to herself where her son had learned so many eloquent words.

"Here she was," he started again without preamble, "sitting behind this huge ornamental desk that made her look even smaller and she had papers to the right of her and her left. She was writing in whatever language she speaks on some of them and in English on others."

Helen interrupted, "You had time to look at her papers?"

"Lots of time, they talked to each other as though I wasn't even in the room."

"Did that bother you?"

"Not really, it's like I said, they operate in another world altogether. But they hired me, and it looks like I'll be the first white boy ever to be employed in this town."

Before his mother could voice her concern, he continued brightly, "One of my jobs is to help unload products at each of her three stores."

"She owns three stores?"

"Yes, three, but I also found out that this isn't unusual. Evidently, there are only a few families that run the whole town. They makeup what they call the family association and pretty much nothing happens without their say so."

"It sounds a bit sinister to me," she said lowering her voice and dipping her last piece of steamed pork dumpling into the small bowl of soy sauce. "Are you sure…"

"I know what you're going to say and I have to agree, I'm not sure, but I'm looking forward to working here and seeing life from their perspective." He saw the look of concern on her face and added, "Don't worry, I'm pretty good at taking care of myself and besides, I'm still fast on my feet, so if all else fails, I'll run up all 40 stairs to the L in a flash and be back home with you before you know."

She smiled as she covered his hand with hers also seeing the time on her watch. "Gracious, speaking of the L, I've got to go. I need to get home to go to the doctor's with your father. His cough is getting bad enough that he's finally allowed me to him to the doctors and he's letting me go along…lucky me," she said as she grabbed her purse and laid money on the table. She saw him start to object and said quickly, "No, it's my treat, that is until you start getting a regular paycheck, and then I'll let you buy."

She kissed him when they reached the sidewalk, and he was not embarrassed. He loved his mother and was always amazed that she could maintain a seemingly normal life while living with a certified drunk like his father while spending days at a time taking care of his two sister's children, trying to keep them quiet so as not to wake their useless grandfather before he was good and ready to get up.

His mother, standing impatiently at the corner waiting for the light to change while watching for the train overhead, felt the old worry creeping into her heart for her boy. The girls gave her few problems, but Scott had put her through her through her paces countless times before and she fervently hoped he would soon tire of this current lifestyle and find something that came with a future. She thanked God every day that at least he wasn't following in his father's footsteps where alcohol was concerned, or at least she prayed he wasn't.

Chapter 4

When Claire stopped in at the Five several weeks later, both Clay and the Duffer were unprepared for her visit.

Duff was in the middle of cleaning out the grease trap under the kitchen sink, always a dirty job, and Clay, equally messy, had washing machine parts strewn all over the laundry tables trying to figure out how they could all fit back in.

"Hello again," she said to Duff's back as he mucked out junk from the silver box on the floor under the sinks.

"He recognized her voice immediately and without turning said, "Grab a cup of coffee there on the counter, and I'll finish this and meet you in the dining room in a jiffy."

She did.

He left his project and plunged his hands into the hot soapy water that was in the kitchen sink and in less time than normal he was sitting next to her with his cup of coffee in hand and a clean apron hiding most of his filth, he hoped. He kept his voice down in hopes that Clay had not heard her arrive. But as luck would have it, Clay came into the dining room looking for more tools and a can of machine oil as Claire began her story. Clay made himself comfortable at the table avoiding the daggers Duff was sending his way.

"She calls herself Madam Zaretski. Madam Sonya Zaretski to be precise, but I never heard anyone call her by her first name. She answers to Madam or Madam Zaretski, nothing else. That young man that's always with her even calls her Madam."

Clay and Duffer looked at each other wondering if they should ask her who that young man was and what she was talking about. After all, it was Johnny she spoke to the last time she was here, so maybe she told him the story. Duffer looked at Clay and raised his eyebrows and Clay took it as a sign to ask her immediately who the young man was. Duffer had meant, "Not now, maybe the young man would come up again and then we'll ask."

He raised his eyebrows again, but this time added the wagging of his head as if to say, "Don't ask about the young man."

Clair seemed to miss all the signals and was saying, "We aren't sure who the young man was. Some of us think it's her son; others just think he's some hanger on or someone she felt sorry for and took pity on, although pity doesn't seem to be part of her makeup."

Before she could begin again, Duffer kindly reminded her that they were not privy to her first conversation and maybe she'd like to start at the beginning and tell them everything. If there were two men who wallowed in stories and gossip, it was the Duffer and Clay, even though they were both in the middle of jobs that needed to be finished, and finished soon.

"That's right," she said, "I guess you don't know what I'm talking about. Do you want the long or the short version?"

Duff glanced at the clock and said a quick, "Give us the long one but after I slip the meatloaves into the oven for supper."

"Isn't it kind of hot for meatloaf?" she asked tentatively when he was gone.

"He's also making baked potatoes and would probably throw in a squash or two if they were in season and heated the place if he could," Clay said looking in the direction of the kitchen.

"He's a nice guy and all, a former Navy cook too, but sometimes. . ." He was about to continue but stopped when Duff came out of the kitchen with a slice of lemon cake for each of them. It was his favorite dessert because it was so simple to make. To accommodate their sizeable supper crowd, Duff usually baked two lemon sheet cakes and then, while they were still hot, poured a heady mixture of lemon juice and sugar over each one. The results were always fabulous.

"No, really, I couldn't," she said. "But thank you for thinking of me. I have to watch my weight."

"You're skinny as a rail," interjected Clay as he slid her piece onto his plate without asking.

"That's because you have to be very thin if you want to be an excellent dancer."

A-hah! Thought Duff, I knew she walked like a dancer the first time she came. I'm right again, of course.

"What kind of dancer are you?" asked Clay as he started on her piece of cake ignoring the glare from the cook.

"Ballet."

Neither man knew what to say, neither knowing a thing about ballet, so Duff asked, "So who did you say this Madam person was?"

"Well," she began with a sign of resignation running a finger around and around the rim of her coffee cup as she spoke. "She says she's Russian, has a thick accent and claimes to have been a great ballerina in her own country, but because she lived during some mass starvation in her homeland, she became too weak to dance. Now she gives Russian Ballet lessons over on the Gold Coast, you know, north by the Oak Street beach?" Before either men could answer she continued, "Well, it's not really in the nice part of the classy neighborhood, it's more like on the fringes. Anyway, she has this upstairs studio, and she teaches only Russian ballet."

"So," asked Duff. who had no fear of entering boldly into uncharted water, "I thought ballet was French, isn't it?"

"Oh no, it originally started in Italy, it was the French that gave actual names to the moves."

"I thought you said it was Russian," Clay inquired as he put down his fork."

"Russian ballet is ballet, but not French ballet." She seemed satisfied with the answer, and neither man was genuinely interested in understanding what she had just said, so they moved on.

"And the young man?" Queried Duffer.

"Ah, yes. Well, first of all, no one has any idea how old Madam is because she wears a great deal of dark eye makeup, a thick foundation on her face and always dresses in black; she's a dramatic theater type. She's also short and uses a cane not to use it to walk necessarily; it's more like an authority stick. She beats the time out on the floor with it.

This young man kind of looks like she does, short and stout, and it's no telling how old he is; he could be anywhere between twenty and forty. But then she could be somewhere between forty and sixty." She continued after a quick breath, "He calls her Madam instead of Mother, and he's very devoted to her. If he's not her son, they have to be related somehow. Most people would call him challenged."

"Challenged?" Clay asked scraping his plate. "What kind of challenge, a duel?"

"You know," she said looking confused as to the right word to use, "challenged, like mentally handicapped. Most of the time he has to be told very carefully what to do, and he stammers, but as I said, he's devoted to Madam and is constantly running errands for her. His name is Leonid, Russian like she is, I think." She thought about her last comment and added, "But then he would be, I mean if he were her son."

"Would be what?" asked Clay using his wet finger to get the rest of the cake off of the plate."

"Russian," she said.

The three came to a verbal stand-still, none seem to know which way the conversation was going. All they knew for sure was that she was a ballerina whose teacher was a strange old lady who had a son or maybe not and they were Russian, or something.

But why would she be looking for lodging at the Five? Wondered Duff.

They all sipped their coffee in silence until Duff ventured into uncharted waters again and said rather soothingly, "You never told us why you are thinking of moving in with us. You are thinking of that, aren't you?" The hope in his voice was evident to everyone but Claire.

"Oh yes. Things are getting too strange at the studio. I did tell you I lived there, didn't I?

"You poor lass," Clay said with more Irish lilt in his voice than Duff had ever heard. "Be you having a difficult time there?"

That's it, Duffer thought. He'll be singing Danny Boy soon if I don't jump in.

"More coffee anyone? Claire?" She nodded, so Duffer asked with all the innocence he could muster, "Clay, would you do the honors?"

As Clay fumed out of the room Duff turned to Claire and asked, "You never did tell us why you want to move in here, you know."

"That's right, sorry. I guess I told that other guy. What was his name again?"

"Johnny, but that's not important," Duffer responded. "Tell me your story from the start, oh look," he said with resignation, "here's Clay with the coffee already."

Clay slopped Duff's coffee down carelessly, but he carefully laid a napkin down on the table before he placed Claire's cup in front of her, taking great pains to make sure to position the cup's handle was to the right. She took a tiny sip of the hot liquid and smiled at Clay as she said, "Thank you so much."

He almost giggled but was saved from embarrassing himself as she once again began her narrative. "Ever since I was a little girl I've wanted to dance. My parents didn't take me seriously and insisted that I could have ballet lessons only if my grades were good and if I put half of any money I received, you know birthday and Christmas money, in the bank for my college fund. I complied with their wishes and by the time I was a junior in high school I had a pretty good account built up. College was not in any plans I had for my future, but my parents insisted that I find a few local schools and apply. When I was a junior, they sent for information on grants and other cash incentives from state and federal coffers so if I would be accepted somewhere, my freshman year costs would be covered. I still only wanted to dance, but I still had a year to go in their house, so I complied." She looked at Duff, "I've changed my mind, do you think you could get me a small sliver of that cake?"

Clay turned his head to innocently look out of the dining room window at the empty lot next door as though the accumulated trash and weeds were the most beautiful things he had ever seen, making it difficult for Duffer to leave the room again on another errand. He knew as soon as he went out that Clay would turn on his limited Irish charm and try to make personal inroads.

"Here, let me get it for you," Duff said in a tight voice directed at Clay's back, "but promise me that you wait until I get back before you continue your most interesting story," he said looking directly at the woman who had swept him off his feet.

"I promise," she said while crossing her heart and looking at him with her enormous blue eyes.

"I'll hurry." His words said in a near whisper, and Clay rolled his eyes.

Before Clay could turn his chair back around and continue his conversation with this striking girl, to his amazement Duffer returned with the cake on their best plate.

"I shouldn't be eating this, but it looked so good and I am so hungry."

Another awkward moment, should the two men inquire into her personal life or not? Neither knew what to say so silence reigned again.

When Johnny came into the dining room he was amazed the three of them were all just sitting and staring at the walls.

"Hi," he said as they all turned to look at him simultaneously. "Am I missing something?"

"Um, not really," said Duff rising from his chair. "Can I get you some coffee, some cake?"

"Sure, why not. I've no place to go." He sat down next to Claire, but a little too close for Duff's liking. As he hurried into the kitchen, Duff berated himself under his breath for inviting Johnny into their conversation. He didn't need any more competition. Clay was enough with his sudden heavy Irish brogue and interest and now here's Johnny who, by any standards, was no longer seeing Sandy and was obviously interested in Claire. "Not again," said Duff under his breath, "I've already lost Jane to some guy who just walked into her life and managed to marry her within six months, oh no, this woman is mine."

The down-and-out man that Scott usually saw on the main street struggling with construction objects was now sitting on the steps in front of the Chinese Hardware store. He seemed oblivious to the crime he was committing according to the Chinese brothers who ran the place and set their own rules.

"Hey," he said when he reached the man, surprised there hadn't already been a confrontation with one of the elderly Chinese brothers, "You're taking a risk sitting here," he said as soon as he reached the steps.

"What, a risk of being run over by hundreds of tourists? If you'll notice, young man," he said opening his arms wide, "there doesn't seem to be many in town this morning, so I think I'm safe."

"You're safe until one of those brothers looks out and sees you. They are adamant that no one enjoys the comfort of their steps." Scott reached down and offered his hand, "Here, if you need to sit, I was just going to Feida's, I could sport you a green tea if you wanted one, or if you just want to sit, you could do it there."

"Well, that would be nice. I guess you're not as unfriendly as I thought."

"Unfriendly," asked Scott almost stopping right there on the sidewalk to have it out with this weirdo.

"Okay, maybe not unfriendly, but aloof, you know, better than me."

"Just what do you mean by that?" Scott inquired as he mentally changed the older man's sentence to 'other than I.' "His mother had been a stickler when it came to proper grammar, and Scott found out he followed in her footsteps, making mental corrections all day.

They had arrived at Feida's, and Scott pushed the door open, and they walked into the front part of the building where the bakery was. Scott moved to the display cases that were overflowing with pastries. "Do you want something to eat?" he enquired. The man was staring at everything in the three cases, row by row, as if he hadn't seen food for months.

"I'd buy you one of their real breakfasts, but I don't know how to order it, and I'm not sure you'd like it. I've never tried the slimy stuff myself, but it looks disgusting-I think they're some kind of see-through dumpling."

The young girl behind the counter was losing patience with the two men seemingly not being able to make up their minds, and she was looking at the group that had come in after they had as if to wait on them if they didn't decide quickly.

"I'll have one of those," Scott pointed to a steamed bun, and my friend here will have…"

"One of those and one of those and one of those," he said, his eyes gleaming.

"We'll also like two pots of tea, and we'll eat in the back." He paid for their food with money his mother had slipped him before she left last time. He knew she would have approved of how he used it; she was big into good works.

Scott paid the girl, and he led the way to the crowded back room where there was no seating. Several men moved together at their tables only when the woman who took their order arrived with their breakfast pastries. She said something in their native language and the men moved over without comment. The two men squeezed into a spot at one of the large tables as the tiny Asian girl placed their order in front of them, spoke to a man at their table and then retreated to get their teas.

The older guy looked around at all the men and asked in a low voice, "So what is this, some type of men's breakfast club?"

"Oddly enough, you're right in a way. See," Scott lowered his voice, "notice most of them have on white shirts and black pants?"

"A dress code?"

"In a way, you can say it is. Almost all of these men work in restaurants outside of the city, both near and some almost an hour away. I was talking to one guy last week who said that he was one of the waiters and the guy next to him was the cook and the third guy was the owner of the one restaurant furthest away from where they all worked. If we're still here at ten, you'll see the different van's lining up outside, and then each man gets on the one going to 'their' restaurant so they can all ride out into the suburbs to start their day. If you notice, it's not only here they do it, vans arrive to load employees that are waiting outside of all three bakeries. I don't know if it's a matter of space that they don't all gather at one place, or if the vans go different places, I plan to find out though."

"So that's why they look so gloomy, they're going to work."

"I suppose," Scott said, "I guess I never thought about it that way. I just thought Asian people always look gloomy, or maybe just thoughtful, I don't know."

His companion laughed at that one, spraying the flakey pastry crumbs on his shirt.

"So," Scott ventured, "have you ever had a job?"

"Ha!" he exploded spraying more crumbs, "I was born working."

"What do you mean?"

"I mean I was born on a dairy farm in the beautiful state of South

Dakota and learned how to work very early in life. You're hardly out of diapers when you're collecting eggs and helping in the barn."

"You had cows?"

"We milked almost 75 cows!"

"Is that a lot?" Scott knew he sounded stupid, but in a way, he was trying to build up the old guy.

"Seventy-five was more than enough because when you have that many cows, you also have seventy-five calves, more or less."

"Is that like a requirement?"

"Is what like a requirement?"

"The number of cows is often equal to the number of calves."

The homeless man almost choked on his final bite with laughter. When he caught his breath again, he said, "A cow doesn't give milk until she's had a calf." Seeing the dumb look on the younger man's face he continued, "A cow comes into heat about once a year and when she's bred, it takes about ten months for her to have a calf. That's when her milk comes in abundantly, and she'll give milk until the time when she's bred again."

"Does the calf drink the milk too?"

The older man realized he had a real city boy by his side so he explained, "No, the calf is given milk replacer for awhile and then, if it's a boy, or what we call a bull, it can be sold at auction, or it can be castrated, which changes its name to a steer, and then sold at auction or kept and sold as beef. You do know what I mean when I say castrated, don't you?" Scott answered with a bravado he did not possess, "Sure, who doesn't," not really sure if his definition was correct or not.

"If it's a," he paused looking for a word, "a girl cow, she's almost always kept on the farm. Sometimes an old cow gets shipped, and the younger one takes her place as soon as she has a calf so they can use her for milking."

This farmer information was entirely new to Scott, and he was having trouble understanding it. "So how long does the average cow live, you know the one that gives the milk?"

"If she's a good milker, she can stay on the farm for years and years, up to fifteen I would imagine."

There was something about that information that pleased Scott.

Farming, he thought, sounded so different than he imagined. He thought it was all driving the tractor in the fields, bouncing up and down on the seat while wearing one of those straw hats and having things like chickens wandering around the yard and pigs in their pens, he'd never thought of the science of raising cows. He was used to milk in cardboard containers that were marked Bowman Dairy without any thought of where it came from and the work involved in getting it to market. As long as he was having a conversation, he decided that this would be an excellent time to continue, "What do you do now since there are no cows in the area?"

"As a matter of interest, sonny, I'm in the middle of a building project."

"Oh yes, and what are you building?" Scott looked up as a woman with several children entered. None of the men moved so the girl in the back that had seated them berated a few of the guys until they squeezed in together to make room at the table.

"Would you like to see it sometime?"

"What? I didn't catch that last part."

"I asked you if you wanted to see it sometime."

"Your project? I'd like to know what it is first," thinking this oddball farmer could be building anything from a barn to a rocket to Mars he was planning on launching some moonlit night.

"Sure, anytime." Scott was hoping that the old guy would get discouraged with his non-committal answers.

"How about later today?" Evidently, the man hadn't understood the tone of Scott's voice.

"Normally that would work for me, but I've just gotten a job, and I start in less than an hour," he said, checking his watch as though to make it official.

"You've got a building project too?"

"Not really, I've just been hired to work here in town."

"But you're not Asian."

"You know, that never crossed my mind," Scott said sarcastically as he gathered his things. "I've got to go, don't want to be late for my first day." He threaded his way between the men jockeying for space in the tan vans that were double parked on the already busy street.

"Hey, kid," the man yelled as Scott headed down the street. "I don't even know your name!"

"It's Scott. And yours?" he asked with a shout.

"Elliot, it's my mother's maiden name."

Scott nodded that he had heard and hurried on down the block not wanting to be late for his first day working for Henry, or was it more for Madam Chang?

The store that Henry ran for his Auntie was at the south end of the last block near the church and it differed from all the other local shops due to its contents. There weren't any ducks hanging in the window or fish swimming in murky tanks. As soon as prospective customers or chatty tourists opened the door, they knew from the uncluttered shelves that this was a place where high-end products were the norm, and the usual gaudy souvenirs were not welcome here. Silence reigned supreme and employees were dressed more like Henry was, in the trendy fashion more familiar to the downtown area, rather than in the usual Asian pants and tops worn elsewhere.

Scott checked his watch as he approached the young girl behind the counter, "Where would I find Henry?" he asked.

"If you mean Mr. Lee," she turned her head slightly and looked sideways up the stairs where he was standing.

"Thanks," he all but whispered and started up the steps.

"I see we have a few things to go over," said Henry with a dismissive tone. "Step into my office please."

His office was also on the top floor, but nowhere near as decorative as his aunts because it was filled with vases of every size, some still in their wooden crates, some half unwrapped. For some reason Scott stood until Henry sat behind his desk and even then waited for permission.

Henry motioned for him to now be seated and began immediately, "You have probably noticed that my aunt, who by the way is my mother's sister, and I have entirely different ways when it comes to doing business in this town, even though we are both from China. She is the generation that still believes in the old feudal system of slaves and landowners. Because she is a major landowner, so to speak, everyone else is a slave in her opinion. She rules with a rod of iron, and many do not like her."

Scott sat mutely not knowing what to say or if he was required to say anything.

Henry continued. "I, on the other hand, have taken on American customs when it comes to doing business. I believe that someone who works for me is an employee and not a slave. I will treat you exactly how you treat me. I expect you to be punctual and to do whatever job I give you. I also expect that you put in a full day's work for a full day's pay. Is that clear?"

"Perfectly," he answered and then ventured, "So what exactly is my job?"

"To begin with, you will be in charge of unloading the truck that comes on Thursdays with my expensive imports. I have already spoken to my other two men, lazy Chinese both of them. Now, about your being in charge, they both speak enough English to understand what you tell them and you are to tell me about any un-cooperation on their part or insubordination, and I will deal with it. It's obvious Henry likes big words, Scott thought to himself as his boss continued. "I suppose you've already noticed that I do not deal in junk like most of the other owners on the block," he made his last statement as he swept the room visually with his arm over the large and expensive vases crowding the room along with intricate pieces of art carved out of large portions of both tan and light green jade.

"I couldn't care less if the average tourist ever walks into my shop. I cater to those discriminating collectors or to the owners of the other shops who are looking for truly fine items and my business dealings are not necessarily limited to the daylight hours."

"I see," Scott responded still unsure of his job.

"So your job will be to supervise the unloading of the truck. It's not a job to be taken lightly. If you've seen what happens when the other trucks are unloaded you will know what I mean. We do not run out and grab stuff to throw on the sidewalk so the truck can continue on down the main street. We have an alley behind the buildings on this side of the street, so things are taken off the truck behind the shop being most careful. The items are then carried very cautiously into the back storeroom where they are circumspectly unpacked and inventoried. If there is the slightest damage to any of the products, they need to be put to one side and then a form filled out and attached to the product. Am I going too fast for you?"

"Not really," Scott said wondering to himself that if the items were to be unloaded and unwrapped downstairs, why was Henry's office crammed full of items still in their crates?

"Good. I hate stupid people who can't take instruction." Henry said as he tugged on his immaculately white shirt sleeve that had ridden up slightly under his expensive suit, the sleeves that ended in expensive gold cuff links with some sort of Chinese symbol embossed in blue on them. He continued.

"You will also be required to do a bit of work in the other two stores my aunt owns, but it will be menial and incidental; your main job is here and you answer to me. I do not expect you to be dressed as flawlessly as I am, but because you represent me, I do expect you to be neat and clean- shaven at all times even though your job will be handling the stock. Because I have faith in you, here's an advance in your pay for new clothes and you will need to find another place to sleep rather than under Mr. Chan's truck in his private lot behind the Three Happiness."

Scott took the envelope hesitantly; amazed by the fact that Henry knew how he lived and where he was sleeping. He also decided that perhaps the family association did have eyes and ears all over their part of the world so he answered, "Thank you," and then he added, "Sir."

"Good, now that we understand each other, let's get started."

CHAPTER 5

Both Sandy and Sarah were deep in conversation when they literally ran into Scott as he was on his way back to Madam Chang's office with her lunch. For some reason unknown to him, he was not only working for her nephew, but he had also become her errand boy and now he was intent on getting her hot and sour soup, that was always ladled into her personal lidded bowl and placed in an insulated container, to her before it got cold and before the order of fried wantons lost their crispness.

"Sorry," they smiled happily. "We are lost in thought and didn't see you, hope we didn't crush your package."

"No problem, I don't think there's any harm done," he said as he checked the bag for leaking soup. He tried to think of something more to say to keep the conversation going with these two attractive girls close to his age but when nothing came he smiled at them once more and hurried on with his mission.

It had been several weeks that he had been working for Henry and so far he had only helped unload and check in two deliveries, the rest of the time he mostly worked for the auntie who was still doing business and treating her employees the old Chinese way, like the slaves Henry mentioned on his first day because she pushed them and him mercilessly. He was now truly in her debt because, until he could find a better place to sleep, she let him stay in a tiny room next to her bookkeeper's office. He slept on the floor but there was a place to hang his Henry-approved clothes which he was required to keep clean at all times and for his shoes that were to be always shining; there would be no gym shoes here.

When Henry didn't need him to help rearrange the displays or haul heavy objects upstairs, auntie had him pricing items in her other two stores and stocking shelves and unloading her own trucks at lightning speed before they blocked even more traffic. He could feel the hatred from the other men unloading the vehicles because of his race, and he knew that even though some of them could speak English, they chose not to when he was around. He would just have to live through it; he needed the job because his graduation money was completely gone.

He had delivered the soup and was just coming out of the back room when he saw the girls he had met on the street earlier, and they asked, "Do you work here?"

He wanted to be flippant and say, "No, I just stopped by to stock the shelves with these strange items for no reason," but instead said, "Yep." Immediately he realized what a juvenile response that had been. Henry would have been displeased. "I mean, yes, can I help you find something?"

"Do you know a lot about Chinatown?"

"That depends, what would you like to know?" He tried to sound more like Henry would.

They lowered their voices, and Sandy asked, "Is this the best place to get things like fans and those hanging red paper decorations that look like paper balls with gold fringe?"

"If you mean stuff like that over there, yeah, I mean yes, and we're also the cheapest place anywhere in town," he whispered as he stepped closer to them.

Both girls walked over to where the lanterns were displayed and asked if he had them in all the sizes that were hanging from the ceiling. "And do you know how many of each you have?"

"That I'll have to check, I'm still kind of new in this store and that woman you see up front speaks only enough English to make a sale or yell at a customer. She yells at them to stop blocking the door or to stop gawking at the barbequed ducks. The bookkeeper knows a lot, so I'll go ask her."

By the time he returned, both girls had their notebooks out and their pens were flying with figures.

"If they have these little ones I think we should get five at least," said the shorter girl called Sandy who looked like she was in charge. "We could attach them to the string of Christmas lights, or we could do like I suggested and glue in paper bottoms and put small candles into each one and hang them on the branches of that tree near the house."

"What if they catch fire and we burn down the house?" The second girl called Sarah asked. "That would not go over well at the end of the party."

"Unless they sent out some Hunky firemen!"

"Sandy, I'm surprised at you. Here you are a practically engaged woman saying things like that."

"Practically engaged doesn't mean a thing. He hasn't called me in weeks, no, I mean months."

"You're kidding! Why didn't you say something sooner?" Sarah had put down her pencil and stared at her sister.

"Because I didn't want to ruin your wedding plans, nor Sophie's either. Maybe when all this is over, I'll make some attempt at finding out if we're still a couple or not."

"Oh no, you won't. You will call Johnny as soon as we get back home! It's not fair to either of you to put your plans on hold just because you're involved with us."

Scott interrupted them with the list of prices and the amounts they carried of each size. "I couldn't help overhear, are these are for some party?"

It had been a casual question, but between the two of them, he learned that it was for an outdoor wedding planned for just two weeks away for an older couple, one of whom was their landlady.

"Phil and Sophie were supposed to get married this spring," Sarah said, "but the groom had a little scare with his heart, so they postponed it until now."

"We've been planning this for months and months and only a few days ago decided it should be an outdoor wedding held at dusk," added Sandy.

"What she means is, after rush hour. We live up on Foster Avenue, and traffic doesn't slow down until after seven."

"And the last thing we need is honking horns and screeching breaks."

While they had been talking they had also been counting out the small lanterns and decided to buy fifteen just to be safe.

"Hey, thanks for the help," they said excitedly dismissing him as they headed for the display of colorful fans on the front counter next to the boxes of rice candy, lottery tickets, and chop-sticks.

"If you need any more information about anything at all, I work every day except Mondays up and down this street." He shouted after them as they left the store, but not sure they were listening. He added anyway, "Name's Scott."

"I haven't seen you around for a while," Elliot or was it Everett said the next morning when Scott was at Feida's having a quick meal of a steamed bun and a red bean paste filled mooncake.

"They keep me hopping, that's for sure," he said while checking his watch. "You still building your, uh, project?"

"That I am, uh, Scott?"

"Scott, yeah that's right." He didn't mention he couldn't remember the older man's name.

"You should come and see it someday, it's just about finished, and if I do say so myself, it's not bad." With that said the older man took a sip of his tea and picked up his pastry trying to figure out what it was. He had more-or-less just pointed to something interesting at the end of the case, and now it was his to eat.

"So, what exactly is it," Scott asked as he poured the last of his tea into his cup and noticed that whatever his name was, had paid for his food.

"It's a house."

He is batty, Scott thought, glad he never got more involved.

"Yep, I've built the only free house on the block, okay it's more the size of a large shed, but it didn't cost me a cent."

"You didn't have to pay for nails and tools?"

"That's right. All the tools and almost all the supplies I needed were in a rusty shed in front of my shed."

Scott wasn't sure if he wanted to finish this conversation and looked at his watch again as if to say, "Wow, is that the time," thinking he might have asked this same thing the last time they were together.

"I know I sound like I'm a little touched in the head, but you've got to see what I've done. Say, when's your next day off? I bet you don't have a lot planned, do you?"

It was true; there was nothing to do on his days off besides washing the few clothes he owned to maintain Henry's rigid standards. Even though he slept in what could be easily called neglected conditions, he found that the fancy Triple Crown restaurant bathrooms across the street were available to take a quick bird bath and if he got to the restaurant early before the crowd arrived, he could even wash his hair in the sink using the hand soap and then dry off under the new automatic dryers. Madam Chang only gave him gave him a tiny place to sleep and to hang a few clothes and nothing else.

Elliot was still looking at him, so Scott finally said. "I'm usually off on Mondays, so I suppose I could stop by."

"Great, I'll pick you up by your truck around nine."

"You knew I used to sleep under that truck too? Is there anyone who didn't know?"

"Outside of Chinatown, probably not, meet me on Monday, and things might change for you."

"Well actually," Scott said as he moved out of the way for the men who were leaving for the vans, "I've moved into the back of one of Madam Chang's stores."

"Nice digs?"

"Hardly."

"Glad to hear it, meet you Monday, let's say nine o'clock by your former truck bed and then I'll give you the tour. Hey, get it, truck bed?"

Scott ignored the lousy pun but nodded yes to Monday as he also left the building behind the restaurant staff. Henry did not like anyone to be late, ever.

The Duffer was smitten: over the moon about Claire. In his euphoria, he forgot this was precisely how he had felt about one of the first women that had ever lived at the Five. Her name was Jane, she called herself Plain Jane, and she was a mess when she arrived with a sad tale to tell. He had been bowled over by his feelings for her but gave her no indication of his infatuation. He was heartbroken when, in less than six months, she had married a man she'd met while they were both working at Brocks Candy only a few blocks away and now they were married and lived in North Dakota. "North Dakota of all places," he muttered under his breath.

"What did you say," asked Clay.

"I said I think we've reached our quota. For female residents I mean. I'm not sure if we'd have room for Claire even if she decided to stay here," he said trying to throw Clay off the scent. Unfortunately, it worked just the opposite.

"And just what would you be saying, that we have no more room? We've got that lovely pink room just waiting for her gentle self to arrive. You know the one I mean, the one the lovely Jane used to have?"

Duff remembered, and he also noticed that Clay was back to his Irish brogue. "I just meant, I thought we were going to cut back on the females we housed. If I remember correctly, you were the main one that didn't want any of them here in the first place."

"Sure and begorin I did mention that a time or two I suppose, but now that I think of it, the ladies seem to add a gentle touch to our humble dwelling."

"Okay, that's enough! You can cut the cutesy talk; it doesn't impress me. Either way, whether you want the 'ladies' here or not, I don't think it's a good idea anymore."

"And where would you have her to go?"

"Who are you talking about?"

"The lovely Claire, that's who, even you don't want to see her staying with that crazy woman, do you? I mean one would suppose that she's probably sleeping on some thin mattress that's just been thrown on the floor and helping with the housekeeping to help pay for her lessons, I mean..."

"All right, all right, don't ride me and don't give me the Cinderella story. We don't know exactly what the conditions are, and I would like to see her find someplace, but just not here."

"Now that surprises me."

Duff stopped his sweeping and asked, "Why should that surprise you?"

"Because I think you're sweet on her already."

"Sweet on her, if there's anybody that's sweet on her it's you with you thick brogue and sashaying ways."

"Sashaying ways, why I've never…"

"Not again," were Johnny's first words. "Why can't you two just get along? What's it about now, something earth-shaking like opening the windows or not, or maybe you're discussing new floor wax?"

"As a matter of fact," said the Duffer, "we were talking about Claire."

"Ah, Claire," Johnny said pausing in his walk to grab a pastry off the counter. "The lovely and lithe Claire, Claire with the beautiful blond hair and the enormous blue eyes…"

The other two men looked at each other realizing they were not the only suitors for her affection.

"Whatever happened to Sandy," Duff asked. "Remember Sandy, the girl you've been trying to marry?"

"I've finally realized that I am the only one between the two of us that wants to get married, so it looks like I'm free to date anyone I choose."

"Does Sandy know?"

"She will if she ever calls. You know what they say, 'you snooze, you lose.' Oh, by the way, I'll not be here Friday night," Johnny said as he twirled around, "I'll be out with the lovely Claire. At least she has time to go to Annetties with me." He made a deep bow and left the two men almost speechless.

"Of all the nerve," said Duff to Clay.

"I heartily agree," echoed Clay, "of all the nerve."

CHAPTER 6

The tension at Sophie's the morning of her wedding was so thick that you could "cut it with a knife," as Sarah kept saying.

"I know it's raining," said Sandy for what seemed the fiftieth time that morning as she balanced on a dining room chair while attempting to reattach one of the red and gold Chinese lanterns to the string of white Christmas lights that Pete had hung earlier that morning. But she did like how he had zig-zagging them over the dining table now that had been pulled out to its fullest length.

Now that Sarah's fiancé Pete, was the manager of a downtown Goldblatt's Department Store, he was able to take time off whenever he liked, even Saturday, the busiest day of the week.

Sarah had bragged that the store he managed was doing so well that his 'little boss,' as Sophie always referred to him to keep him straight from the owner of the company, and who was 'just' the district manager, said he was recommending Pete for a promotion to a district position as soon as one opened.

"Didn't I tell you right from the start that Pete was the one for you darling?" Sophie asked as she surveyed his creative lighting above the table. Sarah hardly looked up, busy as she was elaborately folding the vibrant red cloth napkins and tying a wide gold ribbon around the bottom of each one creating what looked like royal crowns for each place and echoing the red lanterns with their gold fringe above. She tucked a beautiful white place card in each crown. Sarah originally thought about asking Scott to see if there was someone in Chinatown they would hire to write each guest's name in Chinese, but Sandy shot the idea down by saying, "We bought the red lanterns just to add to the red and white theme, we are not making it a Chinese reception, although we are using the traditional red meaning good luck."

"And you Sandy dearest," Sophie added as she stopped just inside the kitchen door to see how her young catering friend was doing and turned to say, "we haven't seen that Johnny of yours for a long time. I trust there's no trouble in paradise, nu?"

Sarah paused in her folding after hearing Sophie's comment to her sister. Whenever Sophie used some of the ageless Jewish words that were part of Sarah's old life, sadly reminding her of the woman who for twenty odd years she considered to be her grandmother. Sarah often thought about the unusual way her own life turned out. A short time back she was 'Jewish Sarah' growing up in a ritzy snob-burb north of the city. A girl with a perfect princess for an older sister and a family that kept kosher in everything they did. Then out of the blue, she found out that not only was she not Jewish, but her birth mother had been a domestic in service for the family that adopted her and a gentile to boot.

"Sarah," said Sandy interrupting her thoughts, "I can't get this thing reattached. Hop up here instead and try, you're taller."

When the final lantern was in place, both girls stepped back, arm in arm, to admire their work.

The white tablecloth gleamed with Sophie's real silverware polished to within an inch of its life, and they flanked the white gold-rimmed plates that were so squeaky clean they reflected the light that was beginning to shine through the large dining room window. There was a stream of tall white taper candles that were resting in their antique candle holders and were streaming down the middle of the table that set for the twenty guests. Everyone who had been invited to the wedding had also been invited to stay for the lavish reception immediately after the outdoor ceremony.

The stunning two-tiered wedding cake stood on a small, round table the girls had grabbed from Sophie's rooms, and under Sandy's touch, it was transformed into a thing of beauty. "Since she's started at that fancy-schmancy school of design," Sophie said beaming, "no one does lace as our Sandy does."

Sophie noticed that the shabby table that had sat next to her well-worn sofa was now covered in lace and tulle and topped with a small circle of red fabric. It was Phil's son Larry, the new owner of the bakery, who had created the impressive dessert. The pure white cake was frosted and covered with the most beautiful white roses whose slight dusting of silver on their petals seemed to glow on their own. Instead of the traditional cake top of a plastic bride and groom, a mound of tiny white frosting roses graced the upper layer, and it too had been sprinkled with silver. "Oy, that Larry," remarked Sophie when she saw the finished product of the table and the cake, "he's something else!"

The girls could hardly wait for the reception to begin to see the old wooden walls, flanked by the two large china cabinets which had all been polished until they gleamed glow as they reflected the soft flicker of candlelight and the gentle blush of the lights in the lanterns above. But that would have to wait for hours seeing there was still plenty to do outside for the actual wedding.

"It's too bad we didn't invite that guy in Chinatown," Sandy innocently mused as she gathered up several pieces of white paper they had not needed for place cards.

"What guy in Chinatown? Not that goofy waiter! He must have been close to a hundred years old, and besides, we're not serving Chinese food tonight."

"You know the one I mean, the young one that helped us with the lanterns. I think he was kind of cute."

"What's kind of cute?" Asked Sophie as she came bustling out of the kitchen.

"The lanterns above the table is what she was talking about," said Sarah before Sandy could answer.

"I'll talk to you later about who is and who is not cute my dear sister" Sarah whispered as she linked arms with Sandy and pulled her out of the room.

The rain stopped mid-morning, and the semi-brown August grass was dry by the time the seven o'clock evening ceremony started.

Sandy, who was using the wedding as an extra credit project for her design school class, couldn't have been more pleased with the results of her weeks of work and was still busy taking endless photos, hoping that some would turn out well when the film came back.

Initially she was going to rent a white archway for everyone to walk through on their way to their seats, but Pete surprised everyone with one he had made himself. Well, almost by himself, he did have a cabinet maker as one of his best friends, and that's why the result was a thing of beauty. They had also increased the standard size so Sandy had them move it to the front of the chairs now for not only the pastor to stand under, but also Phil and Sophie. Sandy wondered what they were going to do with after the wedding and thought if worse came to worse they could always put it permanently somewhere in the yard and plant vines on each side with a bench in the middle. It's too bad they never put in a garden.

Months ago in Sandy's 3-D mock-up of the old house, complete with its outdoor wedding in the side lawn, that she had made to get extra credit, she had carefully glued a piece of lace over the top of the curved archway. The lace had been a part of the dining room curtains that Sophie and her first husband Otto purchased on their honeymoon in Germany. Sophie was so touched when she realized the smart way Sandy had included the curtains, like a blessing from the first husband that this marriage should be, she cried at the project's unveiling that night on her dining room table.

Now the actual curtains were draped artfully over the new archway, caught up here and there by small bouquets of gold and purple mums; and it stood beautifully awaiting the bride and groom.

Phil, the next groom that he was, had rented the white chairs which Sandy had practically covered in tulle with a matching bouquet attached to the back of each chair to match the look and colors of the archway.

They had considered rolling out a white carpet that led from the house to the archway, but Sophie, worried about falling, decided that the mowed lawn was just as good. "Better!" she said.

Some of the guests started to arrive a good forty-five minutes before the wedding, creating a situation that never crossed either Sandy's or Sarah's mind. The girls didn't want anyone in the dining room so they could keep the decorations a secret until the reception. They didn't want anyone to see where the actual wedding would take place on the side of the house, and they didn't want them just milling around the center hall. They couldn't use Sophie's apartment because it was full of extra decorations, dresses and her suitcases that needed to be loaded into the limo after the wedding. As Sarah fled upstairs to find her sister to help figure out what to do she passed Pete coming out of the dining room cautiously carrying a half-full bowl of punch with some plastic cups sticking out of his pockets to the front porch where the guests were sitting.

"I love you," Sarah said as he hurried past and saw what he had done. "And thank you!"

"I'll fill them up with punch and some nuts and mints and entertain them for a while with stories about what goes on behind the scenes at Goldblatz, but you'd better hurry and get dressed, I'll be lucky if I can even think of a half an hour of stories."

"I love you," she whispered to herself as he retreated outside. "I love you so much," she added as she fled up the stairs, falling in love with him all over again and even more anxious for their wedding to take place.

And now it was seven, time to begin. The traffic had thinned; the guests had arrived and seated in their beautiful chairs. A gentle breeze wafted across the lawn and the evening turned balmy and golden, and the long white tapers in their generous candelabras on each side of the archway provided a soft romantic glow to the evening, aided by the sun shining its final rays of light as it headed behind the buildings to the west. Pastor Anderson was sitting with Phil in the back porch of the old house along with his two sons, Danny and Larry, who were acting as his two best men and be would accompany him to the front. Meanwhile, the girls were making sure that Sophie had the traditional items by asking, "Something old?"

"My dress, but it's not too old, I bought it for my neighbor's daughter's wedding a few years…"

They interrupted what could have been a long story about the dress and the wedding.

"Something new?"

"That's easy, my shoes. Did I tell you that I put them in the freezer with a bag of water in them so it could freeze and …"

"Sophie, we don't need the long answers now, the ceremony is about to begin."

"Oh, so what else?" She sounded slightly miffed.

"I've forgotten, where were we?" asked Sarah running a hand down her pretty dress to make sure it was hanging right.

"Something borrowed," added Sandy. "Sophie do you have something borrowed on?"

"It's funny you should ask." She stopped their purposely seeing if they wanted her to continue or not.

Sarah checked her watch and then quickly asked, "So what is it."

"This will not be a short answer, so you might not want to know." She smiled innocently.

"We want to know," said Sarah, "but could you hurry a bit. I think our guests are getting restless.

"So, whose wedding is this after all," asked Sophie softly.

"True. Okay, we'll take a deep breath and slow down, now tell us what do you have that's borrowed?"

"You know the Jewel grocery store down the street, the one with the good sales on day-old produce?"

"Oh no," thought both sisters. This is not going to be a short answer.

"Well, remember Denise?"

"The check out girl at the Jewel whose husband left her and their two little kids to start a new life with someone else?" Sarah asked with resignation in her voice.

"That's the one. Well, when we were talking the other day, and I told her about the wedding she started to cry and then came around the counter to hug me. She's such a sweet girl, but that husband of hers…"

"Sophie, please!"

"Anyway," Sophie added, "I must have mentioned the part about something borrowed, and she just reached into her pocket and gave me a lucky stone."

"Did you say a stone?" asked Sarah as she stepped behind her sister to adjust the strap on the back of Sandy's dress."

"Yes, I said stone. Denise's daughter gave it to her because she had picked it up off the street and thought it was beautiful. She told Denise that it was for her because it looked just like a 'mommy heart.' Because of that Denise puts it in her uniform pocket every day she works to remind herself why she puts in the long hours, sore feet and all."

Both girls paused briefly to smile soft, sappy smiles reflecting the kindness of strangers when Sarah remembered and recited quickly, "Something old, something new, something borrowed, okay, something blue?"

"Never you mind about something blue," said Sophie, blushing slightly and turning on her heel to start down the hall having the last word on what could have been the most exciting conversation of all.

Sarah and Sandy had chosen matching soft sage sheath dresses for the occasion, and each carried a bouquet of yellow mums and purple stocks and assorted greens and babies breath with trailings of lavender, yellow, soft green and pink ribbons cascading nearly to the floor.

As the canned wedding music filled the side yard with surprising depth, Sarah couldn't help but think of their former housemate, Jilly. She would have loved this day and would have added her zany touches here and there to the whole production. She hoped Jilly was happy living in New York working for an off-Broadway company as their official dresser, but she did miss her so. Maybe after their wedding, Phil and Sophie would go back into the rooming house business, and the place would be full of renters again. She was so deep in thought that Sandy had to elbow her before she realized that Pete had changed the music tape from the rich classical selections that had been playing to the wedding march and they needed to accompany Sophie down the aisle.

Sophie had just stepped out onto the front steps of the beautiful old red brick building with the four corner turrets that she and Otto purchased so long ago and turned into a rooming house so young people would have a place to live that was inexpensive and safe. There had been many happy memories in that house, but Otto was gone, and it was time to move on with her life.

Later, everyone said that Sophie looked radiant in her soft lavender dress and flowing fall bouquet that matched her two maids of honor. Sophie herself liked her new bone colored open-toed beige shoes that she shopped for until she finally found some that not only looked good but fit her so well that she would be able to wear them for years. No one knew that she had put them in the freezer overnight with a slightly filled water balloon in each one that she had placed down by the toes.

Sophie had heard somewhere that when the balloons expanded as the water froze, they also expanded the shoes a bit. Now that she had them on, they did feel more comfortable, and it made her smiled broadly to know it worked.

As the three of them started down the aisle and she saw her beloved waiting for her, her mind wandered back to shoes. Phil is just like an old pair of shoes; she thought happily as she walked steadily between Sarah and Sandy. She smiled again as she realized that he was a dear man that she had known practically all her life, her sister's husband for many years and now a man who had fallen in love again, this time with her.

"Thank you sister," Sophie said softly as she neared the end of the chairs and the friends and family sitting in them. "I will be good to your man." She winked skyward.

With the girls on each side, Sophie heard the words she had heard at numerous wedding ceremonies, "who gives this woman in marriage?"

"We do," her maids of honor said as they each, in turn, kissed her cheeks with tears of happiness threatening to ruin their mascara.

Phil's sons stood proudly next to their father when the minister asked unconventionally, "And who gives this man?"

"We do," said his son as they too kissed their father's cheeks and stepped aside making room for Sophie whom they also surprisingly kissed lightly. Phil took her hands in his and thought, this is my Sophie with the beautiful smile and the lavender dress and the radiant glow that could be seen across the street at the diner if anyone had taken the time to look up from their bitter coffee and their dried meatloaf blue plate special. Nothing like Sophie's cooking, no sir, she was quite a hand when it came to food, especially those veal roll-up things stuffed with. . .

She promised to love and cherish him as long as they both lived and he promised to be the kind of man who would love her to the end of his days.

Family and friends, the listeners to this gentle exchange understood that with the physical troubles this couple had already experienced during the last six months, the years might be short, but they would be good. There was love in this marriage, and it showed in both word and deed and on their faces.

When Phil slipped the beautiful diamond ring onto her finger and she, in turn, placed a ring on his, the tenderness of the moment was interrupted as the #22 bus blew its horn, and an arm snaked out of the driver's window and waved. The couple smiled and said I do together, adding a lovely kiss for the rest of the traffic that had all suddenly taken an interest in the goings-on in the side yard of that beautiful red brick building that looked like it could be an exclusive or private club.

As the wedding party made their way into the house that had also been decorated from top to bottom with yards and yards of tulle and fall flowers, especially the stairway that wound its way up to the second floor, they could also smell the mesmerizing smells of the meal to come. Sarah left Pete's side to link arms with her sister. "I know this is not the time, but you should have invited Johnny. You should at least have let him know what was happening," she whispered.

"You're right," Sandy said looking at the room filling with all Sophie and Phil's special people.

"It was very small of me to not even call him. I don't know what I was thinking."

"You were thinking that maybe he should be the one calling you," Sarah said as she led her down the hall to get out of the way of the people entering the house and waiting to go into the dining room

"Listen, Sandy, this wedding is over, mine is far away, you are excelling in design school, so what's the problem, why have you two lost touch? I thought this was a forever thing between you."

"I did too, but let's not talk about it now. I promise that I'll call Johnny first thing tomorrow. Will that make you happy?"

"More importantly, will it make you happy?"

Because there were people that had to leave right after the wedding supper, Sophie decided to throw her beautiful bouquet before the meal instead of after. She had initially thought that she'd walk up eight or ten stairs and stand dramatically backward on the hall steps and hang on to the railing to throw the bouquet in the traditional manner. But a moment of dizziness made her decide to just throw it forward, like pitching one of those Chicago famous sixteen-inch softballs underhand. To make it 'legal' she closed her eyes, hung on tightly to the railing and tossed it into the crowd, right to Sarah.

As soon as she caught it she handed it to her sister with the command, "Call him."

When the crowd had finally gone, stuffed with food and cake, Sophie and Phil's limo arrived, and they were gone too.

Everyone assumed they were going directly to the gorgeous Palmer House on prestigious Michigan Avenue, and then on for two weeks in Miami Beach where they had both family and friends. No one knew they were making one stop first that had been prearranged between them and the driver days ago.

By having to backtrack some, it was very dark by the time they arrived at the Ridgewood Cemetery on Milwaukee Avenue. As they arrived, the caretaker came out of his little office to tell them the cemetery was closing and that he was on his way home,

"You'll have to leave and come back tomorrow," he said as he stepped back into the building. They heard another voice as a different young man pushed his way forward.

"Aunt Sophie! Congratulations! Let me introduce our new guy, name's Bill, and he hates working nights," he added as he elbowed the new employee in jest.

Needless to say, Bill was confused as to why a well-dressed older couple would want to visit a cemetery so late at in the evening, but Wally explained that this was his kind of great aunt with her new husband and they had arranged to stop by the cemetery for personal reasons.

Wally quickly led them to the cemetery's golf cart which he had just washed and even added a little bit of wedding finery around the top. It took only minutes for Wally to drive them to each of the graves and then gave them a moment of privacy at each site while parking the golf cart so the lights could shine on them, but not too clearly. When this rite of passage was concluded, both Phil and Sophie felt the blessing of their former spouses, and they arrived back on the golf cart holding hands and smiling because they had settled something that was important to both of them.

Sophie kissed her kind-of-nephew, actually more of a distant cousin and then thanked Wally for the surprise decorations on the cart.

"It's a bit unusual, nu?"

"Unusual? Definitely! But Chris will be glad you liked them, she's the one who did it."

"So, how is your lovely bride?"

"She's expecting our third any day."

"Three, how wonderful! I was just telling one of my lodgers…"

"Sophie, darling," Phil said knowing that if they didn't leave now it could be a long time before they arrived at the hotel and it had been a long day for them both.

"You're right Phil. Give that wife of yours a big kiss from me," she said as she looked at her new husband, "No, I mean give her a big kiss from us, and kiss the children too."

As Phil was steering her towards the limo, she was still able to shout back, "Come see us soon and bring the children and the new baby. We're still in the same place, Foster Avenue!"

CHAPTER 7

As Scott rolled over Monday morning, he was painfully aware of where he was. This sleeping arrangement was not working out, his sleeping in this small space that was hardly bigger than a closet just off the office area. Sure, thanks to Madam Changs' 'generosity,' he was relatively safe, and he was dry and out of the weather, but he was still sleeping on a hard surface with limited bathroom facilities making him feel more like an unwanted dog. He thought again about the offer the Five had made just the previous week. Duff said their door was always open offering 'three hots and a cot' and maybe he should consider moving there. He'd have a whole room of his own, a decent bed and full laundry and bathroom facilities. There would also be some people his age and in the same financial condition as he was, but something kept him in Chinatown. Of course, one of his biggest concerns was if he did move north, public transportation costs would eat into his small weekly packet of cash that Henry gave him, and he would have quite a commute changing L's or buses at least once each way.

It was a little past seven, and as he opened his door there was already a buzz of language he didn't understand, and his nose was once again filled with the bizarre combination smells of heavy incense, pickled fish and sour cabbage kimchi brewing in its barrel behind the fish counter.

"Oh well," he said to himself, "no use complaining." As soon as the words were spoken, he realized they were the very words his mother had used on many occasions, usually occasions that included his father in some way.

He hurriedly dressed to avoid running into Madam Chang and

having her assign a few things for him to do. She wouldn't care if it was his day off, the first one he'd had for weeks, because in her eyes he was forever the slave and she his master, even though she agreed that technically Henry was in charge. It must be an Asian thing; he thought to himself while crossing the already busy street to the restaurant to wash and change. If it was someone other than his aunt, Henry would have to watch his own back, as it was, this woman had her tiny hands in everyone's lives and business whether they knew or liked it or not.

By nine o'clock Scott was dressed and washed and had grabbed a quick bite and was leaning against the truck that once served as his temporary home. Right on time, he saw the old guy come loping down the sidewalk towards him.

"Great day, huh?" he shouted over the noise of the L overhead.

"I suppose so Elli..."

"That's right. Elliot, just like that Chicago Ness guy."

Scott was embarrassed that he had forgotten the guy's name but grateful for the clue on how to remember it in future; if there was a future with Elliot Ness.

"Have we got far to go?" he asked as they immediately began to walk briskly east toward Lake Michigan.

"Blocks, only blocks," the guy said as he quickly picked up speed and strode ahead of Scott like a man on a critical mission.

"Looks like August is going to be hot," Scott added trying to make conversation with the man well ahead of him in case it might slow him down. "They say August is going to be hot all month, and dry." He added raising his voice.

Elliot wasn't answering so Scott broke into a trot to keep up. This neighborhood, like many Chicago neighborhoods, changed within a block from decent and even up-scale to that's far enough, turn around. This was becoming one of those 'turn-around and go home areas.' A half of a block later they turned into a dark alley in a derelict neighborhood. Scott paused briefly pretending he was out of breath as he surveyed the area for safety, "You're sure this is the place?" he asked as he looked around at the old houses whose windows were either covered with plywood or broken in various places. More than several lots were devoid of any structures at all, just piles of cement blocks, weeds and a few scraggly trees growing up through the rusted floorboards of a burned out car. Siding hung off the houses whose aging backs faced the alley that was also overflowing with debris. Anything with a semi-flat surface was covered with graffiti, some quite creative, much of it just brainless and crude. There were two ancient dumpsters that were rusting in place, and there was a stolen newspaper box upside down and leaning against a smashed garbage can. It looked like the whole block had been the site of a small but violent war and now it was virtually abandoned and no doubt condemned. For a place that was so close to the heart of the city and only blocks away from the busy Stevenson expressway, it was eerily quiet.

Elliot must have sensed Scott's trepidation, so he said brightly, "Hey, I know the neighborhood has a lot to be desired, but it's relatively safe. Clancy, the cop, comes through here all the time and the house in the front is one of those drug rehabilitation houses run by some church group, and it has some decent people in it, so that helps. It also helps that the few residents who have cars park them in the front and not back here, can't say as I blame 'em."

Scott took his eyes off the mess all around him and looked to where Elliot was pointing with his outstretched arm.

Despite the weeds, this yard was a fraction better than the others. There were still piles of junk along the fence that ran between the houses, and Elliot's building project was indeed behind an old rusty shed which itself was behind the old three-story building whose back steps were tilting precariously, I'd park in the front too, thought Scott.

The recently built shed didn't scream 'new' because the pieces of wood Elliot had used were old to begin with and their sizes varied along with their various hues, but anyone could tell there had been activity in the area because all the late summer grass had been trodden down to bare ground. There was a window on the side of the building that looked a little crooked, and it covered with what looked like the Sunday comics.

The old guy waded through the bits of junk here and there by the well-worn path and motioned for Scott to follow. When Elliot reached the door of the shed, he opened it and for Scott to follow him and take the tour. As Scott reached the entrance to Elliot's creation and looked in, the scene almost took his breath away. As though he was in a trance, Scott stepped partway into the one-room structure that was a riot of color bordering on psychedelic due to the chaos of vivid designs of the various pieces of billboard pieces. Scott noticed there was another window on the other side, this one smaller and straighter and between the colored comics on the windows and the various designs on the walls, it was difficult to stay inside surrounded by what could be described best as a bad drug trip.

"Holy buckets," he turned in circles taking it all in. So this is what you did with all those pieces of billboards and signs you were always carrying. Wow, it sure is…colorful."

"Well, you have to admit the studs break it up a little and I didn't want to put the printed side on the outside, I might as well put up a sign that said, new place going up-please add graffiti if you can find room and break in whenever you want. I know its wild, but I plan to insulate the place before winter."

"Are you going to spend the winter in here?"

"Why not, you see that orange metal thing that looks like a giant funnel?"

"Yeah, I think you were carrying it past me the first time I ever saw you."

"And you asked if I needed help with it."

"And you growled 'no' if I remember."

"Just checking you out sonny, had to make sure I could trust you."

"Trust me with what?"

"With my secret here. You see, I figured that maybe you'd ask me once, but would you ask me twice if you could help."

"As I remember I asked you more than a couple of times."

"And that's exactly why I decided you were okay and that you might want to see what I did with all the stuff."

"So now I see what you've done with the pieces of wood, but what are you gonna use that funnel for?"

Elliot smiled widely and shared, "That funnel thing is the reason I did this project."

"But, what is it?"

"I wondered that too, but I picked it up because I thought it would make a great chimney. You know, it seems to be some kind of metal and I thought that during the winter I could somehow attach it, so it stuck out above the roof line by drilling holes on each side near its top and threading in a metal rod. This way the chimney could rest on the roof and hang down inside. I figured I'd dig a deep pit in the dirt directly underneath it and make a fire to keep the place warm and it would pull out all the smoke."

It was hard to disagree with the guy's logic, but Scott wasn't sure it was a good idea. "Don't you think the fire might heat the pipe and then burn the roof around the hole and then the entire building?"

"You know, I thought about that and that's why I haven't put it up yet. I've been trying to think of something to put between the wood on the roof and the pipe going through it, any ideas?"

No one had ever asked Scott to solve a problem before and this was the first time he realized the sad fact. He couldn't remember any time in his life that anyone asked his opinion on any problem solving, not even his mother.

Surprisingly, that one question about how to make the roof safe from the hot metal led to an entire morning of conversation between the odd duo. As they sat on chairs outside of the shed, one wobbly wooden one and one rusty metal one, they exhausted ideas about the chimney, the conversation eventually led to Elliot's plan for a place to keep food cold.

"I remember back in South Dakota my father dug a hole a few feet down into the ground next to the house and then slid a tin liner he had made to fit down into it." Elliot relayed the information while staring skyward as though the details were written in the clouds. "It must have been next to the back door at our farmhouse, but I can't remember for sure, I was very young. I don't remember much about our ice box in our kitchen that we had when I was in grammar school except that every once in a while my mother would bolt out of the chair in the living room after a busy day and run into the kitchen. The next word we heard was usually "Rats!" as she carefully carried out a pan, full to the top, with melted ice and then mopping up the water she had spilled."

Continuing his perusal of the sky, he was back to his original thought. "He put a piece of wood over it when he finished, you know, kind of like a lid, and then a heavy blanket that he folded over and over on top of the wood. I remember my mom putting the milk and cream and butter and other things that had to be kept cold in the earth box. It must have worked because the stuff was always cold when it came out. Dad was always going on about the earth being a constant 40 degrees taking sideways credit for its success. After his accident, he was unable to bend down to get anything out or put anything in the box, and I think that's when we got our first icebox."

Elliot returned to staring at the clouds, and Scott checked his watch to see if he should be going thinking if he asked about the old guy's father the conversation would continue well into the afternoon. He still had his laundry to do. He was surprised that it was almost one o'clock and even more surprised that he had a pleasant morning with Elliot who wasn't too weird when you got to know him. They had spent the morning discussing chimneys and life while sitting near a cold campfire. Elliot had also buried an old washtub up to its top rim in the dirt and by the amount of ash in the bottom of the tub; he must have used it often. "I found the old grill grate off one of those new fancy round grills that someone had thrown out in the garbage," he said giving the nod to the grate in question that was hanging on the side of the shed. "It just fits, so we've been using it ever since to cook on. It's funny," he mused, "the grill I got the grate off of was rusted out at the bottom, but the grate looked practically new."

"Did you say 'we' just now when you talked about cooking? That would be you and someone from the house?"

"Nah, me and Leroy. You'll meet him in a minute; he should be around shortly with lunch." The words were hardly out of the old guy's mouth when a noisy pickup chugged to a stop. It took a bit of banging to get the truck door to open, and one of the fenders was about to fall off, but when the door finally opened, a man about Elliot's age joined them on their rickety old chairs while passing out hamburgers and chocolate malts from Wimpy's.

"Hey Leroy, this here is the young guy I told you about. This here is Scott."

"Happy to know you," the man with skin the color of maple syrup took Scott's hand and shook it with a firm grip. "Elliot here give you a tour yet?" he asked as he jerked his head in the direction of the shed.

"Oh yes, I got my tour, and I have to say it's not a bad building, despite the colorful insides and the price was right."

"I always tell him the only place that would be cheaper is jail!" Leroy laughed at his joke.

As soon as Johnny left the building kitted out in a new dark suit and what looked like a new white shirt and silver tie, both the Duffer and Clay were mute. Both were thinking their thoughts about this Lothario who had spirited off the most beautiful woman they had ever seen, and worse yet, he did it right under their noses.

Several residents past by the two silent men as they came into the dining room to snag a pastry and coffee before heading to bed. Thankfully they took their snacks down to the end of the room where a large television had been installed, thanks to their friends at the Goodwill store. Even though Pete no longer worked at their favorite thrift store, they had made friends with the new manager and he always kept an eye out for whatever was on their current list of things for which they were looking.

Clay lowered his voice even though the television was blaring and there was a discussion among the guys as to how much more aluminum foil it would take to get the rabbit ear antenna to get better reception. As one of the men passed them on his way to the kitchen to get some more foil, Clay asked Duffer, "So, what do you think?"

"What do you mean, what do I think, about what?" His response had a note of resentment in it.

"You know, I mean, Johnny taking out our sweet darling Claire. Whatever happened to that girlfriend of his, Sandy something? Weren't they on their way to getting married?"

Tony had a table set and ready when Johnny came in with his date. It had been a while since any of the residents or even Johnny had seen the other co-founder of the Five, Tony, who now owned this restaurant that was left to him in the original owner's will and which was now the talk of the town. It was a popular place before Tony took over, but now, even customers with a reservation often waited an hour to be seated.

As the owner strode through the doors that lead out from the state-of-the-art kitchen, Johnny noticed that Tony was decked out as well as the restaurant was. Now his tall, slim friend was dressing more like a real Italian wearing a shiny sharkskin suit, narrow tie, and narrow, black shoes. He had managed to recreate the look of the original owner who had been a true Italian and beautiful to look at with his longish silver hair and polished suit and pinky ring.

The restaurant no longer boasted an overload of plastic grape vines in every nook and cranny because there was now a feeling of elegance and refinement as soon as diners entered the room. Tony had hired a professional decorator from a firm who painted the walls a beautiful reddish brown that was complimented by the soft brown cloth tablecloths and dark green cloth napkins. Expensive pictures were expertly spaced down the walls, each with its light above illuminating the painting's details and lending a romantic touch to the room. The obviously expensive carpet was replete with similar colors and results were stunning, making Annetties a restaurant that felt more like an elegant mansion somewhere; quiet, refined and very expensive.

"Johnny," he said grabbing his old friend's hand. "Great to see you, it's been a long time, and this is?" He looked at Claire, surprised it wasn't the woman Johnny had tried unsuccessfully to bring to the restaurant several times so he could propose.

"This is Claire." Johnny offered no more explanation because he realized that he wasn't really sure what to say. He couldn't say that she was a ballerina, but sleeping on the studio floor and he didn't want to bring up Sandy, so it was the only answer that came to mind and he didn't add anything to it; at least not this time.

"Well, kids."

Who's he calling 'kids?' thought Johnny.

"Right this way," continued their host. As the couple followed, Tony led them to a lovely table complete with a spotless tablecloth that had a candle burning in its etched glass bowl, surrounded by fresh flowers. Johnny took note that it wasn't the table by the kitchen door like the Duffer said it would be and he smiled widely as he filed that bit of information away so he could use it tomorrow when he'd let it accidentally slip out while talking to the two weirdest guys he'd ever know.

Tony took the smile to mean Johnny was happy to be out with Claire and Claire took the smile to mean Johnny thought more of this date and her than she wanted him to.

The couple talked their way through the dinner hardly aware of the delicious cold borscht soup that had been served as an appetizer in tall and fragile glasses with a dollop of sour cream crowning the ruby red creation as it sat on a small serving plate to which a doily was added. They also gave only faint notice as their waiter brought the ingredients for a Caesar salad and dramatically prepared it in front of them.

Johnny praised the tenderness of the veal steak medallions and potatoes Lorraine but only briefly as to not to interrupt Claire's unraveling of her complicated life.

"Between you and those guys at the Five I can't remember what I've told who."

"That's okay," Johnny said generously, "start anywhere you like. I'll stop you if I've already heard it."

"Okay, that's fair." She told him all about wanting to be a ballet dancer her entire life with the ambition of moving to Paris someday to take French ballet lessons at the Centre de Danse de la Cite Universitaire. "That's probably why I stayed with Madam Zaretski so long. I mean, with her being a ballet teacher all these years and a ballerina herself I figured I had an in for future dancing or schooling. I would dearly love to become a Master of Dance anywhere, and I have worked long and hard to achieve my goal. This food," she looked down at her salad, "will be the most food I've eaten for years at one meal. I'll have to starve all week to lose this."

She saw the disappointed look on Johnny's face and added quickly, "But it's worth every bite. I've never had such a wonderful dinner with such glorious food."

It was then that Johnny knew they wouldn't be having any of the luscious desserts for which the restaurant was now famous. No tiramisu, or gelato with fig cookies, no cannoli's and certainly none of the Pignoli Nut Pie that was loaded with white pine nuts and was the restaurant's signature dessert. And no coffee to go with their delectable visit to dessert Nirvana that Annette's served with a lemon slice rubbed around the cup's rim before drinking.

Claire continued by telling him that she was beginning to suspect that her dance master was putting her on.

"What do you mean, putting you on?"

"I mean I almost never get dance auditions."

"And why do you think that is?"

"I've been asking that myself. The other twelve girls in class have been accepted to dance all over the city, three just last year in the Nutcracker that was performed at McCormick Place. One was a mouse, and the other two were snowflakes. I think I've grown too tall for ballet," she admitted while practically whispering the information.

This was an awkward spot for Johnny. He suspected that it might be her height, or she might not be good enough and that her dance master was just kind, or maybe she danced just fine, and the teacher had an ulterior motive. Either way, he was tired of talking about Claire and thinking of his missed dessert.

Claire had gone quiet, and Johnny suddenly realized that she had.

"I'm sorry," he said, "I was lost in thought."

"Anything interesting?" she asked with just a hint of sarcasm in her voice.

"It might be, and this is way off the subject, so I'll apologize beforehand, and this doesn't solve any of your dance problems, but we are desperately in need of a bookkeeper, actually a person to handle all of our assorted book work and the IRS and I was thinking that you might be the perfect one for the job." Before she could object he added, "Not that I would like to see, you give up your career, no, no, that's too important, but if you could give us say, twenty hours a week you could work and continue dancing. That way you'd have a little income, you did say you had a degree didn't you?"

"Yes, I have my degree," she said sounding a bit like her nose was slightly out of joint. After a pause, she inquired, "Would that include a room?"

"Certainly, certainly, we'd throw in a nice room with a soft bed and all the comforts of a home away from home." He was starting to sound like a used car salesmen who would soon be offering all sorts of perks, but he didn't care. All he wanted to do was go home and have this evening ended. Claire was beautiful, that was for sure, and her eyes were ones to get lost in, but there didn't seem to be anything or anyone she cared to talk about as much as herself. He knew all about her family and the girls at the school and her ambitions and the strange dance master and her son/not son and her health and on and on.

She even went on at length about the ballet originally starting in Italy, but because the French gave the poses actual names, it became French and then she explained at length the difference between Russian and French ballet much to his growing boredom. She hadn't even asked how his schooling was going or how much he had left before he graduated with a Business Degree and what he was going to do with it. He never even got a chance to drop his father's name to prove he was really someone himself and that he was going places.

It was late when the phone in the hall at Sophie's' rang, and Sandy padded out to answer it while leaving a trail of assorted scraps of colored paper behind her and some were still sticking to her robe and fuzzy pink slippers.

"Hello," she said as she noticed a blob of glue on her hand and was trying to wipe it off with a tissue from her pocket.

"Hi sweetheart, let's elope."

"Who is this?" she asked while giggling.

CHAPTER 8

Scott was spending more time with both Elliot and Leroy, and it was usually during the evening, Scott's time off. Henry had started closing his store promptly at 6 o'clock each evening even though there were tourists still coming into town for supper and shopping. Scott knew this was a bone of contention between him and his aunt, but Henry was adamant about closing early, and when Madam Chang interrogated Scott about it one morning, he felt like the proverbial ham in between two pieces of rough bread. Or perhaps it was more like being the filling in a steamed dumpling, stuck in the middle with the outsides getting hotter. He hated being in the middle of anything. That's why he worked hard when he lived at home to not be in the middle between his sainted mother and his loser father. He didn't take sides then, and he didn't want to take sides now.

As Auntie Chang sipped her morning tea, she innocently inquired, "My sister's boy, Henry," Scott had the feeling she was trying too hard to sound casual. "His business is good."

Was this a question or something rhetorical, he thought to himself, but he didn't answer.

She delicately folded her hands around her elaborate cup that was made without a handle for the drinker to warm their hands while enjoying the hot liquid. Looking directly at him she asked, "Between my nephew and me, you know I am your highest boss?" She paused for his reaction.

"I pretty well figured that out early, yes you are."

As she lowered her head to stare into her cup, she shared, "Henry has always thought that life owed him a living. Even as a child he acted more like an emperor rather than the second child of a relatively poor family. If you know anything about the Chinese," she looked up briefly, "we are restricted to having only one child. Our country is already overrun with people and the idea is that if two people only have one child for the next generation or so, eventually the population will decrease and our cities will not be so very crowed."

Madam Chang put her tea down on the leather blotter that covered over half of her desk and began to pace around the room. Scott got the impression that she did this often while pondering a problem because she scarcely looked where she was going, but never came close to bumping into any of the valuable art pieces.

"This is wrong of Henry to close his shop, my shop, early. Does he think that only rich people come during the daylight hours? Where does he go each evening? What does he do? What is pulling him away from his duties?"

Scott waited before he answered any of her questions, not wanting to get involved in the conversation or the problem. He didn't have to wait very long before she got to the part that included him.

"Scott," she said pronouncing it more like Sot, "do you have answers for me?"

"About where he goes and what he does?"

"Yes, I noticed that you are not around anymore in the evenings and I want to know if you and he are up to something."

"Hardly," Scott answered, trying to keep the dislike out of his voice. "Henry and I are employer and employee, and that's all. At six o'clock we all leave, and Henry stands at the top of the stairs, says good night, and watches us go. What he does after that, I haven't a clue."

Madam Chang had come to a stop in front of the magnificent carved art piece which depicted what Scott thought must have been a village somewhere in China. It was a scene that was replete with meticulously carved houses, boats on the water, intricate people going about their daily tasks and even birds in flight through the tiny clouds.

"Sot, I have a preposition for you." She looked directly at him.

He wondered if he should tell her that the word she meant was proposition, not preposition. He let it slid.

"All right," he answered slowly, wondering if he wanted to get involved.

"I want you to stay late one evening, make something up, some excuse, and see what he says and does."

"That's going to be pretty hard. My work is usually finished around five, and I am more or less just hanging around until six." He saw the disapproving look on her hard little face, so he added, "I mean, I help with the dusting and sweeping and such, but my official job is over, you know, the unpacking and logging in of the freight." He hoped he had covered his trail.

"Then you and I will have to work together."

Scott groaned inwardly while she continued plotting, walking her familiar path around the furniture mumbling to herself.

"I will send word that I will be coming to talk to him after he is closed." By the set of her tiny red lips, Scott could tell she liked the way this was shaping up. "I will wait until nearly seven before I arrive, giving him a chance to feel safe and continue what he does every night that I do not know."

She seemed to forget that this would be during Scott's time off and it would delay his supper by several hours. But then why would she care? She seldom thought of anyone else and how her decisions impacted their lives. After all, he reminded himself, I am no more than a slave, okay, he mused to himself, maybe I've moved up to the unwanted dog position.

"What do you propose I do while waiting for your arrival?" He asked the question as carefully as he could while trying to keep the sarcasm or the challenge out of his voice.

"I do not care. Dust some more." Now that she had a plan, she was all business and more or less dismissed him.

Dare he ask when this would be or just wait for her last-minute announcement? He took a chance and asked. I'm sorry madam, which night would you want this to be?

"Tonight, of course, weren't you listening? You may go."

"Thank you," he said as he headed for the door and his shoes which he had carefully placed on the mat in the hall. He all but backed out of the room.

By the time Scott changed his clothes and arrived at the shed, Leroy had already gone home, and Elliot was busy poking at the campfire. The evening was one of those soft summer nights that felt like velvet and brought thoughts of dates and convertibles to mind and long rides down the beautiful Lake Shore Drive, sometimes called the outer drive or as Chicagoans simply put it, The Drive.

"Well son, I thought you weren't coming tonight, kept your supper warm just in case you changed your mind though."

"I had every intention to come earlier, but that auntie woman made me stay late so she could spy on Henry. Honestly, how did she think it would work by keeping me around? If Henry is up to something, he certainly wouldn't be doing it while I was there."

"Do you think Henry is up to something?"

"I have no doubt of it."

"Because?" asked Elliot as he used a small shovel and reached deeply into the coals and drew out a square package of aluminum foil.

"Because I've noticed that some of the vases that I had unpacked that were in perfect condition when they arrived are now on Henry's office floor broken to pieces."

"What do you think that means?"

"You know what?" Scott said as he stood staring into the fire, "I don't care. I just don't want to get involved."

"Ever have a fire-roasted potato?"

"I can't say as I have," said Scott as he made his way to the rusty chair he claimed as his.

"It's the best thing there is," Elliot said as he laid the package on the ground. It's gonna need some butter though, why don't you reach down and get some."

"Reach down where?" Scott thought for a few seconds and then said, "You put in the cold box didn't you?"

"Did it yesterday and so far, so good, it's over there by the old shed covered with a folded blanket."

The cold box was not the only improvement that Elliot had made.

He had nailed on an old piece of wood across the side of the metal shed that fronted the new structure by about twelve feet. There were long nails protruding every foot or two acting as hooks so the grill grate Elliot used when cooking was hanging there as well as an assortment of pots and pans and lids and a smattering of utensils for flipping and turning food.

"You've been busy. Where did you get all this stuff?"

"Are you speaking of my cookware?"

"More or less."

"That's all thanks to Leroy. He's a first class garbage picker and dumpster diver."

"He got this stuff out of the garbage?"

"Do not disparage garbage young son, haven't you heard that one man's trash is another man's treasure?"

"Sure I heard it, but I thought it meant more like house trash, you know, old books and odds and ends that were still in good condition and not covered with yesterday's supper and wet coffee grounds."

"Allow me to enlighten you about trash and garbage," Elliot said as Scott was returning with the butter from the cold box.

"Hey, that box works great! Butter's nice and cold. So what was it you were saying about garbage?"

"Trash and garbage."

"Okay, trash and garbage. How do you eat this?" He asked while attempting to open the steaming hot package.

"First of all, be warned, the potatoes are very hot. Not like the potatoes of the old days though. Those we just buried in the coals until they turned black. The only trouble was not only was there only a few tablespoons of potato in the middle that was eatable because it wasn't part of the burned outside, and they had a nasty habit of exploding in your hands and burning your face when you took them out of the fire. Aluminum foil has given new life to the roasted potato, but it's still very hot."

"You're not kidding," said Scott as he laid the package back on the ground. "I suppose you don't have any hot pads?" Scott meant it to be a facetious question, but Elliot said, sure, right inside the shed."

"Which one?"

"The new one, naturally, the old one is just full of old rusted stuff that I use to create amazing things."

Sure enough, more surprises. There on an old green table that wasn't there before and stood leaning a bit on its side were assorted dishes and towels and hot pads. There was even silverware standing in an empty coffee can.

When Scott returned and sat down with his hot pad, he picked up his potatoes again without saying a word.

"As I was saying," began Elliot again smiling slightly, "the difference between trash and…"

"I get it, you don't have to explain. So where exactly did Leroy find all this stuff?"

"In a dumpster," the old guy responded with a now growing smile filling his face. Scott was getting tired of waiting for the story, so Elliot explained, "You see, Leroy lives down on 47th and Cicero Avenue. He and his brother-in-law kind of own a used furniture store."

"Kind of?"

"It's a long story, and it's a sad story, but I'll let him tell you sometime. Anyway," he continued, "Leroy grew up pretty poor in the south, Mississippi I think, and he was the ninth child out of fifteen, and the whole family knew how to squeeze every drop of anything out of anything, so Leroy's been a garba…uh, trash observer all his life. He says that it's the first thing he notices- trash. It could be a house for sale with a pile of stuff in front of it or a dumpster in one of those upwardly mobile neighborhoods where people start out but don't stay for very long because the husband gets a better job or a transfer to somewhere else. He says that a lot of people would rather throw stuff away than haul it with them. Point, in fact, that's how their store got started. He brought so much stuff home using that old rickety truck of his that their house and garage were both full to overflowing. So when his brother-in-law suggested they use the other side of his auto parts building as a used furniture store, Leroy jumped at it. Made his wife Ruby happy too, not only did she get her house back, but it gave Leroy something to do so he wasn't under her feet all day."

"He didn't have a job before?"

"He never really talks a lot about his past, but I get the impression that he might be a war veteran with a little pension money coming his way or maybe he gets some kind of disability check from a former job; ever notice that he kind of walks to one side, like he needs a front end alignment?"

"Maybe he gets two checks, one from each place. Maybe he's loaded with money and just pretends to be poor." Scott was trying to balance the hot foil package on his knees as he attempted to pull it open.

"And just why would he do that?" Elliot watched with interest to see if Scott would be successful at his task or end up dumping the entire thing on the ground.

"You know the old saying; once you're rich, you can never be poor," Scott said as he slid a pot holder over his hand to see if that would work to grab the foil.

"But that's just the opposite of what you said," corrected Elliot. "Do you think he's rich pretending to be poor?"

"Oh yeah, I guess you're right, now that I think about it, the saying is once you've been poor, you can never be rich. Sorry about that."

Scott finally had the package open at one end where he added butter and the salt that was sitting between them on the ground and pushed his fork into the steaming potato and took a tiny bite.

"Anyway," he said pulling in his breath trying to cool the hot food in his mouth, "I don't know a man yet that wouldn't want a better truck than the one Leroy drives. I think if he was rich that he'd upgrade to one that he could at least get out of without practically destroying the door and the fender falling off; wow," he added digging fully into the delicious surprise, "what did you put on these potatoes? They are the best I've ever eaten."

"They come with a large dollop of hunger. Do you realize that it's almost nine o'clock?"

"Each day is getting shorter and shorter, pretty soon it will be dark at four, and it's hard to know just what time it is anymore. So it's nine o'clock, already?"

"Will you turn into a pumpkin if you stay out later?"

"In a way, yes. It's more like I'll turn into homeless again, The Great Madam's stores close at nine thirty, and I have no way to get in after the door is locked."

"Then you'd better hurry back to mama."

"You mean Madam."

"No, I mean mama. She's got you all tied up and dependent on her you know."

"Yeah, I guess she does. She gives me only enough, so I have to depend on myself for the rest. She wants me to be clean but doesn't offer any facilities. Even Henry wants me tidy and clean-shaven but offers me no facilities. What do these people want from me?"

"And have you ever figured out why they would need to hire a white boy?"

Elliott's question got him to thinking again. "Yeah, I keep asking myself why they would hire the only white boy in town? I think it's because Madam Chang is out to ruin my life so she can find out what her nephew is up to and when she does she will just fire me and say it was because I'm white and that's why she involves me in her crazy schemes. When they turn out badly, she'll blame me."

"Got her little lap dog working overtime?"

"More or less, you'd have no idea what she's working on now."

"And she's got you right in the middle of it?"

"Pretty much, but I have no choice, she's got my job in the palm of her hand."

"And the job is still important to you?"

"You know, it really isn't anymore. I guess I'm getting tired of my big adventure and the work is getting boring, and I'm getting tired of being bossed around by not only one person, but two."

To his surprise Elliot did not encourage him to leave, not only did he encourage him to stay, but to get more involved with the working of Henry's store and the running of the town.

"Do you think I can come out of this in one piece?" asked Scott as he licked the butter off his fingers. "First of all, there's one controlling auntie, and one egomaniac nephew and I think it might be a bad idea to get between them."

"But this might turn out differently than you think. I think I would stay because it could be fun to see what's going on between them. You can always quit when it's over or even tomorrow if you're tired of the espionage."

"True," Scott said as he rose from his chair. "Either way, I've got to get back before I'm locked out."

"You know that my door is always open if you need a place to sleep. Leroy's brought over two twin beds complete with mattresses."

"Thanks, I'll remember that," Scott said as he looked at the shadowy shapes around him. "Wish me luck," he said as he stepped out into the dark alley. "Hopefully I'll see you tomorrow."

Snaking down the alley and staying in the middle of the road, Scott arrived at the store just as Madam was locking the door. "I thought it went well tonight," she said as she pulled the door to make sure the ancient lock held. "Tomorrow I have another plan."

"Well, there you go," muttered Scott as he headed down an isle full of groceries to the back room. "Another exciting day of adventure and probably no sleep tonight worrying about it, great, just great. I hope she's not planning on including me again."

Just as he thought, Madam was sitting in the desk opposite the bookkeeper the following morning. As usual, she was berating her employee about some earth-shaking mistake she must have made somewhere. It seemed like Madam was always scolding someone, at least it sounded like that. Maybe it was just the language and how they spoke it, but everyone sounded angry all the time.

"Ah, Sot," she said turning away from the messy desk and standing, "I must see you now upstairs. I must speak to you." Evidently, she hadn't slept well either because she penciled on one eyebrow a little higher than the other giving her face an inquisitive look.

Scott's answer was his first act of rebellion against Madam and the whole of Chinatown. "I can meet you in about 20 minutes, I have to go across the street to begin my day," he nodded to his kit bag and towel.

"Why you do not use the bathroom here? Why you go across the street to that bad family? I have a bathroom that you should use, not there, they do not like me, they jealous."

Madam was once again yelling at or talking to, her bookkeeper. The tiny, everyday woman rose and motioned for Scott to follow her upstairs to show him where the bathroom was. Evidently, it was beneath Madam Chang to do such a menial task herself, and she followed them at a distance. When he was dressed and ready, he opened the door and padded down the hall to her office.

"May I come in," he knocked and asked the door. He knew this was disrespectful, speaking to an elder before she spoke to him, but this morning he did not care. She was sitting behind her desk, but quickly she left it to sit in one of the ornate chairs that was in front of it. "Please Sot, sit down, sit down. Would you like some tea?"

He pushed his luck and said, "Yes, thank you."

She served him herself from her personal teapot using the tiny cups, and Scott knew that whatever she wanted to talk about couldn't be good.

"I have another plan," she said as she looked him squarely in the eyes.

CHAPTER 9

As soon as the Duffer suggested a Labor Day picnic for the following weekend, everyone in the dining room seemed interested. He mentioned it right after serving supper and before the residents started to leave." As long as no one living here has a vehicle," he said standing in the kitchen door, "I thought we could use the fenced-in area behind the building where, when this was a working armory, it's where the guys used to park. And if you haven't already seen it, the new guy at the Goodwill store brought over quite a large charcoal grill, and I thought we could celebrate the last of summer with an old-fashioned barbeque. That is if I can get the charcoal lit, it's never been a talent of mine because we never used charcoal on any ship I was on in the Navy."

No one laughed at his joke, so he continued, "So, Clay, write down charcoal lighter on the list- lots of it."

"You are going to have something suitable for a picnic, aren't you?" Jerry, the new guy, asked as he got up to put his dishes in the bus bucket by the counter that ran under the pass-through window. He made his comment while he was leaving the room, evidently tired of the company.

"Just what do you mean by that," Duff asked before Jerry's could reach the door.

"He means stuff like hamburgers and hot dogs; I'm sure you weren't planning nothing fancy or first class like ribs." Arnold, the other new guy replied from the opposite end of the long row of banquet tables. He had recently made the Five his temporary home and did not seem the least bit grateful for their services. Clay and Arnold had already gone around a few times concerning the running of the place and once it almost led to blows, and now the guy was challenging the menu for what they would be eating at the picnic.

"I think we should be having a little talk with Johnny next time we see him," Clay whispered to Duffer as he dropped his supper dishes in the bus pan while he passed him to enter the kitchen. He's got our Claire so much on his mind that he forgets we have to live with these cheese balls he lets in here."

The Duffer nodded to Clay and continued now that Arnold had gone too. "Okay, I'm thinking hot dogs, the good kind, you know all beef and fixings for a genuine Chicago dog, mustard, onion, tomato, that iridescent green relish, a dill slice, a poppy seed bun and some celery salt. I could throw on a few brats too and serve them with sauerkraut and chopped onion, what does everybody think?"

As Clay came out of the kitchen one of the men was asking, "How about roasting some corn on the cob? Know how to cook it on the fire? We don't want burnt offerings you know."

"Okay," said Duff as he took off his apron, "if this picnic is going to end up being a problem, I just say forget it. I've got enough to do without having to spend an entire morning getting the coals going, and then you guys being ungrateful for the meal." He turned and also left the room.

"Great," said Clay standing and looking down both sides of the table. "What's the matter with you guys? Sure, the Duffer's not the greatest cook in the world, but here you are arguing over a picnic. Don't you remember when you had to fight for every scrap of food you got? Was it so long ago that you've forgotten what it's like to eat out of a dumpster and sleep on the street or a doorway in the rain and the cold?" For a small man, he was growing taller with each statement.

"I say if any of you want to go back to the street, go because no one's stopping you if you care to stay, stop your ever loving complaining. I for one am getting tired of it."

He sat down with a thump spilling some of the coffee he had just brought in from the kitchen.

There was silence for a moment, and then somebody started clapping. Soon the majority of residents were applauding. Duff came in out of the hall and Mr. Albert Rose, usually a quiet elderly man, stood up and said, "On behalf of those here who are grateful for a place to stay and happy there is a man who will not only cook our meals but scours the city for some great food, I say we ignore the naysayers and have a grand picnic. I also think we should have some old-fashioned games, and I will even volunteer to be in charge of them. What do you say?"

He sat down accompanied by more applause.

After the men left, it was just the two friends sitting at the tables with the shopping list between them for the picnic supplies and Clay quietly adding sugar to his coffee.

"Well, it looks like after you said your piece things really changed and now everyone seems to think more highly of the picnic."

"Not an old problem friend. I think they have forgotten what it is to be on the street and to be part of the nightly zombie walk." Clay pulled out the chair next to him and put his feet on it.

"You did say zombie walk, didn't you?" Asked Duff.

"Yup."

"That's all, just yup? What exactly is the zombie walk?"

"First of all, it takes place traditionally between three and five in the morning, that's when it's the coldest. Just where did you say you spent your time when you were out on the street? I don't know anywhere you could have been that you wouldn't know about the walk."

"I've hardly ever slept on the street. I was kind of a transient between friend and casual stranger's couches."

"So you've never had the pleasure of being wet on by a dog to the amusement of their owners or poked by a cop telling you to move it along now? You've never spent days trying to dry out after a sudden rainstorm soaked you to the skin?" Clay's voice was rising, "And you've never been so sick with a cold, and your sinuses were pounding that you just wanted to lie down and die, but there wasn't..."

The Duffer interrupted Clay's tirade, "Okay, okay, so I didn't have it as bad as you did and I've never seen the zombie walk, so what is it for pity sake?"

Clay had gone into the kitchen during Duff's last question to get them each some more coffee and now as he added sugar to the second cup, his friend, whom he knew so little about, sat drumming his fingers on the table while waiting for an answer.

"Well, if you had been one of us you would have been aware there are pretty much two kinds of homeless people, who shall henceforth be referred to by their city name, bums. There are those bums who stay up all night and those bums who try to sleep when it's dark."

Duff sighed deeply knowing this was not going to be an early evening.

Clay took a sip of his coffee. "Now the guys that stayed up most of the night do it for two reasons as far as I can tell. One," he raised a finger and ticked it off with his other hand, "you can sleep warmer during the day when the sun is out, especially if you can find a spot on the grass in Grant Park as the white-collar office workers do. The second reason, he ticked off another finger, "It seems safe to walk the streets at night, you know, walk to stay warm and present a moving target. You know, there are those that get their jollies beating up old bums. And C," he raised a third finger and looked at it strangely, "I mean, three not C, it's too cold at night to sleep anyway."

He stopped as though he had answered the question completely.

"But you didn't mention the zombies."

"Right, sorry." Clay cleared his throat and continued. "So you've got your stay up all night and sleep all day guys, and then there's the sleep at night guys and stay up all day ones."

Duff groaned, "Is this going to go on much longer, I'm getting tired, and I run my food route early tomorrow and the stores like me there on time, especially after a holiday."

"Just hold on, I'm getting to it." Clay deliberately took a slow drink of coffee and placed his cup gently on the table prolonging Duff's agony.

"Some of the advantages of staying up during the day is that you can catch a nap during the daylight hours if you need one, but it's usually a short one, and you don't need to sleep in one place for too long. Cops don't bug you if you don't stay on the ground more than a half hour."
"Who cares about naps, could you just get to the point?"

"I am getting to the point. Now, the other reason for sleeping at night is maybe you've managed to find an abandoned building that's relatively safe. But, it doesn't matter if you're inside or outside, when it gets cold, you can't sleep."

"Even with a blanket and being inside somewhere?"

"There are never enough blankets at three in the morning, inside or outside. And if you remember, a street person has nowhere safe to leave anything, so they have to carry everything they own with them wherever they go, that's one of the reasons they don't have a lot of bedding." Before the Duffer could interrupt again, Clay added, "The lucky guys with the sleeping bags have them only because they were in the right place at the right time when the vans came, and they're light enough and small enough to carry around."

Duff yawned and asked, "Are we ever going to get around to the zombie walk and what do you mean the guys with the sleeping bags were in the right place at the right time?"

"Whoa bucko, I'm getting to all of that."

"How about soon Clay, I really need to go to bed." He checked his watch, "It's late you know."

"Hold your horses; I'm getting to it. But first I want to tell you about the vans." Clay shot his friend a look that said, listen to this and then I'll tell you what you want to know. "Every once in a while a van, which usually belongs to some church group in the suburbs or a medical facility or a general all-around do-gooder will pick out a neighborhood at random and pass out stuff. Sometimes it's clean needles for drug addicts, which I do not understand, and sometimes its food or blankets or backpacks, hats and mittens or medicine, you know, aspirin or that pink stuff for your stomach and other mild things. Sometimes you hit the jackpot, and it's..."

"Sleeping bags," the Duffer yelled as though he had scored a touchdown becoming punchy as he got sleepier.

"Yes," Clay added pointedly, "sleeping bags. The trouble is, none of the vans frequent the same place twice, so it's all a matter of chance."

"So, are we going to get around to the zombie walk tonight or should I ask you tomorrow? I've all but lost interest, and I'm beginning to feel like a zombie."

"Now you've got it. The walk takes place when the night sleepers can't sleep anymore because they are so cold and they decide it's better to get up and walk then to freeze to death where they are. Most of them are only working on a few hours of sleep, and they're cold, and they're hungry and most of all, they're really cranky."

"And they look like zombies?"

"Yes! Yes, they look like the half-dead creatures they are who are practically sleepwalking to find another place to lie down and at this point, and they don't care where."

"And is there such a place?"

"Not often, and that's why these guys are sick and every one of them has a chronic cough and they're always tired, exhausted, dog tired, and all they want is a shower, clean clothes, something to eat and then a good long nap in a warm place on a soft bed."

"Kind of like you were when you first came here?"

"Exactly, I would have done anything to stay here."

"And as I remember, we all thought you had died in your room."

"If I remember the story they told later," said Clay, "you were the only one who thought I was dead. Remember you even called your friend, what was his name, Lenny?"

"No, Leon. He and his wife used to own the cleaners over on Clark Street."

"Well. Whoever he was I was spared a funeral thanks to him."

"You should have told us you slept soundly." Duff had folded his hands and leaned across the table speaking like a doctor would if bringing bad news. "After all," he intoned, "it was three days that you were in your room without coming out."

"I told you," Clay said, draining the last of the coffee into his mouth, "I did come out, but it was during the night when I woke up. I used the bathroom, ate some food and went back to bed for more blissful sleep. Speaking of sleep, I thought you were going to bed."

"Oh no, thanks to you I've found my second wind and now I'm not tired anymore. I should wake you up early tomorrow for keeping me up so late and for that three-day dead stunt you pulled on me. Don't you remember that I got razzed pretty good for a couple of months for thinking there was a dead body in your room?"

"Well now," Clay was dipping into his Irish accent again, "aren't ya glad laddie that I was alive, who else would be telling you about the walk of the zombies?"

"There is that, but anyway, what do you think of the picnic idea? Think it will fly?"

Clay looked down at the crumpled list which he had been smoothing all through their conversation, "I think it will be grand. Do you think we need to pass it by Johnny?"

"That might be a little hard because he never seems to be around anymore," Duff answered as he stood and gathered both their cups. "He's probably out with Claire, smitten by her beautiful eyes and lissome figure and could care less about us."

They both sighed as though on cue as they added their dishes to the bus bucket, turned out the dining room light and retreated to their own rooms, each thinking their own thoughts about beautiful Claire and that cad and former friend Johnny.

"Sophie, enough, you are by far the biggest second-guesser in the world. Don't worry; we'll call them back later. Right now I suggest we go over to that little place we found last week and have a bite to eat. Aren't you hungry, Sweetheart?"

Sophie hung up the pay phone and joined Phil on the bus bench. "You don't mean that place with all those seagulls in the parking lot and the girls in those pirate costumes?"

"No, no, I mean that nice little restaurant a few blocks from the beach with that good coffee, those delicious pastries, and that melt-in-your-mouth corned beef."

"Corned beef this early Phil," she looked at her watch and saw it was only eight o'clock in the morning. "I think you're doctor would disagree with corned beef altogether."

"There's the answer," she said as she gently punched her husband on the arm. "That's why the girls didn't answer. It's after nine back home, and they're both out for the day. Sandy must have had an early class, and Sarah is at the phone company. See, there's no reason to worry." She struggled to get off the bench taking her illogical thinking about the Chicago-Florida time zones with her.

Phil thought momentarily about correcting her confusion about the time, the fact that the girls were actually an hour behind them, but he let it go so she wouldn't have another opportunity to worry, instead he asked, "Do you think they might have some leftover corned beef at that second place that they've maybe made hash out of and would serve some of it with eggs?"

She was holding his arm as they walked toward the corner among shops that were painted bright pink and blue and salmon, each one featuring some kind of seafood something or other, some with thousands of oyster shells attached to the base of their buildings like traditional brickwork, "I think," she said kindly, "it would be better just to enjoy where we are and eat something native this morning and skip the corned beef altogether."

He sighed and agreed, and when they reached the corner where the beach shop was with sky-high windows full of swimsuits and swim fins and surfboards and thousands of tee shirts, they crossed the street to catch the bus.

The sun was already warm and the day lay entirely ahead. Florida wasn't as bad they decided the previous night. The sunrises were breathtaking; the people open and friendly and there didn't seem to be the hustle and bustle or the street noise of Chicago. If anyone had a job down here, they didn't seem to be in a hurry to get there, and there weren't any L trains that slid by every fifteen minutes, breaks squealing with each stop. They were just another elderly couple, arm in arm, enjoying another beautiful Southland morning and making plans on what to take home for souvenirs while trying to remember which relative they were supposed to have dinner with tonight.

"I'm still not crazy about this four o'clock early bird supper everybody eats down here," said Phil as they seated themselves on the bus. "But I really like that game, um…"

"Shuffleboard?" She filled in.

"Yes, I could play that all the time."

"You already do Phil." She chided him kindly.

"I don't think there are any courts in Chicago, do you?"

"I've never heard of one, so maybe you'd better see if you can find a partner this afternoon for another game or two."

"I might just do that, but only if…"

"If what?"

"If you buy one of those colorful summer dresses at one of those beach shops. And one of those big purses that look like they're made out of reeds or something. And then buy one of those colorful scarves and tie it to the handle as everyone does down here and maybe some big sunglasses."

"Why indeed would I want to do all that?"

"Well, for one thing, I wouldn't feel so out of place wearing these shorts and my flashy shirt and you in your sturdy Chicago practical pantsuit."

To Sophie, it sounded like the beginning of what could be their first argument. An entire block passed by before she said, "I wouldn't want you to feel out of place with me, so," now was the time she could turn it into an argument or keep the peace. She decided to keep the peace. "Like I was saying, why not go a little native? If you want me to get a sundress, I think there's another one of those stores near the restaurant. We'll pop in, buy a dress and I'll change in the bathroom while you order breakfast."

"And you'll get the scarf and the big purse and the sunglasses?"

"Yes dear, I will." She sighed softly. "But not the sunglasses, unless they have some large enough to fit over the glasses I wear all the time."

"But at least we'd be starting," he said.

"Starting what?"

"Going native." He winked at her and squeezed her arm. "This could be fun you know!"

Chapter 10

Scott's mother was waiting for him at Henry's store when he arrived. She remembered he said that he was not allowed to enter the front door so she walked down the alley that was behind the long row of stores and bordered by the Stevenson Expressway to the east.

When she reached the back of Henry's store, she stopped and sat on the steps and watched the hundreds of early morning vehicles jockey for space on the Stevenson. Her face was contorted with grief, and there was no way for her to pretend the news she had for Scott was good in any way.

He saw her sitting and waiting for him while she wiped a flow of tears from her eyes and her face. He broke into a run and slipped onto the step beside her. As he slid his young arm around her, he asked, "What's wrong, mom? Somebody die?"

She loosed another torrent of tears and when they were finally spent she tried to speak, haltingly at first then, after a shuttering breath said, "Your father served me with divorce papers yesterday."

There was silence between them that was broken by his mother's renewed sobs. Scott checked his watch, hoping his mother wouldn't notice and saw it was time he was to be inside at work. The next decision he had to make was easy.

"Wait here a minute mom; I need to go in and talk to Henry for a moment." He was gone before she could object.

"Lisa," he said to the girl at the front counter, "when Henry comes in, tell him I called in sick today and I won't be at work."

Lisa's face turned from one of friendly greeting to one of concern.

"You realize that Henry doesn't think anyone has any excuse for not coming to work don't you?"

"Yes, I know. But my mother needs me today, and I don't care if he fires me, I need to be with my mom."

She said she'd convey the message to Henry and as he turned to leave she put her hand on his arm, "You a good son."

He nodded and returned out the back door scanning the alley for Henry's red sports car.

"How about a cup of tea?" He asked as he escorted her out of the alley to a less busy bakery at the far end of the Wentworth Avenue that was more for women and children seeing there was never the mass of men in white shirts and black pants there waiting for the vans.

He sat her down in a back booth and promptly returned with a pot of tea and several pastries on a plate.

"So, can you talk now mom? Here, drink some tea."

They sat in silence while they drank their tea, his mother pushing the pastries away. By having her face toward the wall, she was spared the stares of the curious onlooker, and the thought that her son had turned out so sensitive to others needs started her tears flowing again.

Scott, like men everywhere, was uncomfortable with tears, especially his mother's, so he just sat staring out of the little window in the back of the dining area.

"I'm sorry," she said wiping her eyes with a fresh napkin having soaked through her handkerchief. "It's just come as such a shock. I never in all my born days thought he'd leave me."

"But mother," Scott tried to skirt the issue, "it isn't as though he's been the best husband in the world." If he went on at this point, he knew he would say something inappropriate, so he stopped.

"That's just the point. He's been a lousy husband and an even lousier father. I've spent my entire life trying to make up for all of his shortcomings, giving up so much of my own life to do it and what do I get, divorce papers, at this age."

She didn't start crying again, and he was grateful. After a sip of the hot sweetened tea, she continued, stronger than before.

"When I think of the nights I stayed up worrying about him; if he'd make it home safely because he was so drunk, or if he'd get on the wrong bus and ride all over the city before he made it home. I hated his drinking, but I was raised by the kind of family that had the attitude of 'you've made your bed, now lie in it straight,' so I never felt I had any alternative but to stay with him.

She stopped talking, and there was silence except for the noisy chatter of the women having their morning tea and discussing their day.

"What can I do to help? Do the girls know?"

Ellen straightened her shoulders and answered, "Yes, they know. They were there when he came with the papers."

"Did they say anything to him?"

"Not a word. But then he didn't stay. He just came home around six with hat in hand, gave me the papers and turned and left."

"I opened the envelope, and if it wasn't for the girls being there, I don't know what I would have done. You know," she looked at him as she had another sip of tea, "I've always told you that the Lord cares for his own and this is proof. Normally neither of the girls would have been there at that time of day, they have their own families needing supper and all, but this night we had made a date to go out for dinner, just the three of us. I mean," she looked directly at him, "this is the first time we've ever done this. Can you see how God planned it all?"

Scott could see that his mother might be making something up to bolster her faith, but on the other hand, it could have been more than coincidence. To get off the subject of God, Scott asked, "So, what are your plans?"

"Right now I have no plans. Both the girls want me to move in with them, but I wouldn't do that."

"I don't blame you; you don't need to be a full-time babysitter for anyone."

"Now Scott, it's not just that, although I did think of that. They have their own families, and I think that since I'm still more than able to take care of myself that I'll stay at the apartment until this is all over."

"Do you have any idea how long that will be?"

"No, no idea whatsoever."

"And my father, where will be staying?"

"He, my son, will be staying with the girlfriend that he's had for over four years."

"What?"

"Yes, four years. I suspected something but didn't pursue anything because you know how bad your father's temper is. I just dismissed it thinking it would blow over like the other ones, but it didn't."

"Do you know who she is?"

"Not really, just somebody that is connected with the tavern. I don't know if she works there or is just a frequent flier. Either way, she can have him."

She blotted her eyes and asked, "Don't you have to be at work today? I'm so sorry; I was so lost in my thoughts that I completely forgot it was a workday."

"I've taken the day off, and before you can say anything, I took it off because I have not had any time off since I started months ago."

"Are you sure it's all right? I mean, won't your boss…"

"Don't worry about my boss. He isn't in a position to say anything. His auntie suspects him of doing something she doesn't know about, and he's on a hot seat of his own making." Scott changed the subject and asked, "And what's on your agenda today?"

"I'm pretty well free today. I guess that's why I came down to see you. That and since you don't have a phone or someplace I can contact you, I thought I'd take the day off and come and tell you my news in person. After all, there's no big lout asleep in my bedroom because he'd gotten home late again last night. No, I have the day."

"Then finish your tea and come with me. I want you to meet someone."

"Oh Scott," was all she got out before he said, "No arguments now, I've wanted you to meet Elliot for a long time now, and there is no better time than the present. You'll like him, he's taken me under his wing, and he's a nice guy. I think he's even a Christian like you, at least he acts more like you do than anyone I know."

Elliot was surprised to see Scott and even more surprised that he had brought someone with him.

Scott was surprised to see new lawn furniture between the two sheds.

"Well now," said Elliot, "it's a good thing today is not my washing day, you could have found me in less than decent circumstances. And who is this lovely lady you've brought along?" Elliot had stepped up to meet Scott's mother with an open hand and welcoming expression.

"I'd like to introduce you to my mother, Elliot, this in my mom, Ellen. Mom this is Elliot Ness."

Ellen looked surprised that anyone would name their son after one of the prohibition's most famous men.

"Actually it's Nussbaum, but it was easier for Scott to remember my first name if he thought my last name was Ness. I am delighted to meet you; won't you please come and try out my new deluxe lawn furniture?"

As he led them to the gaudy furniture that sported cushions of vivid aqua and pink flowers and bright green leaves he explained, "I was as surprised as you about this furniture."

"First of all," Scott interrupted, "let me catch my mom up as to why you're living here. I know I've told her about you as a person, but come to think of it, I don't know why you're living here."

"No guesses either?"

As they seated themselves on the ultra-cushy patio chairs, Elliot walked to the cold box and got on his hands and knees and produced some orange juice which he poured into matching glasses and placed on the patio table in front of them. "I'd include some ice, but I haven't figured out how to make a freezer yet."

When they were all sitting drinking their juice, Ellen grateful that Scott hadn't said why she was there, Elliot began his explanation.

"I'm originally from South Dakota, a farm boy from way back. If it weren't for a woman I loved with every fiber of my being, I wouldn't be here today."

"A woman from here?" Scott asked as his mother shot him a warning look. "Don't worry mom, if Elliot doesn't want to answer anything he doesn't."

"That's right, I believe in open relationships, there were too many closed ones where I grew up; no one knew what the problems were about and no one dared asked; everything was always one big secret. We lived lives of second-guessing, always afraid to ask for the truth to be told; I have no idea why we did that either."

Ellen nodded in agreement while Elliot continued. "I fell in love with a girl back home, and we planned to marry as soon as I graduated from a college known for their advanced agriculture programs. I was going to help my parents by staying on the farm and contributing the updated information I had learned at school.

"We had two houses on the same acre that had been there for several generations, one large and one smaller. The idea behind them was that the retiring family, or should I say the family whose kids were grown and gone lived in the more modest house and the child who was married with kids, who wanted to be a farmer and carry out the family business, lived in the big house. That way it could be continued over and over throughout the generations, each family contributing to the other.

"Anyway, we had the wedding date set and all the plans made and the invitations printed and ready to be mailed. We'd even ordered the cake and had a deposit down on our honeymoon hotel. Then my older brother came home from the Air Force while I was finishing my last semester at Ag. school, in less than two weeks they were married and moved to his base in California. I was devastated when my parents called and told me. It threw me for such a loop I almost didn't graduate. I didn't care about anything for a while, and if it hadn't been for a professor of mine who gave me the Dutch uncle speech, I would have slunk away and ended up no telling where spending a life feeling sorry for myself."

Elliot went silent and Scott decided it was too personal to ask any more questions. Ellen thought different and said, "How long did it take to get over the hurt and pain?"

"I don't know if I have even yet. It's been well over thirty years, and it still haunts me. But not as bad as when it first happened. I'm able now to see the possible negative side of our relationship, or you might call it the everyday side. You know how it is when you remember old boyfriends or girlfriends you always remember them in glowing terms and always paint a rosy picture in your mind as to how your relationship would have been. At some point, you realize that your memories qualify as fantasy and that's all. No one could guarantee any relationship would last or be happy."

Ellen was staring at her orange juice and quietly added, "My husband filed for divorce and brought the papers over for me to sign last night." Because she had made the statement so casually, Scott was not sure she said it.

Unknowing what to say about Ellen's matter of fact statement, Elliot continued his narrative. "When I first got the news about my fiancé and my brother, I couldn't believe it, and I didn't know how to deal with it. Here I was with only a semester to go, and I thought I was all set in life. She was a farm girl and perfect for the life we planned to live. But suddenly, out of the blue, it was over."

"It's odd you said, out of the blue. I've been awake all night thinking of that very thing. Is this divorce something out of the blue, or did I know it was coming?"

"I think that if you look back on your marriage, you might have seen the signs, but didn't want to acknowledge them. You know, not wanting to rock an unsteady boat? May I ask how you feel about it this morning?"

Scott was beginning to feel like the preverbal third wheel and said, "Hey, since it's early, I'll walk over to that little cafe and get us some coffee." When he saw the look on Elliot's face, he knew what he was going to say. "And don't tell us you can brew some up over the fire, remember, I've had your coffee, and it certainly leaves something to be desired."

"Fine then, go," said Elliot teased as he reached for his wallet.

"Nope, these are on me," Scott said as he turned to leave. "You still take your coffee black, mom?"

"Not today. Today I need a little cream and sugar if you don't mind."

"Black, Elliot?"

"Not today for me either, I'll try what your mom's having."

No sooner had Scott left when their conversation continued about marriage and love and betrayal.

"Did you ever see them again?" asked Ellen."

"A few times, but they mainly stayed in California because my brother was a Lifer."

"What does that mean, a Lifer?"

"It means that he kept re-enlisting for over twenty-five years making a career of the Air Force. They're still in California even though he's finally retired. I guess they're living in splendor from the way they write in their Christmas cards to the folks. Either way, after it happened, I couldn't stay on the farm any longer after I graduated and did what I had initially planned to do with my parents, so I waited for a little while and then decided to leave to find my way in the world so to speak.

"What did you do then, what did your parents do?"

"What could they do? They saw my heart was broken along with my spirit, but there was nothing anyone could do about the pain or the circumstances that led up to it. For a while we all pretended nothing had happened, but as I said, my heart was no longer in farming, and after a long talk with my younger brother, who, by the way had bought his own farm nearby and promised to help dad out, I left South Dakota and moved around the country for a few years."

"Did you mean you traveled the country, or did you say you moved around the country?"

"Very insightful of you to notice the words, Ellen, I got around, however, I could. I hitched rides; I rode the rails, I took a bus when I earned some money washing dishes in some dive in some dinky little town."

"You were running away."

"You might say that."

"I only asked that because it's what I'd like to do, just run away and be someone else for a while."

"And who would you like to be, just for a while?"

"I don't know, maybe a housewife with a loving and caring husband that has a day job and comes home each night and helps me do the dishes while we discuss our day, or maybe a single woman who has a job downtown doing something interesting that paid well and I'd meet some exciting people who I'd go on break with and gossip about the new floorwalker."

"Floorwalker? I don't think they have those anymore!"

"I suppose not, see I'm showing my age. But I never thought that at my age I would be divorced either." She twisted her tissue to shreds as her eyes filled with tears.

"Life throws us curves all the time," Elliot said as he grabbed a napkin and gave it to her. "Your son tells me you're a Christian. What kind of a Christian are you?"

"What do you mean what kind? How many kinds are there?" She dabbed her eyes but didn't look at him.

"My mother always said 'In this world, there are believers, non-believers and make believers.'"

Ellen sat in her gaudy chair and thought about the statement as Elliot brought out more juice and filled her glass.

"We won't have room for coffee after this," Ellen commented while staring at her full glass of juice. "And I'm afraid I had too much tea this morning with Scott, although I don't remember drinking any of it. What I'm getting at is, is there a bathroom somewhere that I can use?" She looked around at the house and yard in hope.

"We certainly do have a bathroom, albeit a little seedy, but everything works well, and it's the one I use, and clean," he added. "Here, come with me." He put out his hand and helped her out of the chair. "It's in the house, watch your step though when you get to the stairs. I've shored them up as best as I can, but, as you can plainly see, they still list to one side."

"Thank you," she said as she resumed her seat at the table. "It must make living in the shed easier that you have a bathroom to use. Do you use the kitchen too? It certainly is messy."

"Not as a rule. I try to stay as independent as possible by supplying my own needs."

"I like the sound of that. Maybe I'd like to try a bit of independence too."

"Whatever you do, go slowly. The decisions you make now can affect the rest of your life."

"Like the ones you made that landed you here."

"Exactly."

"So, Mr. Ness," she said teasingly, "what do you think I should do first?"

"I think the most important thing is to decide if you're a believer or make-believe, it will make all the difference in the world."

"You are a very wise man you know. And just the person I needed to talk to today. I believe my son has found a valuable friend in you, thank you."

"My pleasure," he said as he stood and dramatically bowed low.

"Do I want to know what you two are talking about," asked Scott as he gingerly walked across the grass holding three to-go cups of coffee.

"We're talking about life, and getting on with it," his mother said and then drained her glass of juice.

CHAPTER 11

Thankfully Labor Day dawned bright and sunny, and the Duffer was busy in the dining room laying out his vast supply of picnic foods on several banquet tables. He hummed with joy as he arranged the items in their proper order; the charcoal and lighter and plenty of matches on one end of the table and the other end that was groaning with six beautiful Texas watermelons and all manner of picnic food in between. By nature, he was a talker and a sharer of everything he knew, but the money he used for the purchase of this meal was his secret and his alone and needed it to stay that way.

No one knew or could remember the fund that had been initially factored into the budget that allowed his department a specific payment of money into the kitchen fund each month. It was growing nicely now that he had contracted with grocery stores and restaurants around the city for their out-of-date products and leftovers. His goal was a new van, well, not brand new, but nicer than the piece of junk he was driving now. Nothing says turn-off like a VW hippie van, flowers and all, pulling up at the back door of some of the most popular places to glean their extra food. As far as anyone was concerned, he fed the residents entirely on someone else's food and there were a few naysayers to his menus, but it would be worth it at the end. He could see the vehicle now, something tan with the Five's logo on the doors. That could be an opportunity in itself, creating a logo.

He was laying out the buns next to the ketchup and mustard when Clay made him jump as he cleared his throat to get Duffer's attention.

"How many times do I have to tell you, Clay, don't ever do that!"

"Sorry, at least I didn't come up behind you and yell 'boo'."

"It's a good thing you didn't. I would have probably automatically knocked you down, and that wouldn't be pretty. I was deep in thought about this picnic, want to make sure I have everything we need, gonna put those two knuckle brains in their place."

"You don't mean Jerry and Arnold? Don't worry about them. They're the kind of losers that are always looking for an argument. I'm sure everyone else is just looking forward to a nice day and good food."

"I hope you're right; everyone's signed up to come. Here, help me put these brats and dogs and the polish sausage on a tray. Put them next to the buns, notice I got both white poppy seed buns for the Chicago dogs and the wheat buns for the brats and enough kinds of mustard to satisfy anyone thinking they had gourmet status."

"Where do you want all this other stuff?" Clay gestured at the fresh cucumbers and tomatoes and onions that were piled near the vibrantly colored sweet relish, the gallon jar of kosher dills and the celery salt.

"Put them there by the mustard. I've got absolutely gallons of iced tea in the fridge that's just the way I like it, nice and sweet just like the glorious nectar you get in Georgia and throughout the south, yum. And whatever you do, don't tell anyone about the corn."

"What corn?"

"That's right; you don't know about my surprise. If my good friend, you glance underneath the table you will notice a gunny sack that is quite lumpy." The Duff lowered his voice and practically whispered into Clay's ear, "It's full of beautiful farm fresh corn. Glorious corn on the cob just waiting to be roasted and then slathered in melted butter." Duff started humming again as he walked down the length of the table rearranging the food as he went and smiling to himself.

The charcoal finally lit after using a can and a half of charcoal lighter on the weak flame; the last squirt almost singeing off Clay's eyebrows. Since the day was so beautiful the men of the five dragged banquet tables and chairs outside and sat them close to the building in the shade and to the far side of the new basketball hoop that was installed just that morning.

Albert Rose kept his word and had a basketball hoop up before the day began, thanks to their friends at the thrift store and an old ladder he found in the back and some tools they jury-rigged to get it up, and he was busy signing up men for teams. It got him off the proverbial hook because there were very few games he could think of that would be interesting to grown men. Everything he knew about games he remembered from the ones he had played with his children, certainly not suitable for grown men and Al decided that his investment of a new ball would advance his status there at the Five as long as he was a resident.

Neither Sarah nor Sandy were home for the long Labor Day weekend, and neither were their landlords. Sophie and Phil had met some new people from the shuffleboard set and had decided to extend their Miami honeymoon by another week. "Besides," said Sophie shouting into the phone so Sandy could here all the way from Florida, "Phil doesn't want to miss the last tournament for shuffleboard. He's in the final four," she said proudly," and I've got to get all the wear out of my new Florida clothes before we come home. They'd look silly up there."

Sarah and Pete spent the long weekend with her parents on Chicago's North Shore so Pete could be introduced to the important people at the club and friends of Sarah's family and Sarah and her mom spent their time making wedding reservations and plans with the country club. "One has to book a year in advance, darling," Sarah's mother said with her country club voice, "if one wants to get the date and the amenities one wants."

While the women, even the Perfect Princess sister, who was remarkably friendly, made plans, the men played golf arranging to meet at dinner time for the club's traditional outdoor steak and lobster buffet. Pete worked hard to not be amazed at the nonchalance with which club members swaggered through their day. No one mentioned green fees, the clubs and cart rental or the lunch costs or the had-to-be expensive evening buffet. All charges were merely signed away in almost a careless fashion. It made him feel oddly uncomfortable.

Sarah noticed that Sandy must be working on yet another extra credit project for design school judging from the small scraps of craft wood near her door. Other then the four of them, Sandy, Sophie and

Phil and herself, there was no one else that was currently living at the rooming house.

Carl, a former resident, had finally found the love of his life or was it the one who loved his cool car as much as he did and he had moved farther into the city to be near her. They heard it cost him a fortune to garage his car.

No one knew where Tex had gone. They had heard he lost his job in the suburbs working for that contractor and that he was either living in some Chicago flophouse and probably frequenting every bar and tavern that played country music so he could drink himself to the floor. It was always possible that he had managed to hoodwink his former wife into sending him a ticket back to Texas.

Sarah stood in front of the glass in the front door and watched as mounds of colorful fall leaves gathered by the front steps that led up to the porch and with every blast of the August wind they swirled up and down the stairs as though waiting to get into the house. She imagined that even to a casual passerby the place probably looked empty, lonely and forlorn, kind of like the way she felt and her melancholy mood surprised her. She and Pete had a marvelous time with her family. Well, she certainly had, but Pete seemed uneasy with the lifestyle. He'll learn to love it, I'm sure, she mused. These friends of my family can do great things for him; they can open doors if he lets them.

The picnic, much due to Duff and Clay's efforts was a complete success and even Jerry gave them a backhand compliment when he said it wasn't as bad as it could have been. But now there were piles of corncobs and garbage bags full of watermelon rinds to gather together along with two overflowing garbage cans that needed to be hauled to the alley for pickup. The basketball was forlornly rolling around the back lot, and when the Duffer picked it up and asked Clay if he wanted to play H-O-R-S-E, Clay said: "Absolutely not."

"It's not that I'm tired, mind, it's just that you're about three feet taller than I am and it wouldn't be fair now would it?"

"Okay little guy, I'll let you out of this one, but I think you are just too tired and old to play."

"Okay, I won't argue with you there. I am tired, and it seems like ten years ago that I helped out at Annetties with those fancy-schmancy parties instead of just last year. It didn't seem to bother me then to be on my feet all night. Now all I want to do is to sit down and put my feet up."

"Not so fast, we still have to get this garbage to the back curb."

"Not me sonny, find one of those young lads to do it."

"Good idea," said Duff as he also walked away from the full cans into the building where several guys were lounging around the television, two of which were moving the rabbit ears trying to get in a better picture.

"I think we've done enough today," Duff said as he headed to the television area. "Let's take it easy the rest of tonight. Anything good on TV?" he asked one of the guys giving directions to the antenna man. "Has anyone seen the TV guide?" Duff asked the general populace then he remembered and said, "Wait a minute, its Monday right, and we are not watching Green Acres tonight. After a hard day of cooking a superb meal, I get to pick, and I pick The Avengers."

As he made himself comfortable he added loudly, "Don't anyone even think of a late supper, the kitchen's closed on account of illness, this guy is sick of cooking."

Several pillows hit him at the same time.

Much to the surprise of Ellen's girls, she turned down both their invitations to their Labor Day family picnics, even though one was going to be quite an affair, sponsored by her son-in-law's shop's union. This union celebrated every holiday with a lavish party, paid in part by their union dues, but for Labor Day they went all out. The free picnic was held at a nearby public park and the day was full of eating and drinking and game playing. Men and boys alike teamed up for sixteen-inch softball while the children did the three-legged sack race, the balloon toss and the relay race carrying a raw egg on a spoon. The highlight of the kid's games was the one where the kids had to run down to a pile of clothes and put on an entire outfit, shoes, hats and all, and then run back in order for the next teammate to put the clothes on and run down and change again. It was even funnier when a very small boy was just ahead of a very large boy who had difficulty fitting into the clothes the small boy had chosen. As long as the clothes were on the body somewhere it counted, so many a large child ended up with jeans on their arms and a belt around their neck and a shirt worn like a hat.

Moms would sit on the sidelines of the picnic and tend their babies and visit, thankful for the rest.

Ellen, Scott, and Elliot spent Labor Day downtown at the lakefront enjoying people watching and eating the picnic lunch Ellen had packed. They sat on a blanket that Leroy had given to Elliot on the beautiful grounds of Grant Park as they waited for the orchestra to begin Chicago's final outdoor concert that would go well into the night followed by spectacular fireworks. Ellen was happier than Scott had ever seen his mother, and he figured Elliot was the reason why. They seemed to have many things in common, and he was able to help more than Scott could, seeing they were more the same age.

It was another soft, velvet night and Scott did not return to Chinatown, but rode home with his mother and stayed in his sister's room that night listening to the L's rumble as it passed close by on its infrequent holiday schedule.

Elliot thought of walking, it wasn't far to where his little shed stood, but he knew he'd never get across the eight lanes of traffic by the Field Museum and besides, anyone who walked in the city after dark in his neighborhood was taking his life in his own hands. He reluctantly back-tracked and took the red line the short distance to Chinatown thinking about the seemingly endless summer nights he had spent deep in the South Dakota farmlands while the train rocked gently back and forth. Elliot could see, as he closed his eyes, the massive fields of oats that undulated in the wind, golden and ready for harvest. He reluctantly thought about the woman he had loved with all his heart as she pushed her way unbidden into his thoughts; and how she broke his heart so carelessly and how it changed his life forever.

Tuesday morning Sarah was still half asleep when she opened her door to go down the hall to the bathroom. It had been late last night when Pete dropped her off, and though she was still half asleep, she thought she had seen someone slip through Sandy's door that wasn't her sister. She wondered if it was Jilly come back for a visit, or maybe New York didn't work out, and she was back for good. If that were the case, things would liven up around Sophie's now; maybe even Friends Together Night could start again with Jilly entertaining with some of her stage friends after supper. Wait a minute; Sandy didn't know Jilly, why would she be bunking in with her when there were all the other rooms standing empty. But the girl who slipped into Sandy's room had the same dark hair as Jilly. Oh no, she thought, I hope Sandy hadn't tried to dye her pretty blond hair only to have it turn out badly. She worried about this as she closed the bathroom door, looking for telltale signs of hair dye in the sink and on the towels.

Only minutes later when she opened the door, the hall was deserted. She slipped up to Sandy's door and put her ear to it but didn't hear a thing-strange, had she gone back to bed? She thought of knocking to talk to her sister and check out her theory, but Sarah had overslept, and she would barely make it to work as it was. Traffic would be heavy this morning now that vacations were over and everyone was back at work. She'd find out anyway in eight hours or so when she got back home, interested in finding out why her sister was in a hair-dying mood.

When Claire walked into the dining room of the Five the following afternoon, neither Duff nor Clay knew what to say. Duff had just carried in a huge quantity of food from his foraging of city restaurants and groceries, and much of his haul was still sitting on the counter. He was taking a break with his feet up in the dining room having the last of the iced tea from the day before in a tall glass filled with ice. Clay had just been commenting about the picnic again when they both stopped and stared at the woman they were both over the moon for.

"Um," she said hesitating before she added "is Johnny here?"

"Nope," said Clay briskly, haven't seen him."

"Is there anything we can do for you?" The Duffer asked. He was still hurt from being upstaged by Johnny, who already had a girlfriend

"Well, I, um." she started again. "He wanted me to come in and take a look at the books today."

"Just which books do you mean and who is the 'he' that told you?" Clay was in a foul mood.

"You know, Johnny and the accounting books for this place."

Since neither one knew what she was talking about, they remained silent.

She was apparently flustered, but began tentatively, "When he took me out for dinner last week he asked me to look over the books to see if I wanted to do some bookkeeping for this place." She hurried on, "And he said I could have a room here if I took the job."

More silence and two faces made of stone. "So, could I see the books and then maybe the room?"

Each man was trying to figure out exactly what she was saying, finding it difficult to grasp what this sudden announcement meant. Did Johnny plan to have her working here so he could be nearer to her? Didn't he realize there were others that liked her as much as he did? How could he be so insensitive?

No, this couldn't be good, both men thought in unison. Finally, the Duff broke the silence by asking, "Which would you like to see first, the room or the books?"

"I suppose the room," she said in the small voice of someone afraid of their surroundings. "That is if you think it's a good idea for me to stay here. You seem to have a lot more men than women."

"Right now," answered Duff, "we don't have any women at all. It would just be you. Do you think you could handle it?" He knew there was a cruel note to his voice and he didn't care.

Claire melted in front of them, tearing up while she reached for a chair. As she sat, she said through her tears, "I have no other place to go, I've run away from Madams. I think she's crazy and that son of hers gives me the creeps. I didn't want to get physically hurt, and if I can't stay here, I don't know where I'll go or what I'll do."

The tears were fully flowing now, and Clay got up to retrieve a few napkins from the serving counter.

"There, there lass, there's no call for waterworks. I'm sure we can work something out. After all, if Johnny wants you here, I guess that's where you need to be. It's just that he hasn't said anything to us about you. I guess you two have been seeing a lot of each other; we certainly haven't seen much of him lately, nothing at all over the long weekend."

She raised her head and said, "I haven't seen him since we went out to that fancy place for supper well over a week ago."

Now the Duffer instantly joined Clay at her side. Both men pulled out chairs simultaneously and sat down near her and Duff asked with a voice full of care, "Would you like some iced tea? It's left over from the picnic yesterday, but it's still good, nice and cold and sweet."

"Sweet? On no, thank you. I don't dare."

Duff had forgotten that she didn't eat anything sweet, or didn't eat anything at all."

"Well then," asked Clay in a soothing tone, "how about a big glass of ice water? It would hit the spot on this warm day."

"Okay," she said while hiccuping. "Thank you, that would be nice."

If there ever was an instant transformation, it occurred that late morning to both the Duffer and Clay. Suddenly all was forgiven where Johnny was concerned, and they were back in the running for her affections.

"I think we should start by showing you the pretty room," said Clay as he put his arm under hers to help her up." It's a soft shade of pink, but if you'd like us to paint it blue, we'd be happy to; anything to keep our new accountant happy." He led her out the door to the four rooms that had been set up for women while Duff trailed behind talking about getting the account books and meeting her in the office. Clay noticed he said meeting her and not him when mentioning the next confab.

The Five now had a genuine degree-wielding accountant sitting at her desk with Duff in a chair next to hers forgetting all about fixing lunch for the few residents who were hanging around the Five, yet to find employment. Duff wasn't about to give up his seat close to Claire using the excuse that it was vital that he explained his complicated system of income and outcome in the food department while not wanting her to be aware of his actual food budget.

"Johnny is the one that will show you how to do all the other accounts, you know, utilities and such and insurance and who pays what, you do know that we're privately funded, don't you?" He asked before she got to the kitchen money. "And we ask all of our residents if we can share in their welfare food stamps. I'm not sure if it's legal or not, but it makes a huge difference in our food budget."

Claire looks startled as though wondering what she was getting herself into, welfare fraud?

"Speaking of Johnny," asked Clay as he came into the office to see when Duff was going to start lunch, "anybody know where he is? I haven't seen him for several days."

"I have no idea," said Claire distracted and anxious to ask Duffer about the welfare thing.

Sarah was worn to a frazzle when she returned from work. "I can hardly believe it," she said while kicking off her shoes in the hallway and entering the dining room to talk to Sandy as they decided what to fix for supper seeing they were the only ones there.

"I got called into the office today and do you know what they wanted?"

"Nope, what?" said Sandy as she rummaged through the fridge to see what they could make out of the assorted leftovers.

"They wanted to promote me. Can you believe it?"

"Why not?" Sandy said straightening up. "There is nothing in that fridge that is worth eating, and we've got to clean it out this weekend before Phil and Sophie get back. We were both gone too long over the weekend, and everything is spoiled. By the way, have a nice time at the country club?"

Sometimes Sarah wasn't sure if her sister's comments about her rich adoptive parents were a dig at them because they were wealthy, so she answered cautiously.

"We had a great time. There was a picnic at the club and Pete, and my dad played golf with two of my dad's friends. Mom and I," she looked over to see if Sandy winced when she used the word mom, "mom and I," she continued, "did a lot of planning for the wedding. The perfect princess sister was even friendly," she added to help lighten the situation.

"That sounds like fun, you planning a big wedding?" Sandy took a wilted head of lettuce out of the fridge and frowned.

"Kind of, I think we're figuring on 300."

"Did you say 300?" She threw the lettuce in the garbage can.

"Um, yeah, why?"

"No reason, I mean some people like big weddings, I prefer small ones, say, four people."

"Four people? What are you talking about? And why didn't you dye your hair?"

"Why would I dye my hair?"

"No reason. What were you saying?"

"I said, do you remember that older couple, Vivian and Leon McKee?"

"Are they the ones that own the cleaners on Clark where we first met?"

"Now that you mention it, yes that is where we met, and they are the ones."

"I didn't get to know them too well, I mean it was Pete and my first date, and I was feeling awkward, I didn't want to be considered his date, just his friend." Sarah was leaning against the counter as Sandy closed the refrigerator door and faced her.

"Well," she hesitated, "look before I say any more you have to pinky swear that you will not tell anyone. Like my sister I need you to swear not to tell anyone...yet."

"What are you talking about? Pinky, swear about what?"

"About the fact that last Friday Leon and Vivian and I and..."

The phone rang in the hall and Sarah ran for it saying, 'Hold that thought."

Minutes later Sarah returned beaming saying that Sophie and Phil had just bought their plane tickets home, but they were flying to Tennessee first to see a second or third cousin and then flying out from there. All in all, she said they would be another ten days. "Hey, find anything to eat?"

"How about some cereal? There's a whole shelf full of the stuff." Sandy was taking down the boxes and lining them up on the counter and shaking each container to see how much was left in each one.

"I'm not thinking cereal tonight." Sarah had wandered over to the old-fashioned sideboard and opened the top drawer to see which menus were still there so they could get take-out somewhere.

"Are you interested in Chinese, pizza, ribs, mom's home cooking from the Silver Skillet or something from the Pot and Pan?"

"I'm happy with cereal," said Sandy trying not to smile. "Or we could all go out for fast food and celebrate."

"Believe me," Sarah said as she rummaged through the drawer looking to see if there were any other menus, "fast food is nothing to celebrate."

"No silly, we wouldn't be celebrating fast food, we'd be celebrating something that happened to me over the weekend."

Sarah looked at Sandy's face and guessed, "Something to do with school?"

"No."

"Uh, something to do with Sophie and Phil?"

"No."

"Is it something to do with our mother?"

"Which one?"

"Carol, of course, you ninny. Come on and tell me, I'm out of guesses."

"Okay, but first you have to pinky swear that this will go no further."

"Oh honestly," she locked her little finger with her sisters and said, "I pinky swear."

Sandy was looking like she was about to burst as Johnny walked into the room from the hall in Sandy's pink bathrobe.

Sarah was dumbfounded for only a second before she asked, "Why is Johnny here and why is he wearing your robe? Is this some joke or something? I thought you two were pretty much over."

"We thought so too," he said as he crossed the room and put his arm possessively around Sandy's waist.

"But why are you wearing her robe?" As soon as she asked the question, she was horrified at the answer, and it showed on her face.

"Before you imagine something immoral," Sandy held out her left hand that sported a wide gold band and a thinner band with a small diamond. "We're..."

"You're married! You married Johnny! I can't believe it. You're already married! Now I understand," Sarah said as she sat down hard on a dining room chair. "I thought I saw someone go into your room this morning and I thought it was that girl Jilly I'm always talking about, and then I thought you had dyed your hair, but all the time it was Johnny, wasn't it?"

"If you mean my husband, yes it was."

"I thought you might have seen me, but I wasn't sure," Johnny added as he sat next to Sarah with Sandy sitting on his lap.

Sarah grabbed her sister's hand and asked, "So why all the secrecy?"

"Well, it all just kind of snowballed on us. Johnny thought I didn't care anymore..."

"There's a big surprise," interrupted Sarah good-naturedly.

"Yeah, I know. I took so long dealing with the news my, I mean our mother gave us, and then I was still getting over that Frank thing, and I just didn't want to be involved with anyone in any way, so I threw myself into Sophie's wedding and some extra credit for school. Did I tell you I'm graduating early?"

"Off the subject."

"I suppose it is, but I guess I'm just stalling because I didn't want to hurt you."

"Me?"

Sandy squeezed her hand and said, "You are my sister and a big part of my life now, and I thought that if Johnny and I eloped that it would spare me having to have a wedding with our mom not coming and your mom maybe wanting to pay something towards it and Johnny's parents wanting it at their fancy club, no offense."

"None taken." Sarah dropped Sandy's hand and began pacing the room as Sandy continued.

"So after Johnny got home from his date with the woman he hired as their accountant, he called me and said let's elope," she turned to kiss his cheek and look into his face, "and I said yes right away because it seemed the right thing to do. I did miss him terribly, and it was time to let the past go, so we got our blood tests last Monday, and Leon and Vivian and Johnny and I went to city hall downtown and got married Friday. Leon and Vivian had done the same thing a few years ago, and theirs turned out pretty well. We honeymooned right here at Sophie's because it was such short notice and there was no one else here. And to be truthful, neither one of us has any money."

Sandy stopped talking but looked at her sister for a reaction, "So," she added tentatively, "what do you think, are you angry with me for not telling you or including you in the wedding?"

Sarah sat down again and once again held her sister's hand. "I think you're the most clever and most wonderful sister there is in the whole world." Sarah then stood and closed the gap between them and put her arms around her sister's shoulders and kissed her. "Have you always been this way? This put yourself last way?"

"I don't know how to answer that. I really don't. I just didn't want to make waves with anyone. I know we hurt some feelings and that's why I want you to keep quiet about this until we have a chance to make amends with the people we've disappointed. We just saw no other way to do this, and once I heard Johnny's voice on the phone, I knew I wanted to marry him no matter what and right away."

"Well, I think its swell, a little fast, but swell. Won't Sophie be surprised? Speaking of Sophie, when are they coming back?"

"You were the one who talked to her just now, didn't you say not for another ten days?"

"See how excited I am, I can't think straight. I am so happy for the two or you, have you decided where you are going to live, not at the Five I hope."

"We thought we'd live right here."

"But you only have a twin sized bed, isn't that a little crowded?"

Sandy blushed ever so slightly and said, "Remember there is a bigger room next door to mine and I thought I'd call Sophie and ask if I, I mean if we could have it."

"I see no reason why you shouldn't, get it before they start getting more roomers in here once they return and they're back in the rooming house business. This place could end up being as busy as you said it once was when you first came.

"I don't know about you two," Johnny said, "but I'm starved. I say as long as the Chinese lanterns are still on the ceiling, we should order Chinese. We could fire up those lights, and someone can make tea while I go get the food. Oh, hey Sarah, do you know what Jewish women make for Thanksgiving dinner?" He asked as Sandy now was looking through the take-out menu for supper.

"Should I?"

"No, you're ruining the joke, just answer the question, what do Jewish women make for Thanksgiving dinner?" I don't know, what do they make for Thanksgiving dinner?"

"Reservations!"

"Honestly, get the phone book, and we'll order Chinese. No wait, the number's on the menu. See this is what happens when you surprise me with something out of the blue!"

Chapter 12

"I mean, did you have to get such colorful lawn furniture?" Scott was shaking his head and looking at the wildly floral cushions.

"I had no choice as to color; I told you I picked these up in the alley didn't I?"

"I still can't believe someone would throw these away; they're practically brand new."

"They are completely brand new. But the guy that was tossing them out didn't care. Here, sit down in one my best finds and I'll tell you the whole story."

Scott sat down in the chairs he had meant to ask Elliot about ever since he and his mother had spent the day there. He noticed that Elliot still had the old chairs by the fire, but these new ones sat between the original shed and the old shed and were very comfortable and quite impressive if it wasn't for their shocking colors.

"As I said, Leroy's got me checking out the trash for him and right before Labor Day I was scavenging just west of here in the nicer neighborhoods, you know, little forties-era houses, nice neighborhood? Anyway, I was walking down the alley because it looked like everyone was putting out their garbage and I came to this guy who was pitching some lawn furniture into the alley. I mean pitching the stuff. I stopped, and when he saw me, he said, "It's all going, so if you want it take it. Take her too if you want trouble."

"Well, I stepped aside until his anger was spent and all the furniture was in the middle of the alley. I didn't know what to say, and I was afraid that if I just stood there staring at him that he'd pitch me too. While I was trying to think of what to say, he continued, "I mean it, take it all." He kicked at a cushion that was still in the yard.

"She's not coming back, and she can't have it, and I don't want it. Here, he said, taking the keys out of his pocket and motioning to his garage, take my truck too and haul it away. I don't care anymore."

"I said the only thing I could think of and asked him if he cared to talk about it. I've always thought that was the dumbest thing anyone could ever say, 'want to talk about it?' Well, he did.

He leaned against the garage, and I sat on one of his garbage cans and told me about his young wife and the pool and patio guy.

"He said as her husband he'd done everything for her that she wanted; even repainted the house, inside and out. That wasn't enough evidently because she started wanting new furniture. He told her that if she wanted new furniture, she'd have to find some on a really good sale because she had already gone through most of his savings.

"He added they'd only been married for a little over a year and to this day he couldn't think of why she married him. They met at work, and evidently, she thought he was more important than he was and was making a more substantial salary than he did. She was quite a bit younger than he was and then he told me how difficult it was to live with someone whose values differed so wildly from his. Anyway, when he said to her that she would have to find cheap furniture, she went to the end of season end sale at the pool and patio store and came home with lawn furniture, you know chairs, a table and a whole lot more. He thought she was looking for living room furniture and she brings this stuff home.

"Evidently she had started seeing the guy that worked there on the side, and little by little she started getting more and more lawn furniture. He said the final blow was when he came home early from work and she had all this new stuff out on the lawn, he hated the colors by the way, and she even had a light-up plastic palm tree to go with it. Well, he comes home, and she had patio lights and the palm tree lit, soft Hawaiian music was playing, and she was more than a little surprised when he walked out of the back door and into the yard. Evidently, she just assumed he'd be working late again that night, so she had invited a few of her friends, including the salesman, for a little party. Can you believe he told me all this stuff? But then I suppose he needed to talk to someone, and I guess he thought a stranger would be a good pick.

"Well, he said that not only did he break up her party, but he also broke up with her and sent her packing to her mother's. I just happened to come by the very next day when he was throwing everything away.

"I asked him to reconsider keeping some of it, or returning it, but he was still very angry and said he'd feel better giving it to someone who would appreciate it. He said that while looking at how I was dressed and probably figured I could use it. I hustled home and contacted Leroy who came with his truck and between us we made four trips with the stuff, dropping some of it here and some of it at his store."

"I suppose Leroy got the plastic palm tree."

"Sure did, and the two chaise lounges and some small tables, which I might add he sold right away. I think the few neighbors I've got would have thought I had gone around the bend if I put up a plastic palm tree. Besides, where would I plug it in?"

"True, true, but it sure would have been interesting to see one beside the shed. Or better yet, inside the shed. It would complete your psychedelic drug trip ambiance."

"You might scoff at my ambiance, but you might find yourself living here someday. I'd have to make room for you though because I take the chairs in every night and turn the table upside down, so nobody takes them. By the way, how's your mom doing?"

"Mom? She's okay I think. One of her sisters sent her a train ticket to come and stay with her on the east coast, so she surprised everyone and went. She said she had been invited for an indefinite stay, but I think she'll be back within the month. It's her favorite sister and all, and I hope she can help mom work a few things out, but I think she'll miss the grandkids and be back before the snow flies."

"Speaking of snow flying, have you noticed what Leroy and I have been doing?"

"You mean all that wood stacked up along the fence? When did you guys do that?"

"It's what we've been doing every day for the past week. One of those old trees a couple of blocks down from here had been hit by lightening and was on the ground. I talked to Clancy about cutting it up for firewood."

"Who's Clancy again?"

"Well, it's not his name, but that's what we call the cop that patrols this area. He's a big guy and as black as night. He puts on a big front to scare the gangs, but he's nice, and some nights he stops and sits with us for a while."

"But Clancy isn't a black name is it?"

"Nah, Clancy is more of a salute to the thousands of Irish who were the majority of policemen in cities like New York and Chicago all the way back to the mid eighteen hundreds I believe. Ever heard the words patty wagon? The Irish coined it because lots of them were named Paddy and lots of those Patty's drank a lot so it was natural that the wagon that came to pick them up should be called Paddy's Wagon."

"I've heard it called that all my life and for the first time I know why. Know anything else about them?"

"Nope, just that the lifestyle seemed to have become a family tradition because you can trace many policemen and women back quite a few generations. It's said they had a way with people and they made the best officers. I wouldn't know," Elliot said as he stirred the fire getting it ready for cooking a quick lunch. "It's Monday isn't it?" He added, "You're day off."

"Yep and I've got the whole day, and I have something interesting to tell you about what happened with Henry on Saturday. But before I do, finish your story about what Clancy had to do with this firewood?"

"After the tree went down I asked him what I had to do to get permission to cut it up and take it away, you know, which of the endless city departments would handle something like tree cutting permits, seeing that the project is probably not too high on the city crew's list of things to do."

"I would agree with that. What do they care about this part of town?" Scott added a piece of wood from the stack before putting the grill grate on the fire.

"Exactly what I told Clancy, but he said that I might not want to go to city hall for a permit because someone might come out to make sure the tree needed to be cut and then they'd see my shack and the fact I do not have a building permit taped on the window and then who knows what would happen to me and my little place."

"So what are you going to do?"

"We've already done it. Clancy turned his head the other way, and Leroy brought over an old chainsaw that worked off and on so we've been cutting and hauling the wood over here all week."

"Yep," said Scott, "where's a cop when you need one?"

Elliot laughed and asked "Bacon and eggs all right with you?"

"Sounds great, got any bread that I can toast over the fire?"

"Only if you promise to keep a better eye on it than you did last time, as I remember it was more of a burnt offering than toast."

"If I do mess it up, I'll make up for it with the stuff I bought from the bakery. Good old Feida's, they come through every time with all sorts of good stuff."

Elliot was on his hands and knees reaching for the eggs and bacon down in the cold box before he remembered and asked, "So, what was the problem with Henry Saturday?"

CHAPTER 13

Auntie Chang had finally figured out precisely what her nephew was hiding. He had a woman on the side, and from the looks of it, there was a very good chance that she was probably not Asian.

"I think Henry has fallen into bad company," she told Scott the next morning when he stopped to see what she needed to have done that day. "Why else he no open my store at evenings? He's spending time with a no good hussy who has plans to take him away along with my money."

"And how did you figure that one out?" asked Scott as he stood obediently next to the chair not having been asked to be seated. They were back to slave and owner status.

"What else could it be? He's a good-looking man and a lucky catch. Everyone knows he is going to be very rich someday. But no one in town has seen him with any local girl, so that's why I think she's not Asian."

"Would it be so terrible if she wasn't?"

"It would be a disaster. I promise my sister that I'd watch him carefully. Why did you think I let him run one of my stores and tell him that it's his? He is little emperor, but I am the old queen and still know more how to handle him. I also told my sister that I find nice girl for him, help him settle down, but so far, according to him, none of the girls I show him are his type. I ask just what type his is, and he says he, not interested in girls for now. Things are about to change though." She rubbed her diminutive hands together and continued with a small wicked smile growing on her face. "Little does he know I have a new girl coming right from China sometime in the next month, she already approved by sister, her name Ming Toy, she from Li clan."

Scott noticed when the great Madam Chang got nervous or angry she shortened her sentences and spoke more like a Chinese, leaving out key words and plural words in a sentence. He also hoped this girl who was coming was legal. Due to the number of young people in town who treated her like a queen, Scott had begun to wonder how many of them were legal or if she had smuggled them to the United States, as was common, and now they belonged to her to treat as she liked. Every month it seemed the local Cultural Center, the meeting hall that had been created to preserve cultural identity while providing had new members fresh from China. All of them worked for one of the four ruling families that owned the town, and most of them held very subservient positions.

Madam Chang continued, "As soon as Ming Toy arrives, I introduce; you like her, she good Chinese girl, speaks English, very gentle, like geisha."

Great, though Scott, just what Henry isn't looking for, a geisha from the old country. He despised not only her profession but the entire nation. This will be interesting.

Sandy liked being married; Johnny liked it even more. As they lay in bed, both skipping their day's classes, Johnny wondered aloud, "So, how do you think we should handle things now? I mean, who do we tell first?"

"Well, if you remember," she said while tenderly tracing his face with her finger, "we've already told my sister."

"Okay, that's one, but how about everyone else?"

"Vivian and Leon know too, and they have been sworn to secrecy."

"Great, three down and lots more to go. You know we'll have to tell Sophie and Phil as soon as they return. We couldn't possibly keep up the deception when they get home. And there's your mother and my parents and the people at the Five and…"

"At this moment I don't care," she said now cupping his face in both her hands. "Sarah's gone to work; Sophie and Phil won't be back for another week…"

"Say no more my sweet darling wife," he said softly kissing the ring on her finger that was finally in its proper place.

Lunch was barely over when Leroy's truck pulled up in the alley. As he struggled to get out, Scott walked to the truck and shouted through the passenger window attempting to be heard above the noise of the ancient engine and saying there would be nothing left of the truck if he didn't fix that door. "Every time you slam the driver's door the fender practically falls off." He examined the fender, wiggling it back and forth. "How in the world does this thing hang on, you using some of that new super glue or something?"

Leroy had finally extricated himself from his vehicle, slammed his door to make it latch and walked around to where Scott was doing his examination.

"If it would just fall off I could fix it. But I don't want to pull it off just in case I break something else while doing it."

"Well if that's your story, you'd better stick to it. I'm surprised some cop hasn't pulled you over yet and given you a ticket. Did you realize that it's knocked your headlight sideways too? I'll bet this light doesn't even work anymore. I'm surprised you haven't had an accident with that thing, and the engine makes so much noise you probably wouldn't even hear an ambulance if it pulled up right behind you."

"Don't worry; I'd see the flashing lights and pull over." Leroy looked pleased with his answer.

As the two men walked over to Elliot's outdoor table, Scott added, "I just wouldn't want you to end up in the hospital. Who knows what goes on in there? One of my sister's friends was a nurse, and she worked over at Cook County General. While she was there in the ER, she said she saw enough to make her hair curl. She said because they were always desperately understaffed, she and the other nurses would end up doing the work of the doctors."

"They operated on people? Hey, Elliot, anything cold to drink in the box?" asked Leroy who was preparing for a long, interesting conversation about hospitals and nurses.

"Sure thing, look deep because I think there is still a couple of Cokes."

"Anybody else want one?" asked Leroy as he was leaning into the box on his hands and knees. "There seem to be five cans in here. You know Elliot, there has got to be a way of raising this thing up a bit, I'm getting too old to get on my hands and knees and practically stand on my head to get anything thing out of this thing."

"As soon as you can figure out how to get electricity back here I'd be happy to find a used fridge for you, and we could even have a freezer and make ice too. Of course, you'd have to help me build a bigger shed to hold the fridge and then maybe we could fit in a stove with an oven and maybe install a sink with water and a bathroom and then we could have Thanksgiving dinner here." He turned his attention back to Scott and asked, "So, did they operate on people?"

"Who, the nurses, no they did not operate, but this friend of my sisters delivered several babies by herself the first week she worked there, never having done it before and did it completely alone, well, not completely alone, there was the mother-to-be there too. Anyway, she helped deliver her first baby in the hall, the second one in the elevator and she had hundreds of stories to tell by the time she left Cook County; especially stories about the wildly thrashing patients that the medical crew had to practically sit on so the doctors could examine them or give them a shot to calm them down or knock them out. She said the only thing good that came out of that was the hospital relaxed its stand on nurses wearing dresses for uniforms and let them wear white uniform pants."

Scott stopped his narrative to see if either of the men was still listening because Leroy had turned his chair upside down and was pushing a leg back and forth checking for a loose screw and Elliot was beginning to get involved with the chair, although he was trying to look like he was still interested.

"I believe she was the one who said when the hospitals relaxed their policies on white uniform dresses and caps, they were all happy, but some of them objected to the aqua hot pants with the lime green knee socks."

"If you think the screw is loose, Leroy, there are all kinds of screwdrivers in the old shed, and it wouldn't hurt to check them all while you're at it. I'm sorry Scott, what were you saying about aqua hairnets?"

"I said aqua hot pants."

Both men looked up at the same time, and Leroy asked, "Hot pants on a nurse, which hospital?"

"I didn't think either of you were listening. I said the nurses didn't have to wear those white dress uniforms nor those funny looking caps anymore and now they can wear uniform pants."

Still not with the program Leroy asked, "Why do they wear those funny little hats?"

Elliot filled in the answer this time while turning his chair over. "They each wear the cap designating which nursing school they graduated from. Each school had its own cap design."

"Oh." Leroy had all but lost interest and returned to fiddling with the chair leg.

Elliot, after turning his chair back upright and out of politeness even though was no longer interested asked, "How long did she stay at Cook County?"

"Not long," Scott continued even though he was no longer interested in the rest of the conversation. "I think she went on to Lutheran General, that hospital in the suburbs, and then she became one of the teams of private nurses that took around-the-clock care of some big shot's mama who lived in the new Marina Towers. He was big in cereals or widgets or something."

They sipped their Cokes in silence, each wishing there was ice to go with the pop as Leroy noisily went through the metal box of tools in the old shed.

"I dated a woman once," started Elliot staring at his glass, "who was a nurse. I guess she saw lots of things during her career, much of it I suppose she couldn't talk about, but she said that the one thing that happened that she never forgot was a woman who had driven herself to the ER with a piece of metal stuck clear through her thigh. It seems she had pulled herself up against her parked car to let a car go by, you know like you always have to do on all of those narrow one-way streets? Well, evidently there was a piece of the car's side trim that was flapping in the breeze as the vehicle passed her and it ran clear through her thigh and then broke off as it drove past. She didn't think the driver of the other car knew what happened and being in shock, she calmly drove herself to the hospital and was just standing at the ER desk when an intern noticed her leg and got her into treatment right away."

"Looks like Elliot's saying we'll be taking off that fender of yours today, Leroy," said Scott. "Hope you've got some time on your hands, you know what Elliot can be like when he's got a project."

"Believe me; Ruby would like me gone for the entire day. She's got her church ladies in today sewing stuff or cutting out stamps or rolling bandages or something, and she would like me gone for a long time, and I agreed."

"You hungry? We just ate, but the fire's still hot enough for me to fix some bacon and eggs or you can just wait for the coffee to finish and have some of the pastries Scott brought."

"I think I'll just do the pastries. Ruby always serves those little sandwiches and tiny cakes and tea for the ladies, so I got to eat all the crusts she cut off the bread just now before I came."

"That's all you had to eat, crusts?" Scott was appalled.

"No, they've got filling. Ruby waits to cut the crusts until she's got the sandwiches made. Then she squares them up by cutting off the crusts; says the sandwiches look neater when she does it that way. Either way, I've had my fill of tuna, ham and chicken sandwiches today, not forgetting her new creation of cream cheese and green olive spread."

"And you didn't bring us any? Thanks, pal," Elliot teased. "We'll just have to try some of these interesting looking things in this bakery box. Hey, Scott, grab that sugar off the inside table for Leroy's coffee, will you? Leroy's been cursed with quite a sweet tooth."

After the coffee had been poured and the bakery box practically emptied, Elliot tried to act as though he just remembered and asked what he'd been interested in knowing ever since Scott first mentioned it, "Did you say Henry did something unusual last week?"

"It was the oddest thing," Scott said pouring out a little more coffee for each of them and set the pot on the fire again, but off to the side so it wouldn't continue cooking.

"Henry called me into his office around three on Friday and said that he didn't need me the rest of the day and I could leave early. First of all, that was strange in itself, and then he holds out a hundred dollar bill and tells me to take it to make up for back pay."

"Back pay, for what?" Asked Leroy as he added, "Pass the cream and sugar please."

"That's another thing," said Scott, "he's started drinking that new powered cream and sugar in his coffee."

"What's so odd about that?" Leroy was ready to defend his coffee-drinking position.

"I think what Scott means is that it's unusual for Henry to be drinking coffee in the first place and more unusual for him to be taking both cream and sugar with it, right?"

"I guess I never thought of that coffee vs. tea thing, but now that I do think about it, it is strange he drinks coffee and stranger still that he puts something in it. He's very vain about his looks and I'm sure would do nothing or eat nothing to alter the slim and dashing man-about-town persona he's trying to maintain. I've never actually seen him drink either tea or coffee; he's more of a Mountain Dew guy. There are garbage bags full of cans downstairs for the trash nearly every week. He says he needs it for quick energy."

"So what's your theory?" Elliot's question sounded more intense than his usual off-hand inquiry.

"I don't know, maybe he really is seeing a woman, and she takes cream and sugar in her coffee."

"Do you honestly think Henry would be entertaining in his office after hours?" Elliot asked rather forcefully. "You can be sure that his auntie has spies out everywhere, including you."

"I suppose you're right, I've never seen any signs of anyone except employees and he treats us all the same, as employees."

"So if he only drinks pop, why do you think he's got that new powdered creamer stuff and sugar in his office? Leroy had a point.

"Now that I think of it, no I haven't. But there is a large jar of that powdered creamer on a table in his office, the one the coffee pot's on, and he was brushing some sugar off of his jacket just last week when I went up to his office unannounced to check on some vases that had gone missing. I found that very odd, I mean this guy isn't the spilling kind."

"Hmmm." Elliot looked deep in thought, and Leroy had gone back over to his truck and was pulling on the fender.

"Might as well get this sucker off before I put somebody in the hospital myself," Leroy shouted back to the other two men.

"Listen, Scott," said Elliot under his breath, "why don't you seriously consider moving in here? We'll have plenty of wood for winter," he said looking at the immense pile of logs. "We'll be plenty warm when I figure out how to get that orange funnel chimney up without burning the place down. You've seen and used the bathroom in the house too so you know we've got facilities. It's just an offer, but I really would like to think about it."

They worked on Leroy's truck for the bulk of the afternoon and finally figured out how to get the fender off. When they saw what had to be done to get it to back on, they threw it in the bed of the pickup and Leroy drove them down to his neighborhood to talk to a body man to see if it could be reattached. "Tie it on with string or use some glue on it. I don't care what you do, just make it work," was Leroy's acerbic comment to the mechanic. Elliot always thought that deep down Leroy was a closet tightwad, and what he heard Leroy just say verified the fact.

"Tell you what," Leroy said as they sat on the bench outside Ed's Repair Sh… most the word Shop missing due to a slight misjudgment Ed made while backing a rather large truck into his garage several years ago. Since Ed never seemed to be in much of hurry, no one expected it to look any other way than it did now for the rest of the time Ed owned the shop. All of his customer's thought the sign was appropriate saying "The SH really means, shush, don't wake Ed, he'll get around to your vehicle eventually,"

"Let's walk down to my house and see if the old bags are still there." Leroy started to head down the sidewalk not waiting for his companions.

"There may be some sandwiches left that we could snag and eat while we're waiting for the slowpoke Ed to put that fender back on."

The three men walked the six blocks only to learn that Ruby's ladies were still at the house.

"I'll go in through the kitchen and see what I can grab to eat; you guys wait here."

Leroy was gone before they had a chance to say anything and as they stood looking at the house, they were impressed as to how neat, tidy and well maintained it was.

"Makes you think, doesn't it?" commented Scott. "I would never have figured Leroy's house would look like this; I mean judging by the truck he drives I thought it would be some run-down apartment building somewhere. You know, rusty bikes in the weedy yard and a car without its wheels or rims sitting in the street on cement blocks."

"Kind of where I live now?"

"You know what I mean, you're just temporary, Leroy's' permanent. I was just thinking that this is what my mom would call, judging a book by its cover."

"And she would be right." Elliot shifted to his balance to his other foot, "Hey, mind if I go back to Ed's and sit down; my legs are not what they used to be."

"Sure, go ahead, I'll wait for Leroy."

In only minutes, Leroy appeared at the shop holding a large paper bag and a grin on his face.

"My truck fixed yet? I'd like to get you guys back before rush hour gets any worse."

"Ed said it's almost ready and what have you got in the bag?"

Leroy opened the bag and laid its contents out on the bench next to Elliot.

"We've got hamburger meat, some cheese, and buns. I would have grabbed the ketchup and mustard to go with it, but Ruby would have had a fit if I did. As it is, if the ladies hadn't still been there she would have probably hit the ceiling that I was taking food."

"And," asked Elliot, "what are you planning on doing with the food?"

"I'm treating on supper, of course. I eat enough of your food, and now I'm contributing something to the cause. Is that a problem?"

"None whatsoever my friend, I was just asking."

Ed surprised them all by rolling out the truck with the fender firmly attached. "Ask no questions," he said. "Just be careful with it, and that will be twenty bucks, payable now."

Leroy reluctantly rolled off the money in small bills, and they all piled in, careful where they sat due to old and sharp springs that hid under the thin seat upholstery waiting for a victim.

The cheeseburgers were grilled to perfection and if they would have had some pickles and chips and maybe onion dip, supper would have been even better, but as it stood, everything was delicious and Leroy had brought enough meat so they could each have three burgers. Scott noticed that both the meat and cheese were Government Issue. Occasionally his own family had to go on assistance when his dad was busy drinking up his paycheck, so his mom would have to humble herself and go down to the food bank or on the welfare roll, and during that time they too ate Government meat and cheese and drank powdered milk.

"Not that I want to get rid of you," Elliot asked Scott, "but when do you have to be back at Queen Mama's?"

"You aren't going to believe this, but I have tomorrow off."

"That's strange, isn't it?"

"Yep, it's one of Henry's other ideas. I get the day off, but he needs me to do a little work for him after he closes the shop."

"What kind of work?" Elliot tried to sound casual, but there was worry in his voice." That's just it, I don't know, and none of this is adding up right. I mean, first, it was the little cream and sugar in his coffee that he doesn't drink thing, and then it was the hundred dollar 'back pay,' and now he's giving me the day off so I can do a little work for him tomorrow night."

"What do you think his auntie is going to say when she finds you're not at her beck and call tomorrow?"

"I'm not sure she'll even miss me. There will be no trucks to unload until Thursday, and she's down at the Cultural center whenever she can secretly arranging some big to-do to welcome this new girl from China and introduce her to her nephew. I think that she thinks if she does this introduction thing in front of lots of people he will have to show an interest in her at least. After all, the Chinese are very careful about saving face, and she doesn't think Henry would humiliate her in front of a large crowd and not welcome this new woman into his life and then if auntie had her way, make her his wife."

"Why is it always about women?" Leroy asked as he added more wood to the fire. "I mean, why are they the ones who cause so much trouble?"

"Trouble for whom?" Elliot responded to Leroy's query as he moved his chair a little closer to the fire and changed the subject. "It's gonna be a little chilly tonight I think, and it's time I start thinking seriously about getting that orange chimney up somehow so we can move the party inside."

"Remember, I've got tomorrow off," said Scott as he brushed crumbs from his shirt, "so I could drop by and help, or maybe I'll take you up on your offer and stay so we can get the project going bright and early before I have to leave on Henry's secret mission."

"That will work." Elliot was smiling.

"Leroy, mind if I ask you a question?" Scott had been staring at the fire but glanced sideways at his friend.

"Not at all, ask away."

"I don't know why I just thought of this but do you believe in God?"

"That's a strange question and where did that come from?"

"I don't know. I guess I've been thinking of my mom and how blindsided she was when my dad walked in and said he wanted a divorce. I mean his problems stemmed from a woman, women, and alcohol."

Seeing the questioning looks on his companions faces he added, "No, I don't mean my mom, I mean this other woman he's found. When I stayed with her Labor Day night, she told me what she and Elliot had been talking about. She said Elliot asked her if she was a believer, a non-believer or a make-believer."

"What did she say," interrupted Elliot, trying not to look anxious.

"She said she never thought of it in those terms before. She just assumed that she was a believer because she was a good person and very kind and extremely patient. She never in her life did anything bad to anyone that she could remember and she attended church as often as possible, depending on my father's mood."

"Your father went to church?" Elliot was amazed.

"No, he never darkened the door of one. It's just that if he wanted to do something on Sunday, he wanted my mom to be home so she could go with him or at least be there waiting when he came home."

"I see, kind of a controller?"

"Kind of? He was the ultimate controller. At first, she would try to appease him with an extra special Sunday dinner that she'd put in the oven before we left for church and then serve on the fancy plates when we got home from church. She'd fix all his favorite meats and then add mounds of mashed potatoes and gravy and always a fancy dessert and fresh coffee."

"Let me guess, that didn't work for long." Elliot tucked another piece of wood into the fire.

"You've got that right. We kids got to the place where we hated Sundays because they all ended up the same. Mom would get up early and very quietly get dressed for church. She'd get the meal put in the oven, and we'd get to eat cold cereal on Sunday's because it was quiet and there weren't any smells of frying bacon or sausage to wake him up. We'd sneak out, and by the time we got back he was either gone, or he would have eaten out somewhere just to spite her. Believe me; it was in no way pleasant sitting around the kitchen table eating Sunday dinner with him in the living room staring at us. My sisters and I got to the place where we all found something else to do after service. Sometimes we would say so-and-so invited us over for Sunday dinner and mom would look sad and say okay. I'm not sure if she believed us or not, but after a while, she stopped fixing the big meal and stopped going to church. He had finally won.

"But I've been thinking a lot about what Elliot asked. So, do you believe in God, Leroy?"

CHAPTER 14

They were sitting in their favorite pizza place, neither eating nor talking much. Each of them had things they needed to discuss, but neither was anxious to bring anything up, so they just sat and toyed with their food and watched others eat. The cook kept coming out of the kitchen, quarters in his hand and played the same song over and over on the jukebox in the corner.

"I like the Beach Boys and all," said Pete, "but if he plays Help Me Rhonda one more time I'm going to have to go back there and wring his neck, or at least unplug the music."

Sarah smiled weakly, but the comment did open up a conversation they needed to have. They both realized ever since their luxurious Labor Day weekend on the north shore that something had changed between them.

Even though Sarah wanted to pretend everything was okay, she got up the nerve and finally asked the question that was haunting her, kind of like clearing the preverbal elephant from the room. They both knew it was there, but neither wanted to acknowledge it.

"Is there something wrong Pete, I mean I know something has changed between us, I just don't know what it is, for sure." She had added the last two words giving Pete the idea she did know what the problem was.

Regular feelings had always been for Pete to express, deep feelings were impossible. He'd grown up with a bricklayer dad who went through life with a 'just buck up' attitude. His mother seldom interfered with the way he parented, and she seemed to go along with his attitude of keep doing whatever it was until it was done because that's the way it is. They should have just had their favorite saying painted on the wall so they could repeat it daily, 'Life is Hard, Get Over it.'

Pete often thought of where his life was going and why. Was he still trying to please his father by getting ahead and making something of his life? Was this the life he wanted to lead or was it his father's idea of how things should be? He'd thought about this for a long time, and after the Labor Day weekend, he took the question more seriously. He had been introduced to so many influential people, people who said they could do things for him, people who hinted that there was a bright career out there with him as the star if he'd only give them a call, but after the wedding.

"First of all," he said while taking his napkin off his lap and putting it on the table. He moved his plate of pizza to one side and rested his arms in front of him.

"I don't know how to start this conversation except to say that I was very uncomfortable over the weekend." He paused.

"Which part of it exactly?" She had just the hint of an edge to her voice.

"I'm not sure. Look, sweetheart, I'm still new at this rich man's game, and I felt totally out of place with your family and the country club and that whole jet-set mentality." He saw her wince when he said jet-set, and revised it quickly, "I mean, I didn't have the proper shoes for golf, much less the clubs. I must have been a major embarrassment to your dad."

"Do you really think that? I thought everything was going well."

"Sarah," he took her hands in his, "look at me, please. I don't think you could understand how out of place I felt. I couldn't find a common bond with anyone. They talked about their work, their tan and their stock portfolios and where they had vacationed."

"But you have a job in management."

"Goldblatts? Come on; if I'd of brought it up they would have politely tut-tutted behind their manicured hands."

"I think that's a little cruel."

"No Sarah, I think it was honest. I'm not in the same league they're in. I'm just a humble Gentile trying his best. I come from a plain middle-class family that has always been blue-collar. I don't think I can cut it with your crowd."

They sat there in silence staring at the pizza cooling in the middle of the table.

"I'm sorry Sarah, but it's the truth."

"What do you want to do about it? Break up?"

"I never said that. Besides your mother would kill me, or have me killed if I was the reason the big fancy wedding was called off."

She began to cry without effort, the tears gently sliding down her cheeks. "Now you don't like the wedding we planned?" She wiped her eyes with her napkin and asked, "So, what now?"

"I think we need some breathing room. We both need time to make sure this is the kind of life we want." He had slipped over to her side of the booth remembering he had done the same thing when he asked her to marry him in the very same spot. He held her close and whispered into her hair, "I just don't know. Just give me some time to sort it all out."

She pulled away and tugged on her finger. "You might as well take this," she handed Pete her engagement ring.

"But, I never intended..."

"No, I think we should go to our neutral corners until you decide what we are going to do."

"I never said anything about deciding for the both of us. I just meant that I was having second thoughts."

"Second thoughts about my family and the wedding and my friends, and probably about me? Take me home; I'm not hungry anymore."

She pushed him away to grab her purse.

He opened his wallet and put some money on the table that would not only cover their bill but leave a generous tip. He remembered hearing Help Me Rhonda played again as they made their way out and decided he never liked that song, while at the same time hoping those wouldn't be his exact sentiments someday.

The owner of the pizza place had witnessed the end of the conversation while coming out to sit with the couple she had grown to know and love because of last year's freak snowstorm closing them all in together for several days.

"Oh, oh," she said in Italian, "trouble in paradise."

Sophie and Phil had obviously arrived home seeing the hall was full of suitcases, boxes and bags and even a large woven reed purse with a colorful scarf attached to it leaning up against the stairs.

Sarah could hear the loud conversation in the dining room as soon as she opened the back door and despite the laughter which carried out into the hall, she carefully slipped up the stairs unnoticed, not wanting to face anyone until morning. Even then she thought if she got up early she could avoid them all for the bulk of the day. The incident made her feel even more alone as she opened the door to her room; two newly married couples wallowing in their happiness downstairs and her so completely alone and hopelessly confused upstairs.

"Do I believe in God? Is that what you asked?"

"That's the question on the table, do you believe in God?"

"Do you believe there's someone up there that watches over us and takes care of us more or less?"

"Well," Leroy put his feet closer to the fire and pulled his coat closed. "The answer is simple, yes."

"So you believe there's truly a God who created the human race and the Garden of Eden and everything?"

"I have to."

"Explain please."

"It's a long story, are you sure you don't want to wait until another day? Say sometime warmer?"

"The cold is fine with me, and besides I'm staying here tonight, and I have all day tomorrow off, so shoot."

"All right then," he started in his slow and deliberate way. "We have to go back a few years when I first started the second-hand store with my brother-in-law. Like I told you, we opened it in the other half of his repair shop to get the stuff out of our house and garage. Say, you guys see Ruby's flowers? It's a mighty fine job she does with those flowers."

"Are you stalling?"

"No sir, just wanted to know if you saw her flowers."

"We saw the flowers and were impressed with how nice everything looked, including the house and yard. Hey," Scott looked at Elliot, "why didn't we take a peek at Leroy's store while we were in the neighborhood today?"

"Because Elliot knows the store has moved to a location a couple of miles away, that's why." Leroy glanced at Elliot.

"I thought you said it was right near the house."

"I did, and if you just wait for the story, you'll see why it moved."

"Sorry."

"That's okay, son, the story is worth waiting for."

The stars were starting to come out, and all three men had their feet near the fire keeping warm and enjoying each others company.

"Like I started to say, a few years back I began the store with my brother-in-law. We did well with people coming from all around to buy our stuff. Sometimes people would say they could find the stuff cheaper at the Maxwell Street Market on Saturdays and I'd say, but Maxwell Street doesn't deliver."

"You did?"

"Uh huh. We delivered all over the city. That's when I first bought the truck I'm still driving today. That's the same truck that landed me on the street, homeless for a while."

"Conked out on you and left you stranded, right?"

"Not hardly. Now listen, son, you've got to wait for me to tell the story. Remember I was there."

"Okay, go on, I'll be quiet."

"I'll bet," Elliot said teasingly under his breath.

"Now where was I?"

Elliot said, "You were delivering furniture."

"Oh, right. Anyways, our business was really good. I'd do the fine furniture 'gathering' each night in a different neighborhood. Believe me; I studied each garbage route until I knew exactly where the trucks would be on which day and I would peruse the merchandise the night before the pickup. You know, it's valuable to have that information. If you get to the stuff before anyone else does, you can get some mighty fine things."

"Leroy," Scott interrupted again, "Aren't you getting off the subject."

"Oh yeah, the story. Well, business was good, and Ruby was happy, and my brother-in-law was happy, and I was happy until one day when

I got in early, and I found them sitting on one of the sofa's we had for sale. Not only were they sitting too close together for my comfort but they were involved in a long and what looked like a passionate kiss."

It was silent except for the crackling of the fire as Elliot added several more pieces of wood and held his hands near the flame for warmth.

"Well sir," Leroy started again, "I didn't know what to say so I just sneaked out the side door so they wouldn't see me. When I got home later I asked Ruby how her day had gone and she said 'fine,' and she asked me how my day had gone and I said 'fine.' I waited until after supper and while she was doing the dishes and I was still sitting at the table I confronted her with what I saw.

"I thought that she'd confess and then cry and ask my forgiveness. Well, I was wrong." Leroy had gone silent, poking at the fire with a stick and watching the sparks fly into the dark sky.

Scott wasn't sure if he should interrupt again at this point, but chose to sit and wait for Leroy to begin again while warming his own hands by the dying flames.

"No, she didn't do any of those things, she just stood there with her hands on her hips dripping dishwater on the floor and told me it was my own fault, here she was trying to make a nice home for me and did I appreciate her for doing that? No. And she said I was gone all the time and I said I had to be because her lazy brother-in-law never had time to do anything but occasionally show a few pieces of furniture to someone and arrange delivery and I was the one out making the deliveries. I was the one who was making the business a success, and she couldn't see it."

He paused to slow himself down. After a few deep breaths, he continued.

"So I told her if that's what she thought of me that she could just have that no good piece of genuine garbage and I grabbed my hat and keys and left.

What I didn't realize is that Ruby had parked her car behind my truck and I couldn't get out of the driveway without moving hers. I was not about to go back into the house to ask her to move her car after making such a dramatic exit, so I just took off walking.

"What I didn't plan on was a cold evening. It was spring and some days were pretty nice but the nights were still plenty cold. I was plenty warm from anger for the first mile or so and then I started to get cold, still angry, but cold.

"By this time I was downtown, and I realized that I only had a little bit of cash on me seeing I had gone to the bank to deposit not only the money from the business but also my own money into our personal account. That left me almost nothing and a truck I couldn't use. I had nothing, I mean I guess I didn't plan my getaway very well, but God had me exactly where He wanted me, right in the squeezebox.

By the looks on their faces, both men were fascinated with the story, so Leroy continued.

"I knew the city pretty well, but never figured I'd be spending a night on the street there. I had the choice of a flophouse up on Clark, or the Pacific Garden Mission just south of the loop. I picked the mission because it was not only closer, it was much safer. I had heard others say that to sleep there you had to listen to a sermon, but I figured that would be easy because my mama had us all in church each Sunday when we lived down south. The seventeen of us took up two full rows by ourselves.

"I read the placards on the wall while I was waiting for the preaching and singing to begin. They said stuff like 'Do You Know That Jesus Loves You?' and another one read, 'Do You Have a Mother Who's Praying For You?' That one worked for me because I knew she was. She had always told all us kids that no matter how we turned out, she'd be most proud if we were living a life pleasing to God. Well, that left me out.

"The preacher had a good sermon, and I knew some of the songs. The bulk of the men had come in earlier for the free supper, but I told them that I had just eaten so as soon as I could I took a shower, found a bed and stayed for the night. They're doing a good thing up there, a mighty good thing."

Elliot yawned, and Leroy ignored him. He knew for Scott's sake there was no stopping now.

"The second night I stayed away wasn't so good though. I had thought of calling Ruby to see if she wanted to talk about it or if she even realized I was gone. I decided if she wanted me she'd have to come and find me. So the next night I was north of the city, walked all day and ate some cheap food. I had resigned myself to sleeping on the streets so I was keeping an eye out looking for someplace without rats or crazy people and a spot that looked relatively sheltered from the cold. I didn't find a thing, but I did see an old man who didn't seem to know where or who he was. He was just there sitting on a bench in front of an office building, just sitting there in the cold without a coat on.

"You've both seen those guys that just seem to wander around unaware of anything or anybody. Well, he was one of those guys. He looked pretty old and frail, so I asked him what his name was. He just stared back at me and didn't say a thing. I asked him if he knew where he was or where he lived and he responded by crying. Great, now I had to take care of somebody else as well as myself. I mean, I couldn't just leave the guy sitting out there in the street, especially him without a coat."

Leroy paused to take a drink of the water.

"So now here I am with this old guy, and nowhere for either of us to go, he shivered when I touched him, so I knew I had a fine a warm place for him. We wandered over a few more blocks to look for a spot for both of us now. The only thing we found were three guys breaking into a warehouse in one of those blocks that once was the hub of the neighborhood and now sat vacant and empty. The whole area must have been some warehouse district once.

"Well, they saw us and motioned for us to come closer. I didn't think it was a good idea, but what choice did I have? Even if I had decided to run, the old guy would never have kept up with me so we went closer and we did need to get in out of the cold, soon.

"One of the guys, evidently the leader, wanted to know if they boosted me up if I could slip through the open window near the garage door. I think he asked me because I was agile, and desperate for shelter.

"I said I thought I could, and I intended to beat it out of there as soon as I opened the service door to let them in. If they were breaking and entering, I wanted no part of it.

"So they boosted me up, I climbed in, found my way to the service door in the dark, and let them in. The old guy was still standing outside and once again shivering, so now, so I said that I had to get him somewhere safe and warm and started to leave. They said we didn't have to go and that we had earned the right to stay inside with them for the night to get out of the cold."

"What did you do?" Scott just couldn't resist asking; he was so engrossed with the story.

"I did what anyone else would have done, we stayed, that is we waited just as long as they didn't steal anything. I was worried more about the old guy because he had started to shiver again, you know, almost like tremors or something.

"In order for the other three not to notice his shaking and kick us out I moved him away from where they were and sat him down at an old wooden desk. He put his head down on the surface and moaned softly as his hand started to move, then his body began to shake, and it seemed like it was only seconds before every part of his body was moving so I grabbed him off the chair before he fell off. I found a pile of those blankets garage mechanics used to cover the vehicle seats and wrapped them around him.

"Meanwhile, the other guys had found their way upstairs and had turned the lights on in the offices, so we moved under the stairs trying to become invisible so they would forget about us.

"Now that there was light, it was easy to see that this was once a mechanics garage, probably belonging to some trucking company in the past because the doors were massive and the bays were huge.

"When one of the guys yelled over to see where we'd gone I told them that my friend was really cold and I was trying to warm him up. They seemed to buy it and decided to take three office chairs with wheels out of the one office and have races with them, sitting down and pushing with their feet up and down the hall.

"This was when I realized they were pretty drunk and I started to get worried, and I hoped they weren't armed. That would take this mess and make it a severe problem. The old guy was not getting any better, or warmer either, and then I heard the men talking about starting a fire downstairs to 'warm up' the place for the old guy.

"I wasn't sure if I should say something or not about the possible fire because even though the floor was cement, the walls were very old wood. On the other hand, I didn't know if they wanted my opinion or would even listen. I kept my thoughts to myself but kept an eye on the situation.

"It was a good thing we had moved because they came downstairs and pushed the same desk where the old guy had been out into the middle of the room and grabbed the papers out of the desk drawers and piled them on top to start the fire. Next, one of the guys slammed the wooden chair on the ground, and when it broke, he added that to the top of the pile. Then they went back up to the offices and just grabbed whatever they could that would burn and were tossing it over the railing.

"Chairs splintered as they landed and their parts flew everywhere. Staying was no longer an option. I mean, if it were just me, I probably would have hung around in a back room or somewhere, only to be out of their sight and out of the cold night.

"But this fire was shaping up to be a disaster in the making, and I wanted no part of it. Besides, I had to get the old guy to the police station or a hospital somewhere; I was afraid he would die on me any minute. I started to pray and pray hard. Then something made me say that I needed to take the old guy out before he got any worse and to find him some help. I think they barely heard me because they were passing around a bottle of something in a bag and stoking the fire with more paper and broken office furniture while twirling around on their wheeled office chairs as though this was the most fun they had ever had.

"I managed to get the old guy out, service blankets and all and practically carried him down to the end of the block. There was a bus coming, and when it stopped, I asked if it went anywhere near a hospital or a cop shop. The driver said this was my lucky day because it was only two more stops before the bus would get to the Cook County Hospital.

"We got on and I paid the fares with what change I had left, yes I had only the exact amount of money for two fares." He added as he looked at the other two men. "I started to think this was more than a coincidence and the driver was even kind enough to take us close to the ER entrance and even helped me practically carry the old guy in.

"The old guy, who still hadn't said a word, and I waited for about twenty minutes before a nurse called my name, but I didn't mind. It was warm in the hospital and I think we had both fallen asleep by the time they called us. Now here's the interesting part, you guys still awake?"

"Pretty much," said Scott while Elliot pretended to snore.

"Okay, pay attention; this is where God comes in, I mean besides the bus fare that I didn't have, but 'found' when I needed it. We get this old guy in an examining room, and he starts shaking violently. One of the nurses puts about four blankets on him and started an IV, and hustles out of the room. It wasn't long before the old guy stopped his shaking and relaxed, almost melting into the warm blankets. He was so emaciated that his body made only a small rise in the bed. The nurse said not to go anywhere because she would be right back with some papers for me to fill out. 'This ought to be interesting,' I thought to myself.

"Suddenly it sounded like someone dropped a bomb on the hospital. The gigantic boom we heard broke one of the ER's glass doors; just shattered it and badly cracked the one next to it. The lights flickered and then came back on and within minutes we heard ambulances and fire sirens everywhere and their police scanner had taken on a life of it's own.

"Everybody in the ER was running around confused as to what was going on, no one could hear the scanner, and in what seemed like no time at all, the one working door in the ER opened and EMT's rushed in with stretchers, endless stretchers full of bodies and lines of ambulances kept disgorging their victims.

"The old man and I were pretty much forgotten with all the chaos, and I started to close the curtain around the old man's bed because I couldn't stand to look at the people who were being wheeled by, but something macabre drew me to watch. As I stood watching, people of all ages with burns all over their bodies and the few clothes they still had on that were black with soot were now being wheeled in examining rooms and then directly upstairs, many screaming in pain. Others were bleeding profusely, and the hospital staff had to watch their step because places on the floor were getting fairly slippery, some sticky with blood."

Scott felt as though they were sitting around a campfire telling ghost stories; the look on Leroy's face was hauntingly animated as he spoke.

"In addition to the chaos of bodies and carts in motion, there was also the unmistakable heartbreaking cries that would crescendo into screams of pain rising above the din adding another frightening layer to the already mind-numbing horror. A mother walked slowly past as though she was in a trance cradling a completely quiet baby in her arms, both mother and child were eerily quiet, they looked like two ghosts walking by. When I couldn't take the carnage anymore, I closed the curtains and pulled the old metal chair next to the bed so I could hold the old man's hand and I laid my head on the bed and cried. I cried for the people going by, I cried for the mother of that dead baby, I cried for the old man and most of all, I cried for myself. The tears just poured down my face and soaked into the sheets.

"The message at the mission the night before was, 'Are you ready to face eternity?' I knew now that I wasn't. If this was anything like hell was going to be, I did not want to go. After I cried for everyone else, I cried out to God and asked Him to forgive my sins and make me His and hold me close and never, ever let me go. I didn't care what I had to do to qualify; I just knew I had to belong to Him so he would take care of me and not let anything happen to me that He wouldn't be there to help me through."

Leroy stopped talking, the other men listening intently.

Scott wasn't sure Leroy had it in him to finish the story and instead of asking; he got up and got some more wood for the fire. A shooting star raced across the sky, and Leroy began with a voice huskier than before as he leaned into the fire and again warmed his hands.

"Several hours later when it was all finally over, and the hospital had gone quiet, I knew that the exposition was from the fire those guys started at that old garage; the building must have been full of gasoline plus those tanks of acetylene for welding and who knows what other accelerates. I also figured the three guys that were having carefree races with the office chairs were no more; I imagined they died instantly. When the old guy and I had originally gone into that street, it looked vacant and deserted, but evidently, there were families living nearby in the old wooden apartment buildings, and when the garage blew up it no doubt took their buildings with it. I could imagine the resulting fire racing on for blocks, probably destroying everything in its path for a long way. It must have thrown the city into chaos, and every hospital must have witnessed the same chaotic scene in their ER's, and I'll bet people thought the world was coming to an end."

Leroy shifted in his chair and just as the other men thought he had finished, he continued, but in a voice that was hoarse with fatigue and emotion.

"All through the night, ambulances brought people in, but some were unrelated to the explosion and fire, and I had finally crawled into bed with the old guy out of sheer exhaustion and fell into a sound sleep. It must have been hours later when I felt him moving, and I reluctantly woke up and found I was still holding his hand. His color was much better, and he was looking at me. I smiled at him, and he raised his head a bit and smiled the sweetest smile directly at me. That was it; after that, he gently put his head back down on his pillow, closed his eyes and died. He was still smiling.

"Now before you say anything or jump to any conclusions, I just want to say that after all these years I still don't know what to think."

"Think about what, the explosion? It was from the fire, right?" Scott wasn't sure if Leroy was even listening now that his long narrative was finished.

Leroy sighed deeply and continued. "Yes, the explosion was caused by the fire. The detailed newspaper coverage the next day made me think all over again that we could have been right in the middle of that. We could have been blown sky high along with those three guys and who knows how many others or possibly have died from extensive burns like that baby. If it weren't for that old guy, I would have been blown sky-high with the other guys.

Leroy took another deep breath and blew it out slowly. "Because the ER staff got busy again in the early hours of the morning with a carload of teens who had been in an accident, I didn't bother to tell anyone of the old man's passing until things finally calmed down.

"Since I had gotten enough sleep to take the edge off my exhaustion, I took advantage of the coffee pot at the nurses' station and decided to sit in the ER's waiting room drinking my coffee and watching the sun rise and the maintenance crew board up the door. A new shift had started and the night cleaning crew had mopped the floors several times, so it looked like nothing had happened during the long night of horror. I took my time finishing my coffee before going up to the desk, and I told the new nurse on duty that I had come in with an old man last evening, and to my knowledge he was still in examining room number four and if they hadn't already noticed, he had died during the night. She asked what his name was and I said I didn't know and then she asked what time we checked in and did I remember the name of the nurse who put us in that room? I gave the best answers I could.

"The nurse checked the chart and made some phone calls and finally clicked her pen shut, looked over her half-glasses at me and said there had been no one in room four with that description. She asked me if he was a burn victim and I said no and then she said they had a hectic night and I said yes, and I got ticked with so many questions, so I pushed past her and went to point out to her where he was. Sure enough, there was no one in examining room four, and the room was back to its pristine state that it had been the night before when we arrived and there was no sign of the old man or the mechanic's blankets. The strange thing is I never left the ER after I woke up next to him and I didn't see anyone moving his body at any point since he died."

Elliot had heard bits and pieces of this story before but never this part.

Scott was apparently thinking of possible scenarios and Elliot quietly asked, "Do you think he was an angel?"

"I don't know."

Scott was blown away by Elliot's question. That was something he would never have thought to ask.

"I've thought about that night regularly since it happened and I just don't know. There is a big part of me that says no, no way, yet there is another part of me that wants to believe, have to believe. If it weren't for him, I probably would have stayed in the garage, having no other place to go and I would have died. Worse yet, I would have died before I talked to God and got things straight.

"Yes, he could have been someone sent by God, or not. If I got it wrong, and he wasn't a messenger, why would he smile knowingly at me before he died and then just disappear?"

"So is that why you believe in God?"

"Partially, the other part has to do with Ruby. I realized that if I now wanted to honor God in my life, I had to go back and apologize to my wife."

"Apologize, what for? She was the one stepping out on you." Scott said with resentment.

"Yes, I know that, but I felt Jesus wanted me to apologize and see what He would do with it."

"And what did He do?" asked Elliot with a grin on his face.

"He healed my marriage and started me back to wanting to know Him better with a weekly Bible study in our home with others searching to understand Him better, which made Ruby glad and she finally apologized to me and asked my forgiveness. We've been pretty happy since then, as long as we put God absolutely first in all we do.

"Now, young fella, you can see why I believe in God. He did a work in my heart that I will never forget as long as I live."

"What happened to your shop and your brother-in-law?" Scott just couldn't resist asking even though it was very late now.

Leroy smiled a big grin. "Why, that woman of mine, the day after I got home, marched over to the shop, told the guy off and started calling around looking for another place for our store. I was so proud of her that I changed the name from Pretty Good Used Furniture to Ruby's Very Good Used Furniture and business has been thriving ever since."

"Remarkable," whispered Elliot, and then added, "Praise His holy name."

Scott stood, stretched and said he'd better head to bed because he had a lot to think about, adding, "Great, now not only do I have Henry to worry about, I've got angels to think about."

"Think hard and long," Leroy said as he started his noisy truck with the fender looking like it was ready to fall off again if he hit a big enough pothole.

"I'm going in the house for a minute to the bathroom, and then I'm going straight to bed. Which bed did you say was mine?" asked Scott.

"The one on the left, it's got all the blankets you can need, and I think you'll be comfortable, after all, you'll be sleeping on one of Ruby's Very Good Used Furniture beds. By the way, you're not under any obligation to stay here; I just wanted you to know you were welcome to stay whenever you like."

"Thanks," said Scott as he turned towards the house.

Elliot was looking down the alley at a car making its way carefully to avoid all the obstacles. "I think I see Clancy coming down the alley, think I'll go out and have a word with him and thank him for the wood." Elliot winked.

"Okay, night."

"Good night."

Scott was not the only one who would have something to think about tonight, Elliot had his own demons that he was facing.

In just minutes Elliot poked his head in the shed door and said, "Clancy's asked me to do a little ride along with him tonight. I shouldn't be more than an hour or two. Lock the door, and I'll use my key to get in. Sleep well."

CHAPTER 15

Claire was good at her job; you had to give her that much. She worked on the books for several days, and she had Duff on the carpet several times for his questionable kitchen accounts. He started to bring coffee in for her each time he was summoned for another session, and occasionally he would bring in a piece of fruit or a tiny sliver of something sweet to try to get on her good side.

"Mr. Duff," she would say, "you know I don't eat sweets. How dare you bring that delicious looking bit of pie in here?" But each time he returned he noticed with satisfaction that the plate was empty.

She berated not only the Duffer but also Clay and even Johnny when he finally strolled in a week later.

"Look who's back Clay, I think I recognize him from somewhere. How about you, ever seen him before?"

Before Clay could say something funny to Johnny, Claire was standing at the dining room door tapping her foot and holding a sheaf of papers.

"I'd like to see you in my office, Mr. Sinclair, we have a few accounts to discuss," she said before she turned on her heel and left.

"Look who's in trouble now," Duffer sing-songed when she was out of earshot.

"What's up with her? What did you guys do to the lovely Claire? How long has she been like this?"

"Ever since you brought her here, we thought you two were going out for a romantic supper, not conducting a job interview." Clay was visibly upset about this new arrangement and wanted Johnny to know he was to blame for it.

"What's the matter boys, this beautiful woman jerking you around a bit?"

"Just wait lover boy," Clay said under his breath, "it's your turn next."

Scott was right about his mother; she was back in less than two weeks. Scott had been checking the apartment every one of his days off and this time when he unlocked the kitchen door he smelled something that made him think of apple pie.

"Mom?"

"In here honey."

She was sitting in the living room with a box of pictures on her lap and small piles of photos surrounding her on the floor.

"What cha doing?"

"I just pulled an apple pie out of the oven to cool, and now I'm going through some old pictures. I'm putting them in piles for each of you and if you can I'd like for you to come over when the girls are here, and you can all pick and choose and trade any pictures you'd like."

"Why are you doing this? Why are you giving them to us?" Scott was worried about what his mother might have decided when she was out East with her sister.

"You're not moving east are you?"

She heard the tiny quiver in his voice and added quickly, "Gracious no, why would I do that?"

"Well you're getting rid of everything, so I thought you might be moving."

"You're right about one thing, I am moving, but I'm not leaving the area. I still think this is the greatest city anywhere, you know how much I love Chicago, you know, that toddling town?"

"So do you have a place already?"

"Oh my no, I haven't gotten that far, I just know I have to leave this place." She looked around the living room sadly. "I'm going to miss the old place, but the neighborhood's getting much worse and now I'm here by myself, and I don't feel safe, especially with the L going by and it's only me that's here."

"Do you want me to move back in with you? I'm living with Elliot now, but I could come back in a flash. I would even quit my job if you needed me to."

Ellen chuckled at his words.

"Did I say something funny?"

"Not at all, I am just so impressed by your maturity. You are not my little boy any longer; you're growing into quite a young man."

"I can't take all the credit. Elliot and Leroy have taught me so much in such a short time. You'll never guess the story Leroy told us, I was fascinated."

"Fascinated? I can't wait to hear what the story was about."

"I don't know if I tell you that it would do the story justice. I mean, it's just amazing, and it got me thinking about a lot of things."

"Well, when you're ready to share it, let me know, I think I'd love to hear it."

"When are you going to start the process of moving?"

"I've already started." She pointed at the piles of pictures surrounding her."

"That's a slow start, isn't it?"

"It's not the only thing I'm doing. I've already talked to the super and told him I'd be out by the first of the year."

"But you don't know where you're going?"

"No, I don't, but God knows, and He'll show me when its time" Ellen expected the customary wry smile from her son but this time he simply said, "After Leroy's story, I would bet you're right."

"I haven't got unlimited income you know. In fact, I have no income at all, remember, all these years I was the housewife, and your father was the breadwinner. Now there's no bread coming in, and I'm living off the money I was able to squirrel away."

"You know mom, I never thought about that. What are you going to do? Aren't you kind of old to be getting a job? You know what I mean when I said old, right? I simply mean isn't it going to be hard to find something that pays more than minimum wage."

"I would imagine it will be. I haven't been in the job market for a good twenty years, but when the time comes, God will take care of that too."

"I suppose I've never told you this before, but I appreciate it that you're a mother with a strong faith."

"Thank you. My faith has been my salvation in a crummy and unhappy situation. I always thought God would bring something good out of it, but I can't see anything yet, but maybe that's not the point, I don't know. I know I've grown closer to my savior because of the trials I've experienced. He's never failed to give me the peace I needed."

"Listen mom, I'd love to pursue this conversation more, but I've got to get back to the shed, Elliot, and Leroy and I are heading to a new pizza place for lunch, heard of Pizza Uno?"

"I don't think so, is it new?"

"It's new to us, hey wanna come?"

"I don't know I've got these pictures to finish."

"That's the poorest excuse I've ever heard. Grab your coat and come on. I know Elliot will be happy to see you. He asks about you all the time."

"Really?"

"Yeah, strange huh?"

She didn't respond, but she did put the box of pictures down on the floor and said, "I'll just grab my purse."

"Great, the guys are going to be surprised."

"Just where is this place?" she asked as she was buttoning her coat.

"Over on Ohio and Wabash, I think."

"New place?"

"Nah, Leroy says it's been there since the forties, but then Leroy's facts don't always jibe with the truth. Sometimes I think he just makes them up."

Ellen laughed, suddenly feeling happier than she had been for years as she checked the oven one more time to make sure she had turned it off.

Henry had gone high-class. Or, thought Scott, low class. Either way, his auntie was not going to like the change. Scott had been given two days off in a row and when he returned he was surprised at the changes.

Miss Lee at the front counter motioned him over as she kept an eye on the office door upstairs at the top of the elegant new white staircases.

"Watch your step today Sot. Strange things are going on, and I am very uneasy."

"What kind of things?" He lowered his voice to match hers.

"You and I are the only employees left for one thing."

"Really, how does he plan to run this place with just the two of us?"

"He told me two days ago when he fired the other people that worked here that you and I were the only ones he needed or trusted. I worried about what the 'or trusted' part meant. The changes he's starting to make are making me concerned."

"Whoa, you mean he let everyone else go except for us, that is something of concern. What did his auntie say?"

"Madam Chang does not know what's going on here. She is planning a big celebration to welcome Ming Toy to the community. She has a big party for this girl planned as soon as she gets here followed closely by a wedding if she has anything to say about it."

"When will that be, does anyone know?"

"Madam Chang thinks that it will be soon."

"Scott, you're here." Henry was standing at the top of the stairs, and they were both thinking the same thing at the same time, how long had he been there and what had he heard?

"I need to see you a minute, have a good time during your time off?" He motioned Scott upstairs, and he kept up his friendly banter.

The change in Henry was hard to believe. Gone was the formal tailored black suit and the shiny shoes and the white on a white shirt with the gold cuff links. In its place was leather. Expensive but tight leather pants, a black tee shirt, and a leather vest and it looked like he was well on his way to growing a Fu Manchu mustache along with growing his hair out.

"Great to see you," he said as he headed to his desk without waiting for a response expecting Scott to follow. "Things have changed since you've been here. I'm sure Miss Lee has told you that you and she are the only ones left. I chose you both because you're hard workers and loyal."

Loyal, what's that about, Miss Lee used the word trusted, but somehow the word stupid might fit the situation better thought Scott, wary of the recent changes to both his employer and business in general. He stood mute; learning well from Madam Auntie that being quiet was always the best response to situations like this.

"Since you were gone," Henry began, "I've changed a few things here as you can see. First of all, I've upgraded my already exclusive inventory."

"I thought it was already pretty special." Scott decided to take a chance to see what he could find out for Elliot.

"Yes it was fine, for the tourist's trade but I have a new and exciting source that supplies me with specialty items for the genuine Chinese porcelain vase collectors." He walked deliberately over to a stunning vase that stood over five feet in height and said, "I'll bet you didn't know that there are a series of huge vases, sometimes in this striking blue and white, that used to stand in long rows in the Chinese palaces. Appropriately enough they were called solder vases because their job was to stand well-spaced and quietly like soldiers. I have recently learned that China was already exporting these beauties back in the eleventh and twelfth centuries during the Sung era."

Henry walked over to an impressive porcelain vase that had an incredible luminescence about it. Scott looked closer and saw Chinese hunting scenes combined with what looked like European baroque images. Henry continued, stroking the vase as he said,

"Once you learn the history of these rare vases you'll think of cities like Lisbon, Spain, Portugal, Holland and England, all countries that imported these stunning vases from China throughout the centuries going all the way back to the twelfth century."

There was a new arrogance in Henry's attitude as he motioned for Scott to sit down on his new furniture and as he sat Henry continued as though revealing some vitally valuable information, "Did you know Marco Polo was the first one to use the word porcelain? You knew he was from Venice didn't you?" Not waiting for Scott to answer he continued as he paced the room while giving his impromptu tutorial.

"Evidently the translucent vases looked similar to shells that native-born people used as currency in parts of Asia, India, and Africa and they called the look 'porca' in Polo's native country. The word must somehow have morphed into the new word, porcelain."

It's like he's reciting something he's just learned at the library, like he was reading off a page, thought Scott.

Without waiting for a comment Henry continued the long history lesson. "Marco traveled to China along with his father and uncle in 1271, and they didn't return for 20 years. Of course, it didn't help that for some reason he was held as a prisoner in Genoa, but it was during that prison time that he wrote his influential travel books."

"Did Marco ever return to his own country?"

"I really haven't any idea but I could go on and on and tell you about the Jesuit missionary who toured Jingdezhen in the early seventeen hundreds and said that after the vases were baked, they then passed through the hands of seventy workmen with each person painting only one particular stroke or object before passing it on to the next person. Now you can see why I need these vases handled with extreme care; they are literally priceless and I'm getting in some beauties for my special clients. Notice they are in two pieces," he said as he lifted the top third off of the base.

Scott looked dutifully, trying to look impressed.

"Because it isn't possible to do something this massive in one piece on a potter's wheel, they're made in two adjoining pieces. They fit into the kiln better that way too." His hand slipped from the neck of the vase to what looked like a porcelain rope around the bottom half that rested between the two sections when they were together securely. "This 'collar' is always added to the vase in order for the two pieces to fit together. Once they are fired individually, they are attached with a substance and then they hold together, the collar acting as a stabilizer."

Scott knew he had seen vases like this before and now he realized they were the set of matching vases standing on either side of the large window in auntie's office. He was also floored that Henry should be so knowledgeable about vases, but then he realized that just like Henry to absorb everything he could to set him above everyone on every subject. Oh yes, it was very important that Henry looked good, really good all the time.

Henry continued, "From now on, all this delicate stock will be sent up to my office and you will leave it in its packing crates and I will do the job of unpacking. I need to make sure everything is exactly right.

Now you know that some of these exquisite vases I'm now privy to are worth a small fortune." Henry smiled that creepy smile of his.

"And do you have anything else for me to do besides trying to get huge vases up the stairs without breaking them?"

Henry walked to a back wall and pushed a large red button on the back wall that hadn't been there before.

"It's a dumbwaiter I've had installed." Seeing the question on his face Henry explained.

"A dumbwaiter is a small elevator; they used to use it to take food from the basement kitchens to the upper floors of ritzy houses. I've had this oversize one put in to carry my vases up to me for my inspections and private showings up here."

"Wow, that's cool." Scott admiration was real as he looked inside the elevator.

"That will help big time. So, let me get this straight. I unload the vases and check them off the inventory sheets and then shoot them up to you?"

"Not necessarily, I will give you the new company's name and anything we get in from them you can just send right up to me, these are the ones you'll have to sign for, and then I'll have to sign for, and I don't want to take any chances of breakage. All the other things you can do like you usually do, unpack, check and then put them in the back room so I can place the items where I want them in the shop. Got it?"

"You bet, but what do you want me to do when there are no shipments coming in?"

"I need you to spend more time with my aunt, see what she's up to, what she's planning."

Scott almost groaned outwardly.

"Okay, do you want me to go over now?"

"Definitely, and take notes and listen to everything she says. I need to know everything she even thinks. Listen and report back to me when you hear something. Don't just stand there, go, go."

Miss Lee shrugged her shoulders ever so slightly and raised her eyebrows as he passed her on his way out.

"I think this old guy has fun playing mind games with the tourists."

Scott was putting a few more pieces of wood on the fire while Elliot, his mom, and Leroy were devouring the lemon cake Ellen had brought along. She had made several trips by now, and several without Scott's knowledge.

"What kind of mind games, dear?" His mother was pouring more coffee for Leroy.

"Well, he's a funny little man, to begin with. He's tiny and wrinkled; I mean so wrinkled that when he smiles really big, his eyes practically disappear into his face. Anyway, town was jumping this morning, lots of delivery trucks and lots of tourists. I saw him come out of one of the busy side streets right into the even more hectic traffic on the main drag. He drives a massive car, and I think he gets through traffic by intimidation, that and continually blowing his horn.

"So here he is, driving down the street leaving more and more room between him and the car in front of him. When there's enough room he speeds ahead and all of a sudden he slams on the breaks and the guy behind hits him, not hard and almost no damage. Not only does the guy behind get out of his car, so does this little Chinaman. The little guy starts yelling at the top of his lungs while pointing to a non-existent dent and yelling in whatever language he speaks that the other man has damaged his car and the little guy was going to call the police. In fact, he does. He stood in the street in the middle of the traffic snarl and started to yell, "poweese! Poweese!

"Naturally this unnerved the other driver, so he pulls his wallet out of his pocket and suddenly the disaster was settled with some bills, and they both drove on.

"Miss Lee said this wasn't the first time this had happened. She said he's always thinking of ways to trick people out of their money, so I'm steering clear of him."

"Ah, so Miss Soon Lee still has her job." Elliot said and added, "But if you're down to only the two of you, I would guess he would have to keep her, you can't do it all on your own."

"The way Henry is today, I wouldn't think any decision he made was strange."

"What do you mean strange, what's he doing?" Asked Ellen always concerned for her son.

Elliot answered her question. "Evidently Henry's turned in his 'junior executive of the year' way of dressing for a more edgy look. Scott says he's taken a liking to leather."

"That's not all that he's taken a liking to. Miss Lee caught me by the back door while I was leaving and said that Henry was buying all new furniture for upstairs and it was no longer open to the public. Evidently, he wanted his buyers to be impressed and comfortable."

"By the way Scott, you haven't noticed any tattoos on Henry have you?"

"I don't think so. But then I don't see him in anything but long sleeves. What kind of tattoo do you mean?"

"I mean something that you wouldn't even notice if you weren't looking for it."

"Like what?"

"Like three dots on his right hand."

"Oh those, I thought they were molds or something. Yeah, he's got them, why?"

"No reason."

"You can't just stop there; you have to have a reason why you asked that."

"Okay, I guess you deserve to know, after all, you work for the guy. The other night when I did this ride along with Clancy he was talking about a young group of men who seemed to be forming some group or another."

"To do what?" Ellen was getting interested and worried.

"No one knows. Maybe they're forming some takeover from the old guard."

"I doubt that," Scott said shaking his head no, "there is no way on this green earth that Madam Chang would let him do that. She told me once that even though Henry thinks of himself as a little emperor, she is still the old queen with power over him."

"I hope so, but keep your ear to the ground; I know Clancy would appreciate it."

"Sure, no problem.

Sarah's bags were packed and waiting at the back door of Sophie's. She could not wait to leave.

"Sarah, darling, give your mother our best, and we hope she feels better soon."

"Thanks, Sophie, I'll keep in touch, and I don't know how long I'll be needed, but keep my room for me."

As Sarah hugged her sister, Sandy knew something was not right. It always amazed them both that even though they were separated for twenty years, it was like they were never apart. They finished each other's sentences and seemed to know what the other one was going to say even before she said it. Now Sandy felt that her sister was running away and she looked very sad.

"I won't ask you again," she whispered in her sister's ear, "but please let me help you work out whatever's bothering you. Does Pete know what this is all about?"

When Sandy mentioned Pete Sarah pulled away, smiled and said, "I've got to run, I'll keep in touch" and then she was gone.

"There's something fishy going on," Sophie commented as they watched her back her car up right through the piles of leaves they had just raked and then head over to Eden's expressway on her way home. "Something fishy for sure."

Scott's work day had boiled down to what would be boring to anyone else, but now that Scott had a mission, no two missions, his ears and eyes were open wide to see what he could learn for both Henry and Elliot.

Plans were now finalized for the party at the Cultural Center for Ming Toy who would be arriving at the end of October. Madam wanted to give her a little time to settle in before the big night when she would be introduced to her future husband. Madam had thought about bringing her sister, Henry's mother, over for the big event, but being afraid that she would want to stay in the United States and there would be yet another relative to support, she decided not to, she would send pictures.

"Sot," she said as he appeared at her door, knocking softly. "Where have you been, I have been frantically waiting for you to come. There is much to do now that Ming Toy will be here soon."

As usual, she didn't ask him to sit and virtually ignored him as she thought out loud.

"The plans are all done for the party, but I am still dickering with Feida's for the catering. I can't believe how much they want for an affair. I think I will speak to The Families at the next meeting and then they will have to lower their prices." She smiled to think about not only besting another business financially but making them look cheap at the same time.

"Sot, I need you to make sure Henry's at the party. He is to leave that other woman and take his place at the head of the family." She added slyly, "almost at the head of the family. I have many years yet to live."

"Is there something I can do for you today Madam?"

"What did you say?"

"I asked what I could do for you today."

"You mean after you unload the trucks coming today?"

"Yes, is there anything else I can do to make your life easier?"

She looked at him with narrowed eyes, "What you mean make my life easier? I am not old; I can still work."

She had turned and was looking accusingly at him.

"Yes, I along with everyone else know that you are not old. I just wanted to be of service to you because you have so much to do, I just want to help."

No one had ever spoken to her like that before, and Scott could see her struggle with the offer.

"I have many things still to do, but I think I can find a few things that you can assist me in. Are you sure Henry doesn't need you today, something he needs you to do?"

There was no way Scott was going to say a thing about Henry to his aunt and said, "Nope, not a thing."

"Then you can go downstairs to my other store and ask for their inventory sheets. They will protest, but you must ask, and you must get them. They are getting very sloppy, and I will not have it. Just because

I am planning the biggest party this town has ever seen doesn't mean I don't know everything that's going on."

Sarah's arrival home did not surprise her mother; in fact, Sarah got the impression her mother had been waiting for her.

There were fresh flowers on the table in her old bedroom, and the room looked exactly like she left it. Something about that started Sarah crying. She was still crying when her mother came up moments later and found her with her head buried in the pillows.

As her mom rubbed her back, she said, "This reminds me of all the times your old sister made you angry. You'd always run to your bed and bury your head in the pillows and cry and cry like there was no end of your grief, but it was always temporary."

The tears stopped instantly, and Sarah sat up. "What did you say?"

"Nothing important dear, I just said this is what you used to do when you thought someone slighted you or made you feel bad."

"Pete has made me feel more than badly," she blurted out.

"Pete? I can hardly believe it, he seemed so nice, not your type, but nice."

Stunned Sarah asked, "Did you say he wasn't my type?"

"Now sweetie, I didn't exactly mean to say that."

"But you must have been thinking it."

There was silence as Elizabeth Gold stared out the window before she spoke. "Please don't take this wrong, but it's time to say my piece."

Sarah pushed herself up against her headboard waiting for her mother to continue.

"When I was your age I was seeing a young man of whom my parents disapproved." She held up a finger indicating she had more to say and for Sarah to wait with any comments.

"He was the most wonderful person in my life, and I loved him with all my heart. But," she paused not sure how to continue. "But I knew, and my parents knew that it would never work. For one thing, his father was a factory worker, and his mother was a beautician. Mother sat me down when she saw where it was going and made me realize that our two families could never be on the same level no matter how far we stooped. Don't you see honey, you and Pete are just the same, his father is some steel worker isn't he?"

"Cement I think."

"See what I mean? We have nothing in common with them and to be honest, Pete didn't fit in when you two were here on Labor Day, now did he?" She added patronizingly.

Sarah sighed. "But I love him."

"I'm sure you do, but we've all had several loves before we married the right person."

"Do you mean more like marry the acceptable person when you say the right person?"

"I suppose I do, but it's true."

"What's true?"

"Listen dear; you would have ended up being miserable. When your father and I let you skip your first year of college to pursue a silly career with the phone company we thought you'd come to your senses sooner than you did. Then when you brought Pete home, we didn't know if we should say something right away or let it die naturally."

"Why did you think it would die naturally?"

"Because he's not one of us; he was painfully uncomfortable when he was here, and he wore that dreadful flannel shirt. Surely you could see that he wasn't one of us?"

"Actually if you remember, I hardly saw him at all. We were busy making wedding plans."

Sarah stopped and said, "Oh no, all the wedding plans!"

"Don't give them a second thought darling. I think that Rachel's steady is going to pop the question as soon as he finishes his residency and we can simply transfer all the plans we made to her wedding. See, it all works out." Her mother patted her leg.

"If you don't mind mom, could I be alone for a while?"

"Certainly, I'll have cook bring a supper tray for you so you can give this a really good think and I know you'll make the right decision."

The room went silent when she left but her expensive perfume hung in the air. Sarah's mind was whirling with the things her mother just said; it was as though she had completely erased the man she loved with a few words while eliminating her future to be anywhere but back with her people.

"But," she whispered into the air, "I'm not Jewish."

CHAPTER 16

Claire's reach extended to all parts of the Five. Once she got the books straightened out, she bought a large file cabinet and filled it with individual files concerning everything the Five needed, taxes, utilities, kitchen money, etc. then she began on expenditures.

"So, Mr. Clay," she said as she opened another file. "How many snow shovels did you buy last year and did you use them all? And," she checked another column, "are you going to need more this year? And while you're at it, what is this salt column for, what kind of salt are we talking here and do you have to buy so much?"

Clay took a deep breath and felt as though he was facing his mother once more as she questioned him as to why he was late for supper again. Were you playing with that Mackey kid again? Haven't I told you about that family and why is there a new hole in your pants, do you think I have nothing to do but sew up your clothes, you do have brothers and sisters you know, I can't spend all my time taking care of just you.

"Um," he started badly. "Let's see, I bought two shovels because sometimes Duff helped with the snow and no I don't think I'll need any more this winter but I'd like to keep that open depending on the winter, I'm not sure if that plastic one is going to make it and no, there is no way I can use less salt, the city has laws you know about sidewalks." He finished quickly as though running a sprint, hoping his answers were acceptable.

Evidently, they were because she went on to another subject. "By Thursday I'd like a complete analysis of the condition of the washers, dryers, furnace and water heater and anything else that might be an expensive item that will have to be replaced eventually. If we start putting money away for certain projects when they need to be addressed, we'll already have the money for them."

He had to agree that her thinking was sound and something that would be valuable to do. When he was finally dismissed, he said to Duff, "I still think she's a grand lass, but I think she'd drive any man with a mind of his own absolutely nuts. What I'm wondering is what happened to our sweet and shy Claire, she's becoming a tyrant."

"But you must admit an efficient one and still a lovely tall one." He said dreamily revealing that his love for her deepened daily.

"You have to be completely daft to like that woman," Clay practically hissed to his friend as he also looked over his shoulder to make sure she was nowhere within earshot. Duff was preparing the beef stew for dinner that night. He was busy adding more potatoes to the mix because supper was the time he had the most residents eating at the same time so he threw in more carrots and was eyeing some leftover beets wondering if he gave it some Slavic name he could get away with the addition of the beets.

Duff never had to worry about breakfast because it was always the ready-made pastries that came from the bakery outlet which came individually wrapped. Some weekends he would make pancakes with bacon or sausage, but that was only if one of the stores gave him any breakfast meat, but it was rare. So the standard fallback position was the pile of pastries under the pass-through window. The only residents who were there for lunch were the ones that worked second and third shifts at the surrounding factories, mostly Brocks Candies and the Lay's Potato Chip company but at supper, Duff fed the bulk of the residents, and he fed them relatively well.

"I don't know," Duff said as he sliced some cheese to add to the basket of bread he was getting ready to put out. "There's something about her that fascinates me. She reminds me of my father."

"Holy smoke," said Clay, "I guess I should be thankful for a father that was seldom home because he worked two jobs. I think I would have run away from home at three years old if I had a dad like she is."

"I find her refreshingly organized. Even you have to admit the place is running more smoothly with her here."

"I'll give you that, but I don't dare make a move without her looking over my shoulder. Now she's got me paranoid about buying sidewalk salt, for heaven's sake. I suppose I'll have to ask her highness's permission before I buy a new pair of socks."

"Ha, ha, ha, I seriously don't think she cares about your socks, but" he added with a grin, "she could worry about my socks if she wants to. I would count it a rare privilege."

"I think you're nuts."

"Nuts with love." Duff sighed dramatically.

Ellen had been quietly sitting at the kitchen table circling want ads in the paper, visibly discouraged because there were so few for which she was qualified. As was common for her she bowed her head and prayed, "I know you love me Lord, and I know you've always had a plan for my life, so please give me the patience I need to wait for your direction. I know that when I married Joe I was not looking to you for guidance, and I've paid for it ever since, but Father, I do not want to go one step ahead of you ever again. I will wait for you to lead me, even if that means I'll be living in a box in the middle of the road." She chuckled, "I love you, Father," she added with a smile on her face.

As she got up to refill her coffee, there was a knock on the door. A policeman was standing in the hall back far enough so she could see him clearly through the peephole. She could tell he wasn't new to the job.

"Good morning," she said as she slid the chain off, opened the door and checked his ID.

"Good morning." He checked the piece of paper he was holding. "Are you Ellen West?"

"Yes," she said with a question visible on her face.

"And your husband is Joe West?"

"Yes, but he's not here now. In fact, if you're looking for him he will either be at work or at the tavern at the end of the block." She got ready to close the door when the cop said, "No ma'am, we're not looking for him, we know where he is. We're notifying you of his death and need you to come down to the morgue with us to make a positive identification."

She fell slightly backward and the officer stepped in just in time to help her to the chair that she had recently vacated and was already pulled out. It was the same chair where she had just told God that she would wait for his leading.

"I'm sorry ma'am, but there is no other way to break this kind of news. I know it's rough, but down at the station they tell us just to say it and then give aid."

"I see." Her hands were shaking in her lap.

Officer Richter had been in this situation more times than he liked and it was never any different. Sometimes there was a room full of people, and sometimes, like now, the person was alone. Either way, it was never easy. He knew from long experience that time was on everyone's side. He sat down next to her.

"Is there someone I can call?"

"What?" She looked up at him as though seeing him for the first time.

"Is there someone I can call to come over and be with you, maybe have them meet you at the morgue?"

Ellen had accepted the fact that there was an officer in her kitchen sitting next to her as they sat at her kitchen table, but when he mentioned the morgue, she once again remembered why he was there.

"There are a few people, but I don't know how to contact them."

"Maybe I can help with that. Are they here in the city?"

"Yes, they're here in the city." She felt like she was underwater and everything around her slowed down to a crawl. "I think the officer's name is Clancy. He's one of you; I mean he's a Chicago cop, works down by Chinatown."

"Is that who you want me to contact?"

"I'm sorry, what did you ask?"

"I asked if this officer named Clancy is the one you want me to contact for you."

"No, I'm sorry, I'm having a little trouble putting all this together. Clancy's the one that knows where the one I want is."

"I see, you say his name is Clancy?"

"I don't know," she sighed deeply. "I don't think so, that's just what they call him."

"Who calls him that?"

"Could I just have a moment please?" Without waiting for an answer she rose and went into the bathroom to stare at herself in the mirror. "What's going on Father?" she prayed. "I don't understand what you want from me." Tears started down her cheeks which surprised her; she thought she had cried them all after receiving the divorce papers. They weren't tears for Joe, not really, they were more tears of regret as to what could have been, but now it was over, Joe was dead.

She held a washcloth under the cold water and dabbed at her eyes. When she opened the door the officer had gone, but he had left the door open and she noticed the kitchen curtains had been closed, had he done that so the L riders would not be privy to his visit?

"Okay Sarge, I'll tell her." His voice drifted in from the hall.

"My sergeant knows your guy and is contacting him now. Mind if I join you in a cup of coffee while we wait?" It wasn't standard police procedure, but Richter had been a cop for a long time and knew that some rules were made to be broken. Here was this woman all alone and receiving shocking news and until they found his fellow officer, she needed someone to sit with her.

"No, I wouldn't mind at all, and, and thank you." Unbidden tears started to flow again as her companion looked through the cupboard for another cup.

Badly shaken, she was holding tightly onto her son's hand while Elliot's arm was around her waist as they left the morgue. Elliot had seen the signs of shock many times before and didn't say a thing to either of them, but gently led them to a restaurant nearby." When's the last time you've eaten Ellen?"

"I'm not hungry."

"That isn't what I asked; I asked when the last time was that you ate."

"I don't know, last night?"

"Just as I thought, look, this place is known for their Ruebens, do you like Rubens Ellen?"

"Um, sure, but listen, I'm not hungry."

Ignoring her answer, he asked, "Scott, a Rueben for you too? They come with fries and a pickle."

"Sure, thanks. Mom, are you all right?"

"Yes honey, I'm fine, how are you holding up?"

"I haven't let myself think about it after seeing dad like that, you know, dead, but I think it's going to take us all a long time to be normal again."

"Scott," Elliot interrupted before the conversation became morbid, "Do you think you can stay with your mom tonight?"

"Sure, I'd be glad to."

"And we'll have to let your sister know to mom," Scott added.

She let her breath out slowly and said to no one in particular, "We'll have to let his family know and then start making funeral plans." Seeing the look on Scott's face she replied softly while caressing his cheek, "I have to do this last thing for him; I'm still officially his wife you know."

Elliot was suddenly all business, "Do you want me to go in and tell Henry what happened?"

Scott had completely forgotten about his boss. Elliot had initially found Scott in-between shops delivering an armful of stock from one of aunties shops to another when Clancy dropped him off to tell Scott what happened.

"As soon as we've finished lunch I'll get Clancy to take me back down to Chinatown and straighten everything out for you. I think it wouldn't hurt to ask for a few days off considering."

Ellen, who had seemed to be in a place far away put her hand on Elliot's arm and said, "Thank you for everything. You have been a good friend to both of us during this time."

Their lunch came, and it surprised Ellen that they each ate absolutely everything on their plates.

Elliot was pleased to have an excuse to visit Henry's lair, and Scott was right, Henry was up to something. All new sleek black leather sofas and chairs were delivered to his new private showroom, and they were accented with modern white side tables on which there were glossy black vases sporting vibrant red silk poppies. The place was decorated like an expensive penthouse instead of a shop in Chinatown; there were no traces of Old China anywhere. He also noticed the coffee pot was still on the side table, but now there was no sugar or powdered cream in sight.

Henry tried to be sympathetic when Elliot told him the news, but he seemed relieved that Scott wouldn't be around for a few days. Elliot took note of the three dots on Henry's hand as he shook it to say good-bye.

"Tell Scott to take all the time he needs," Henry called down from his classy showroom which could be seen in all its splendor through the highly ornate white metal railings on the stairs. "I'm sure he'll need a few days," he added absentmindedly.

There was a new full-size General Motor's Jimmy truck sitting in the back of the Five when Duff came back with his truck that was now loaded with donated food. With Thanksgiving only two weeks away, the huge Maurice Lenell's bakery on Harlem Avenue was featuring their discounted Christmas fruitcake seconds, and their famous butter cookies were also marked half price. It didn't matter that the cookies were half-price because they were broken, Duff liked the cans they came in and he especially liked the price, and the residents liked the cookies.

The Duffer had loaded his old VW van with a large stash of bakery products that he hoped to string out to Easter if he played it right and when he pulled into the Five he had to park next to some other vehicle that had taken his parking place. As he thundered into the back of the building, he could hear Claire and Clay's voices in the laundry area.

"Hey," he didn't even pause for the formal 'hello,' but continued. "Who's in my parking place? I have a hard enough time unloading my van, which stopped twice today and I had trouble starting, and now there's someone else by the back door right next to the kitchen. Could we possibly find out who it is and get them to move it?"

He stood with hands on hips waiting for someone to answer. Happily, it was Claire who responded as she moved from around the other side of a washer that had been pulled out with assorted pieces carefully placed on a square blue work cloth next to the wall.

Unlike her usual professional self she linked her arm through his and said as she walked him toward the back door again, "I'd like to have you look at it and see what you think."

"Think, think about what? Somebody just needs to move it."

"Yes," she said taking the keys out of her pants pocket. "I think we should move it and we'll only be a half hour at best doing it, Clay."

They decided to drive north of the city to test drive the new panel truck.

"Ride well?" She asked. "The guy that let me take it said this was a new GMC Jimmy and that not only would it be perfect for us, but he's giving us quite a deal."

Duff, who was still in his own kind of shock, felt a little sorry for the poor salesman who had to go up against Claire, she might look like a total innocent, but wave figures in front of her and she was more like a bull ready to rumble.

"As Clay would put it, I think this is grand."

They were northwest of the city heading toward Milwaukee and Devon because the Duffer, unbeknownst to Claire, planned to stop at the Superdawg for a quick bite. He had initially found the tiny drive-in with its carhops while he ambled through several jobs and several friends' apartments until he found the Five. He also wanted to show Claire this Chicago landmark drive-in that had two twelve foot hot dogs on the roof, the boy dog dressed in a leopard skin and flexing his muscles and the female dog in a ruffled skirt and a bow in her hair. She was turned as though admiring her own super dog and winking at him with one eye that lit up only to be matched by his winking at her.

"Let's grab a dog," he said as they pulled into the parking lot.

"But what if we spill, the salesman may renege on some of the deals I did to get this price."

"True, but it would be a shame to get all the way out here and not get a dog."

"I suppose you're right, but I'll just have a diet pop."

Duff parked the Jimmy and turned to look at his passenger. "Isn't about time you join the real world?"

"What did you just ask me?"

"I asked you to stop trying to be somebody that you're not going to be and eat something."

"And just might I ask what that is and what you're talking about and why you're bringing it up now?"

Her face reddened slightly giving her the first healthy glow the Duffer had ever seen.

"Look, Claire," he said as he turned to face her fully. I talked to that madam lady of yours weeks ago, and she said that you were just too tall to dance. She knew it, and she said you knew it and if that's so, why were you still there if there was no future in ballet for you, no future at all."

Surprisingly Claire did not cry even though the hot tears were stinging behind her eyes threatening to fall.

"I can't say as I care that you went behind my back to talk to Madam Zaretski. You had no right to do that. And there is a future for me in dance; I'm going to open my own studio."

"Where, when?" He had her there because up until the very moment the words came out of her mouth she had never thought of teaching locally.

"I suppose I'll start looking for a place as soon as I get the Five's books in order. They were in a terrible mess you know, just terrible." Now she started crying so Duff pulled out of the parking lot before a carhop came out and gave them a menu and a number to put on their window that was partially rolled down and where their tray would rest later holding their food.

He didn't want to hurt her, but he knew he had a few things to say to her before they went back to the Five, so he took the first exit he could find off the Edens and parked at an abandoned Sinclair gas station. This company used a giant green dinosaur as their mascot, and it was looming over them.

He turned to her once more after turning off the vehicle. "I think you should teach dance, anywhere you like, but why did you keep living in that squalid place if you knew you were never going to dance ballet professionally anywhere?"

Her tears had subsided and she was staring out of her window, "I guess I was just afraid."

"Afraid of what?" He asked gently and then added, "You don't seem the type to be afraid of anything or anybody. I know you've got Clay and Johnny and me wrapped around your little finger."

"That's just because your books were a mess and I wanted to do something right for once."

"What do you mean for once?"

She rolled down her window and took a deep breath of cold air. "I'm sure I told you that I've always wanted to dance and my parents made me go to college, right?"

"Right."

"Well, they're both gentle Iowa folks, and it broke their hearts when I moved to Chicago as soon I graduated from Iowa State University. I'm sure that my mom wanted me to move home, find a job nearby and marry some nice dull Iowa farm guy. Well, that didn't happen, or sometimes when I think about it, I didn't want it to happen.

"Maybe it was a form of punishment that I was dishing out, but I resented the fact they were right about ballet. I mean, I'm sure they didn't realize I would grow this tall, they just thought it was something too frivolous even to entertain; a career in dance, I'm sure they thought it was a foolish waste of time.

"Well, I moved to some rat trap downtown and found Madam Zaretski because she was cheap. She was an okay teacher, but by then I had grown to my full height and still I didn't want to give up my dream. Everything just caved in after that. I started doing her simple book work to help pay for my classes, and soon I had moved in and was sleeping in her spare bedroom on a rock-hard bed. That doesn't help with dancing, you know, sleeping badly?"

"I would imagine it didn't." Duff glanced at his watch as she began talking again hoping she hadn't seen him look.

"I didn't like living there. I especially didn't like the after hours. When all the dancers left about eight o'clock, she would lock the downstairs door, come upstairs and put on her garish silk robe and then she'd take off her hair and makeup."

"Okay," he gave her a startled look and carefully continued, "When you said she took off her hair..."

"Yeah, she wore a wig. It's a good thing too because she was bald when she removed it. Well, she wasn't totally bald, but her hair was so thin she looked bald. And what little hair she did have was gray and with her makeup off she looked more like she was eighty than sixty."

Claire had stopped her narrative and Duff thought it was the end of their conversation, but he didn't want the moment to last. He was happy to have her exclusively his, even if it was just for the moment.

"How long were you planning to stay with that weirdo and what were you telling your parents?"

"I told my parents nothing. No, that's wrong; I told them I was in class and dancing. It wasn't a lie, but it wasn't the truth either."

"And at some point, you found out about the Five and came one day to find out more about it."

"Yes," she sighed deeply. "But I am in the same place I was when I was living in the studio, there's not enough for me to do at the Five and I don't have money to open a studio of my own, I don't have much money at all come to think about it."

Claire was hurt as Duff started the truck and completely changing the subject while pulling out into the traffic and asking, "So, according to your figures we can afford this thing?"

"Pretty much, it would be nice to have a little more to put down, but I think we can swing it."

"What if I told you that I've been laying aside some of the kitchen budget for the purchase of a better vehicle myself? He didn't let her answer and continued. "And what if this sum is…"

When he mentioned the figure she smiled and asked, "And just how long have you been laying aside this cash?"

"Ever since I got the job as the cook, let's see, that would be a couple of years."

She had a puzzled look on her face, and he was smiling as they joined the rush hour traffic.

"I'd like to talk to you about a few things when we get back to the Five he said. "Hey, when does this vehicle have to be back at the dealers?"

"I almost forgot about getting it back; I think the salesman said seven tonight."

"Perfect, we'll drop it off and then have a bite to eat somewhere."

"But won't there be supper at the Five and don't you have to cook it?"

"Nah, when we stop to pick up the other van I'll grab Clay and tell him where the soup is for supper and he knows where the sandwich stuff is."

The funeral was over, and Elliot got to meet the entire West family.

He had surprised everyone when he showed up wearing a suit for the occasion. Scott was amazed that a man without any income could find such a nice suit, shirt and shoes at a thrift store and he made a note to ask Elliot if he'd bought them or borrowed the outfit from Leroy. Leroy went to church every Sunday, and he and Ruby went all out to look splendid, so it could easily have been his.

After the family and friends left the house, Ellen was convinced by Elliot to sit down for a while.

"I was so pleased that Ruby and Leroy came today. It was nice to meet her." Ellen said as she sunk down onto the sofa.

Scott thought his mom must be on automatic pilot because she was making small conversation with Elliot and not crying or staring off into space. When Elliot left, Scott brought his mom a cup of coffee and said, "Can I ask you something?"

"She took an exhausted breath and said, "Certainly."

"I mean no disrespect, and I know he was a world-class jerk, but somehow I expected more emotion from you at the funeral." He looked sideways at his mom to see how she took the question.

"Oddly enough, I thought about that too. I didn't feel the need for tears because they would have been tears for me, not your father. He's made his decisions about life and death, and there is nothing I can do for him now. The person that I thought about during the service was, oddly enough, King David of the Bible."

"Did you say, King David?"

"I did."

"And may I ask why?"

"I think it was because he lost someone too."

"And..."

"Well, you remember the story of Bathsheba and David, don't you?"

"Who doesn't?"

"Right, but most people just remember the part about him seeing her taking an outdoor bath and him summoning her to his palace."

"Right so far as I remember."

"And some people might even remember that King David had her husband killed in battle so he could have her exclusively."

"And..."

"And what many people don't remember is that he and Bathsheba conceived a child the night he invited her over, and the child died shortly after birth."

"Okay, I don't remember that part either, but what does that have to do with today?"

"It's just that their baby boy was sickly and David grieved deeply day and night, but as soon as the baby died, David washed and put on clean clothes and ate. His advisers asked why when the baby was sick he hadn't eaten or slept, but now that the baby was dead he stopped his grieving. David answered that he knew he couldn't bring his child back from the dead and it was over. Oddly enough, that's how I felt today. I put years of grief and tears into your father, but now that he's dead, I need to get on with my life and let the past be the past. It also answered the question Elliot asked me months ago if I were a believer, a non-believer or a make-believer. There is no question in my mind; I am a believer, a firm believer that not only did God send his son to die for me, to take the punishment I deserved for my sins but that He will never leave me nor forsake me and I am so thankful for that."

She didn't know where her boldness came from, but while she was on a roll she asked her only son, "So while we're on the subject, which one are you, which of the three in the category are you in?"

CHAPTER 17

Sarah met her sister for lunch downtown on a day when Sandy did not have any classes or obligations shortly after she had gone home to 'take care of her mother.'

It was an awkward conversation, but once Sarah had explained to Sandy what had happened between Pete and her and between Elizabeth and her, Sandy had no solution or opinions to offer.

"This is just wild, just wild. What are you going to do? Don't you love Pete anymore?"

"Of course I love him."

"You don't sound very convincing."

"It's just that, oh I don't know, things are just so complicated."

"Nothing could have been more complicated than Johnny's and my situation."

"Ah but remember, you have an absent mother, I have a very present one who wants me to quit my job, give up Pete and move back to their world."

"And do you want to do any of that?"

"Part of me says no, absolutely no."

"And another part of that is saying maybe to some of it?"

Sarah stirred the ice in her chocolate Coke and struggled with her answer.

"I don't know anymore. I don't know about anything. I mean, my boss just offered me a promotion and a raise at the phone company."

"And it makes you feel pretty proud that you did it all on your own, doesn't it?"

"It does. I skipped going to college right out of high school to prove just that, that I could make it in the world on my own. I mean, honestly, look what I accomplished; I have a promotion waiting for me, a place to live with people I love and a man that loves me with all his heart."

"And the problem is?"

"The problem is my mother. She makes everything I accomplished sound like something that's no more important than learning to tie your shoes."

"But," Sandy put her hand on top of her sister's, "she's not your mother. Remember, our mother is the great absent one."

"It's not that I don't know that, but the only person I've ever called mom is Elizabeth, and they have been very good to me, I think I owe them something, don't you?"

"Yes I do, you owe them something, but not your life, at least not your future life. I mean, what happens if you go back?"

"I suppose it will be just like before, I'll be introduced to all sort of Jewish boys on their way up the ladder and I'll be required to spend Saturday nights at the Country Club. My mother will probably drag me all over making sure I know all the important people and they know me. I saw her do this with Princess Perfect and she ate it up."

"But you're not Princess Perfect, are you?"

"I didn't think I was, but now I'm beginning to wonder. I mean, really."

Their hot beef sandwiches finally came and as they ate Sandy asked, "So, what are you going to say to Pete? You have to tell him something."

"I know and it's really rough. I mean not only do I have to tell Pete, but I also have to let the phone company know when I'll be back to work. I only get a certain number of days for family leave."

"Family leave, whose family?"

"Mine. I told them the same thing I told you and Sophie, that my mom was sick."

"Oh."

"By the way, how are Sophie and Phil?"

"I have never seen either one of them happier. Sophie knows something is fishy about you going back home, you know."

"I knew she'd figure it out. She's a pretty sharp cookie."

"Yes she is, and I think she'd be a great one to talk to about this situation."

"You know, I think you're right. I'll call her tomorrow."

"Call her this afternoon, she and Phil are going shopping for construction materials tomorrow."

"And just why are they doing that?"

"Seems like they've got some new ideas on how to smarten up the old place and they even asked me to give them some advice for sprucing up the inside."

"Well, la-de-da. They'll spruce it up and raise the rent and I won't be able to afford to live there anymore."

"Remember if your mother has anything to do with it, there will be no question about where you'll live. Just think, back in the lap of luxury, and the cost will be giving up so many people you love and everyone here who loves you."

Elliot did not return to the shed until late and Scott was concerned.

"Where in the world have you been and why didn't you leave me a note?"

"Wow, you sound just like my mother."

"Well, you can't blame me for being upset."

"Nothing to worry about, Clancy and I were just out cruising around the city."

"And did you do anything interesting while you were cruising?"

"Nope, not really, Clancy just got talking, and we lost track of time."

"Okay, it that's your story. Henry wants me in early tomorrow because he's going to start training me to deliver stuff to his customers."

"What kind of stuff?" Elliot was suddenly all ears.

"You know, things that are too big for people to carry."

"And just how far do you have to go to deliver the stuff." He tried to sound nonchalant.

"Not too far. Henry already has a service that delivers to places outside the city, so I'm just pretty much local."

"And does auntie know about this delivery at night thing?"

"I have no idea, and I don't plan to be the one who tells her. With this big surprise party next week she's all but forgotten me. Do you know I was gone for over two weeks before she even noticed I had moved out?"

"She must really be involved with this party, but why do you call it a surprise party, Henry knows about it, doesn't he?"

"Oh yes, he knows it's a party, he just doesn't know it's his engagement party."

"What I wouldn't give to be there," said Elliot and then added, "Maybe I'll come and see what happens."

"Not me man, I plan to be far away, so I don't get stuck in the middle of it. I'm sure by the time the nights over both Madam and Henry will be furious with me and in reality, I had nothing to do with any of it, but they'll each need someone to blame. By the way, when are you planning on hooking up the chimney? If you haven't already noticed it's freezing in here."

"Such a crybaby," Elliot said in a teasing voice. "Leroy and I are going to work on it tomorrow. I think we've figured out a way to get it up without burning the place down the first time we use it. But first, we have to shore up those back steps on the house again. If they lean much more we'll have to completely rebuild them because we don't want to lose our bathroom privileges, now do we? You'll also have a surprise next time you're here; we're insulating the place so it will be a lot warmer in here."

"And a lot easier to look at too with the billboards covered, wow, with all that work ahead of you, I would imagine that you're about ready to turn in, aren't you?"

"I thought it would be a good idea; it looks like we've both got a busy day planned, what time did Henry say you were to make the deliveries?"

"He hasn't. I guess I'll find out in the morning. Oh hey, did I tell you that he's paying me a hundred dollars for one night's delivery? These vases must be worth their weight in gold."

"Or something," muttered Elliot as he pulled down his covers and lay down and the soft glow of the streetlight filled the room through the Sunday newspaper comics that covered the windows.

It was a celebration of sorts. The two newlywed couples were out for supper together, and both Sophie and Phil were beaming from ear to ear.

"So," Sophie said as their salads came and they said grace, "Now that both of you will be graduating in December, what plans have you made?"

"I've already been offered a job with a design firm, and Johnny still hasn't decided if he wants to go into partnership with his father's company or he's thinking, just thinking, that he might start his own company."

"Your own company, that is impressive, have you told your parents yet what you're thinking about your career and do they know you're married yet?"

"Well, not exactly," said Johnny buttering a roll.

"What's with not exactly? Either they know, or they don't know, nu?"

"Well, I guess its nu." Johnny smiled at Sophie, but she wasn't buying it.

"So, when are you planning on breaking to them the good news, maybe at the birth of your third child?"

"Now Sophie," Phil said, "This is not our business. Let the young couple decide who to tell and when."

"I'm just asking Phil; I'm not deciding."

"It sounds to me like you'd like to plan their future for them," he said with a smile. "You know, offer them something they can't refuse."

She put down her fork and patted his hand. "Okay, okay, I'll ask, or do you want to wait until dessert?"

"Wait for dessert to ask what?" Johnny looked up from cutting his steak.

"Listen darling Sandy; ever since you came to me that awful night after that terrible thing that happened, you have been special to me, both you and your sister. And after that horrible assault with that disgusting Marshall Field's man, well, we became close, like a family. And if you remember that's when both you and I gave our hearts to God, remember your friend Vivian?"

"How could I forget?" She said softly as Johnny put his arm around her and pulled her close." Exactly," said Sophie. "Life begins new every morning, just look at Phil and me. We were related by marriage for many years, and now we're double related by marriage."

Phil smiled at her allegory as popped a bite of steak into his mouth. "So Sophie darling, are you going to eat or talk?"

"It's up to you."

"Then I say eat, and we'll talk later."

Sandy gave Johnny a loving look that implied, "Aren't they just the sweetest things?"

Scott decided to stay with Elliot the next night after making the delivery for Henry, and he was surprised that the older man was still up and sitting by the fire poking it with a stick and watching the sparks fly. Clancy's squad was parked in the alley, which always made Scott feel safer and now he too was sitting close to the flames keeping warm, his radio a constant buzz of police traffic. Scott wasn't sure if Elliot had any lawful neighbors in the block and he was always worried that the bums who slept in the row of condemned houses along their alley would see Elliot's fire and come over to get warm and spend a few hours doing it, maybe moving right in.

So far it hadn't happened, and he imagined the presence of Clancy's squad car had something to do with that.

"You're up late, aren't you, son?" Clancy was jovial despite the cold.

"Yeah, lucky me," Scott said as he lowered himself in the last chair and warmed his hands by the fire, "I got lost twice, and I finally found the spot."

"Did everything go all right?" asked Elliot trying to sound casual.

"I guess so; once I found the right address I carefully backed Henry's old delivery truck into the driveway and three guys came out and signed the papers and unloaded the vase. Funny thing though…"

"What was that, Scott?" Elliot was losing his ability to sound casual.

"Well, you know how Henry had read chapter and verse to me about some dynasty or another and that at one time it took seventy people to paint one vase? Well, these 'collectors' didn't seem too interested in being careful. I mean, they made a big play at being cautious, but they weren't."

Both Elliot and Clancy sat spellbound as Scott continued innocently.

"So I delivered the vase and drove back to the store, only getting turned around once and there you go. When I got back with the van, Henry said the collector who got the vase called and said everything was in perfect order and then he gave me five one hundred dollars bills for the night."

"Five hundred dollars, did he say why he gave you so much?" Scott remembered that Clancy didn't know that Henry promised him a hundred dollars for the delivery.

"He said that because he got such a huge price for the vase that he could afford to share the wealth. If you two don't mind, I think I'll call it a night, I am just whipped."

"Before you go, I have something to ask you to do." Now Elliot was serious.

"Is it another paying job?"

"Hardly. Do you still have all the money Henry's given you?"

"Um, yeah, why?"

"Is it nearby or did you put it in the night deposit at the bank, maybe into your account?"

"Are you kidding, I've never even thought of putting it into a bank whose employees only speak a smattering of English. My luck they'd ask me if I wanted to contribute it all to some cause and I'd say yes thinking they were asking me if I wanted a higher rate of interest. No, I have it all in that can of peanuts in a box of clothes under my bed in the shed."

Elliot looked more severe than ever. "Scott, Clancy has been telling me that there might be some porcelain fraud stemming from Chinatown and he thinks it might be Henry that's doing it."

"You're not joking are you?"

"No son," Clancy said, "we think he might have conned you to be right in the middle of it."

Scott was silent as he mulled over the news in his head. Things were starting to make sense, Henry's cutting down on employees, putting in the dumb-waiter, making upstairs exclusive, and closing early, not to mention making his aunt believe he had a woman he was seeing. He finally asked both men, "What do I need to do?"

"First of all," said Elliot, "you need to turn over all the money that Henry's given you to Clancy, and I will sign as your witness. Then you need to write a quick affidavit as to your part in all this. Do you understand?"

"Not all of it, but I understand enough not to want to get involved. I mean, could I go to prison because of this?"

"I don't think so," Clancy said as he put his big paw of a hand on Scott's shoulder. "Look at it this way; you've got the entire Chicago police force on your side."

Scott would have felt much better if Clancy had said positively that he wouldn't get into any trouble instead of 'I don't think so,' because it would kill his mother if he went to jail.

Scott had to work the next three days with only one more delivery set for the next week, so it was Elliot who accompanied Ellen to the reading of the will.

"Do I look all right?" she asked for the second time. "I'm so nervous, and I don't know why."

"It must be a little frightening to connect with your husband again in any way. I know I've heard of people in the circumstances like yours, you know estranged, and then having to reconnect in some way when it's all over and they all said that it just felt weird and awkward."

"Yeah, awkward might be right, it's something, and I don't like it."

"Are you expecting anything in the will?"

"What would be there to expect? I think he had a modest life insurance policy through the company and what little he brought home in his paycheck was due to him drinking up the rest, and probably spending more and more of it on her as their relationship deepened."

Elliot deliberately changed the subject as he closed her apartment door after them, making sure it was locked before they headed down the flight of stairs to the door.

"How about having some lunch afterward as long as we have to be downtown?"

She patted his hand, "Let's see how things turn out first."

"Fair enough."

Lunch at the famous, and very expensive Chicago loop restaurant, Henrici's was over. Ellen had been very quiet through the meal, hardly talking at all, relying on the conversations at the other tables to create the ambiance. Elliot ordered coffee for them both and put his hand on hers and squeezed it gently.

"So what now, Mrs. West?"

She breathed deeply, raised both her shoulders and her eyebrows and said, "I have no idea."

"Well, whatever you do, do it slowly."

She turned to look entirely at him and asked with a shaky voice, "Will you help me through this?"

"You know I will. I'll do anything I can to help you make the wisest decisions you can make. Have you decided when you're going to tell Scott?"

"I've been thinking about that during lunch. Do you realize what this means for him? And for the girls?" She added quickly. "This can change his life; this is the opportunity I've always wanted for him."

"Should we celebrate and order dessert?" Elliot was still holding her hand when the waiter returned to the table.

"I think that would be a lovely idea,: she said as though they ate there every day. "I think it should either be Bananas Foster or Cherries Jubilee, What do you think?"

"I think either one would be great and I also think it's your day to start making the decisions. Which one do you want?"

"I think I'll have the Banana's Foster," she told the waiter. : And before we leave, we would like six of your delicious chocolate eclairs and a Linzer tort to go."

"Very good, madam." The waiter putting the accent on the word, 'very.'

"And," she said as she reached for her purse, "I'm paying for the meal. There's no use being flush with cash with more to come and not pay for this meal. After all, you have not only been a good friend to my son, more of a father come to think about it, but you've also been an excellent friend to me." She lowered her voice as she put her head down to avoid his eyes while gently closing her purse.

Elliot wanted to say more but decided that now was too soon. He'd have to keep a close eye on this woman to make sure she didn't get away. It had been a long time since he was so very much in love, and it felt wonderful.

The only four people who lived at the house on Foster Avenue were now all seated by a bank officer in one of their offices; everyone had a smile on their face. Well, maybe not all. Johnny had just about chewed his fingernails down to the nubs with worry about being the new owner of one of the most beautiful and certainly one of the most venerable buildings on Chicago's near north side.

It took them almost an hour to get all the details and paperwork filled out, and while they were waiting for the banker to return to the office Sophie asked, "So Johnny, did you say your mother knows that your father is helping you out financially?"

"She does, and I don't know how she feels about it, but my dad said that since he's trying to put more honesty in their relationship and include her more, he decided to pass it by her before offering it to us."

"But it's still a great deal of money," said Sophie.

"That's what I thought, and I hope we're not making a mistake, no, I mean a huge mistake, by buying it."

"Now honey, you're a smart guy and will do well in your own branch office of your father's business," soothed Sandy. "In a way, it will be a Sinclair and Sinclair company, but one Sinclair will be on Foster Avenue that's all."

"Well, Phil and I think it's a great idea that you're going to make offices out of it."

"Not all offices," Sandy said, "we still have to live somewhere."

"Yeah, because we're putting the offices upstairs, we still plan to live in your old apartment, Sophie. We both agreed it was still the coziest room in the house."

"And so full of happy memories," added Sandy.

"We're also keeping the kitchen and dining room to use as a break room for the employees. Did Sandy tell you she's redoing all the rooms upstairs turning them into professional office space? My girl's got some great ideas."

"Too bad I can't use them for more extra credit, but that part is over. Now I just need to put in a few more weeks and grab my diploma."

"I can't wait to see what you're going to do with the building and I think it's very thoughtful of you to keep the kitchen and dining room, kind of like our Friends Together Nights? And on our first trip back to Chicago when we come back to visit, we will make the old building our first stop." Sophie patted Sandy's hand, and both women were starting to tear up.

"Okay ladies, none of that, we still have a lot of papers to sign."

"See, Phil is the practical one."

"And my dear wife is the tender one."

Chapter 18

The new van sat in the parking lot with both doors proudly bearing the name of The Five, and it's addressed on Armitage Avenue, thanks to city regulations. The necessary information was required by the city of Chicago's commercial truck policies along with the permit number clearly written.

Leave it to Chicago to squeeze another fifty dollars out of a poor working stiff, though Duff as he stood inside starting at this new vehicle. Now what he wanted to do was to come up with a large graphic on the van itself with a new, really neat logo.

He asked everyone who came into the dining room for the rest of the day if they could think of a name and a logo and all he got were suggestions like Grab and Go. Clay said it sounded like a group of bank robbers, and Food Reclamation Van brought hoots of laughter especially from the guy, Jerry, who was having a hard time fitting in.

"Okay, wise guy. What do you suggest we use as a tagline since you know everything," he added.

"Maybe we should have a contest." Clay suggested hoping to diffuse what could end up in a nasty argument between the two men. He looked around for approval of his idea.

"And just what are you thinking of for a prize, a can of beans?" Quipped Jerry, not giving in.

"Funny, ha, ha, so, have you got any better idea?" Clay was once again figuratively pulling his righteous robes around himself, as though Jerry didn't approve of the contest either.

Duff was getting angry. "Give me time; I can do this, just watch."

Duff strode into the kitchen and found a small cardboard box which he placed on the pass-through window between the kitchen and the dining room. He then left the room to see if there was any scrap paper in Claire's office he could cut up for suggestions.

Most of the suggestions he got were terrible and they were still coming in.

"Why would you give someone the power to name your new van?" Asked Claire as she entered the kitchen. "Don't you realize they would undermine your authority if you picked their idea? No, no, no, take the box down, we'll think of something ourselves."

Duffer was amazed that this was the same timid woman who'd only been at the Five for a few months with nothing to say. Evidently living with that ballet master of hers taught her to have a stiff spine when she needs one. He didn't care either way. He was in love whether she was soft as a feather or as hard as a rock. She was everything he ever wanted in a woman. His father would be surprised at his choice. It's a shame he didn't live long enough to meet her, he mused, they would have gotten along famously.

"And by the way," she added, pointing to a large sheet of paper that she had removed from the bulletin board in the hall, "why are we not doing this anymore?"

"Now that's an excellent question," he said as he checked the dates on the columns. "Looks like it's been a while since anyone's signed up."

"Correct me if I'm wrong, but this sign-up sheer is a barter system, right? If I read this correctly when the men work around the place they write down their hours and what they did. And those hours entitle them to buy things in the little store next to my office, right?"

"Exactly," answered Duff while adding, "Yea, things like laundry soap and personal care items and even pillows and blankets or anything else we might have they can buy with their hour-dollars."

"The obvious question would now be, why hasn't anyone signed up to work. . ." she flipped the sheets back to where she could see a few names, "for six weeks?"

"Six weeks you say, hmm."

"With that answer, I can presume that either no one has been keeping track of the hours, or no one needed anything from the store."

"I think it's fair to say that."

"Are both the reasons right or just one?" She inquired staring squarely at him and then added, "If it's just one, which one?"

"You might say both in a way." Before she could start questioning him again, he quickly added, "See, it's summer, and there's isn't a lot to do. You know, no snow to shovel and hardly any lawn to mow."

"So, this is just a list for snow shoveling? I thought that was Clay's job. He's bought enough shovels and salt for an entire crew to clean off and melt snow."

Duffer knew when he was licked, so he sat across from her at the desk and just drummed his fingers on the desk, trying desperately to think of some excuse.

"By the way, since no one's signed up to do anything around here, where's the stuff that's supposed to be in the store? It's all gone."

"Gone?"

"Yes, gone. Vanished, disappeared, missing."

"Well, how about that?"

"Okay," she said pulling out one of her famous clipboards, "From now on, we will take a thorough inventory of the few things we have left in the store. Then we need to resupply, and someone needs to monitor it to make sure things don't walk away. Jerry's not working full time, is he? I think I'll ask him to help."

More like conscripting him to help, he thought. Poor schmuck. But if anyone deserved to be taken down a peg or two, Claire could not have found a better man.

Duff looked into the store later that day, and sure enough, Claire had Jerry working, moving things around and stacking extra furniture pieces making way for new stock while she sat on a stool with her clipboard in handwriting everything down.

"Things going better with Henry and his Auntie?" Elliot asked Scott as Scott slowly picked his way across the yard using the light of the fire to guide his way now that the dark descended early.

"Yeah, things have been pretty quiet at work. Henry's got another delivery for me tomorrow night."

"Do you think Henry suspects that you know what's going on?"

"I hope not."

"Well, let's not worry about it now. I have a few instructions for your from Clancy that he hopes you'll be willing to do."

"Instructions to what exactly?"

"Hold on," Elliot said as he got up and headed for the shed. "I've got them inside, let me grab them for you."

By the time Elliot got back, Scott had put more wood on the fire, and the flames were high and hot.

Elliot held the paper near the fire so he could read it. "It ways here that Clancy wants you to pull the delivery van off the road at some point, climb in the back and get a photo of the vase, or vases. He's included a camera for you, and he needs to take lots of shots to make sure at least one of them will turn out.

He also says that you are to use the flash cubes, so you get a good photo and don't leave any of the bulbs in the truck. He wants you to count them to make sure you've got them all. Henry would be on to us right away if you eve left just one. Do you think you can do that? "I don't see why not. If he asks why it took so long, I'll just tell him I got lost again. Remember I grew up using public transportation and never paid much attention to how I got to a destination. The L would take me to my stop, or the bus would let me out where I wanted to go, and that was that. Now that I have to drive, I get lost all the time."

"Just be very careful and notice everything; where you are, how you got there is the building the same on as before, are there any identifying marks or signs on the building and are you being followed."

Scott thought for a moment and then said, "One thing I did notice from the last time I delivered a vase was a Chinese mark written in chalk on the door of the warehouse. I don't know if it meant anything because I don't read Chinese. For all I know it said this warehouse sold fresh fish."

Elliot ignored his comment and asked. "Was the sign one symbol or a series of symbols?"

"I'm pretty sure it was just one, but the funny part is that I think I've seen it before, I just can't remember where."

"Let it go and that way you'll remember, and when you do, let me know right away."

"Right, no problem."

Scott wondered why Elliot kept including himself when he talked about Henry and the vases. Was he trying to play junior detective or something? I just hope he doesn't get carried away and end up in serious trouble trying to help his friend Clancy solve this case.

"Before we eat, come and see the insulation in the shed. I think Leroy and I did a pretty good job." As Elliot opened the door and stepped aside, he added, "You're not going to believe this. . ."

"Do I want to know?" Scott asked as he stepped closer and looked inside the shed.

By the light of a small table tamp he could see the new insulation, and he also noticed that even the roof was covered with the stuff. Now it was more like one big sleeping bag. Even his voice sounded strange, muffled, kind of like being underwater.

"Wow, don't you think you overdid it? We could smother to death; there's insulation everywhere."

"That's exactly what I said to Leroy, but he said that we could open a window if it got too hot or claustrophobic. By the way, notice anything more?"

"No, I can't say that I do."

"Really? Nothing at all?"

Scott slowly looked around the room trying to see what Elliot meant. "Okay, I see the same beds, the same boxes under the beds, you've moved the old green table that Leroy brought over to stand between the beds. . . Hey, wait a minute, you've covered the spot where you were going to put the chimney, and you've got a new table lamp. That's all I can see."

"Did you notice that the lamp is turned on? We have electricity! And you'll never guess where I found it."

"I can't believe I missed something so obvious, where did you find a place to plug it in? Don't tell me you've tapped into the neighbors?"

"In a way yes. While Leroy went to pick up the insulation, I started working on the back stars of the house. I didn't want your mom to take a tumble when she used the bathroom in the house. When I jacked up the stairs to nail them into the house, I saw an electrical outlet under them hidden from view. When Leroy got back, he drove us to the hardware store, and we picked up a long industrial extension cord and make a hole in the side of the shed wall and strung it through. Then we tested it on the little table lamp that Leroy brought from his store. Do you realize what this means?"

"It means we have a table lamp."

"That and we can get an electric heater."

"Hey, you're right. Just think, now it will be warm for the winter." Scott paused to think and added, "so, who pays for the electricity?"

"That part might be tricky. I think the halfway house in front is owned and run by the state, so I guess they pay for the power. I don't know too much about their operation; I just know that I don't bother them and they don't object to me."

Before Scott could comment on the people in the house, a persistent and niggling thought came to him, just where does Elliot get his money for all these purchases? The shed he built for free, you could tell by the building materials and old nails that went into its construction, but did the patio set really come for some guy who was throwing it out? And what about the money for the insulation and now an electric heater and the lamp? And what about all the food he seemed to have at his disposal in the cold box? For a transient guy, he does pretty well in the money department. Maybe, Scott thought, I shouldn't have given him that cash Henry gave me, no wait I gave him the money well after he got the food and the patio set. Sheesh."

"Hey buddy, you still on this planet?" Elliot was waving his hand in front of Scott's face.

"Sorry, I just spaced out there for a minute."

"I suppose you have a lot to think about." Elliot sat down on his bed.

Scott sat on the other cot and asked, "So you and Clancy honestly think that Henry's dealing in stolen goods?"

"That's what we're trying to determine, and that's why it's so important that you get a picture of the vase, or vases and try to remember everything you see when you make your delivery. And um, check to see if the guys who are getting the delivery have those three dots on their hands too. It might be the most important thing we have to go on."

"Don't you think they'll be wearing gloves. It's getting colder and colder at night, and they just might have gloves on?" Scott had another thought and changed the subject, "You do realize that it's almost Thanksgiving, don't you?"

As a matter of fact, your mother has invited me to your family dinner that she's cooking at her new place. I thought that she would have told you this, didn't she?"

"I haven't seen her for almost two weeks. If you remember, I'm the one working a full-time job now and making night deliveries."

"Hey, now that I'm finished building this place, and we've gotten your mom moved into her new place, I too will be looking for a full-time position too."

"Oh, yeah, doing what?"

"I haven't decided yet. Maybe I'll pick up some expensive government work or perhaps I'll become an international spy. You know, trench coat, dark glasses, and a shifty look?"

"Very funny. I see you more as an under-qualified dishwasher in some all-night dive."

"Where I could be working as an undercover food critic. Yes, I like that."

Sophie was nervously wiping the dining room table for the fourth time since supper. "Phil, sweetheart, go and get that wonderful tart that Larry brought over this afternoon. I think we should have things extra special before Sandy and Johnny come back down. I've wiped the table so put it right in the center, and I'll start the decaf and lay out some plates and forks. I told them to come back down because we had something to discuss with them. I hope they remember." She applied her rag one more time.

"Sophie, please, you're wearing out the table." He gestured to her cloth while heading for the kitchen.

"Sorry. It's just that I'm so nervous, what if they say no?"

"Then they say no and we think of something else."

"But what else is there?"

"Now, sweetheart, we've been over this a hundred times, we will put our trust in God, and He will do what is best, even if we don't understand it."

"I know, I know," she said as she crossed the room to put her arm around him. While kissing him on his cheek, she added, "You, you are my answer man. What would I do without you?"

"Let's hope you don't have to find that out for a very long time."

Sophie was leaning into her husband with her head on his shoulder when the young couple entered the room.

"What's this? Snuggling in the dining room? My, my." Johnny teased while smiling at the elderly couple he had learned to love even though he hadn't known them long. He would always be grateful to Sophie in particular for helping his wife through a rough spot in her life even though she was a virtual stranger at the time. He would never forget her kindness.

"Uh-o, we've been caught red-handed." Sophie said as the young couple sat down across from them, "I thought it would be nice to have a little decaf and some of the pastry Phil's son sent over." Sophie said while retrieving the rich dessert. "What do you think, not too late for decaf, is it?"

"Not if you combine it with anything from Phil's bakery," Sandy said as she rose to help.

"It's Larry's now," said Phil. "And I must say, I like the changes he's made already. It takes someone young, like the two of you, to see the possibilities for change."

"Phil couldn't be more right," added Sophie as she cut generous slices of the raspberry, almost torte for the young people and only a tiny slice each for Phil and herself.

"So, Sandy," queried Sophie nonchalantly when they were all diving into their tort, "how's your sister?"

"I am sad to say that I do not know. Her mother, Elizabeth, made her quit her job and she's taken her to Paris for who knows how long."

As Sophie passed the coffee to the young couple, she added. "I know that when Sarah came to tell me about leaving her job, I asked if she wanted to talk about it. I could tell she was terribly broken up about it, but she clammed up and said that she and her mother were going on a trip and she would be sure to send her rent for a couple of months and not to worry about her."

"I don't think she wants to go to Europe, but I knew she did want to get away somewhere for a while to think about things."

"I think somewhere by herself would have been a better idea. That way she'd be away from everyone who wants to influence her decisions. What she's deciding about Pete isn't any of my business after all." When Sophie made that statement, Phil just rolled his eyes.

"I think what my wife is trying to ask" he paused briefly, "is, did your sister quit her job? I mean, she was just offered a promotion, wasn't she? What does this mean for Pete, is that over too?"

"Sadly, the answer to both of your questions is, yes. It was quite a big promotion, and they were going to send her to their new office building in the suburbs, and yes she quit her job."

"I think she was very foolish to turn it down," Johnny commented as he picked at the crumbs on his plate. "Sarah's going to miss a golden opportunity with a growing company and a rung on the latter going to the top."

"I don't think she had much choice," Sandy said sadly as she cleared the table. "This is what her mother told her she should do and I'm sure her mom will treat her like royalty while they're gone so that she'll 'come to her senses' and come back into the family fold."

Sophie was about to comment, but Phil put his hand on her arm, and she stopped.

Sandy continued. "I honestly don't know what Sarah wants. I was the twin that always had a tough time growing up. I was the one that was raised by our birth mother. She's the one who taught me all sorts of stupid things by her actions. Most of those years were pretty rough, but at least I know who I am today, my goals, my friends, the love of my life."

She smiled at Johnny and blew him a kiss.

Sophie couldn't stop herself and asked. "Do you have any idea what is going on between that nice Pete guy and her?"

"No one knows what's going on between them," said Johnny between sips of coffee. "I had lunch with Pete after class a few days ago, and he's as confused as we are. He lowered his voice and added, "I wonder if he would even give her another chance if she did come back and say sorry."

"Johnny, how could you even think such a thing?" Sandy sat down next to him, surprised by his opinion.

"Now don't get excited, I mean, this is not written in stone, but I got the impression that he was tired of placating her. Tired of being the one to make the changes that would amend his life to the one her mother wanted. Remember how easy it was for her to drop him like a hot rock when she thought he was seeing that red-haired girl that worked for him over at the Goodwill?"

"That's different," Sandy said defending her sister.

"Is it?"

"Now children," Sophie interrupted, "I guess we're not the ones to solve their problems so let's leave it to them. Meanwhile, Phil, is there something you'd like to say?"

"Not me, sweetheart. You seem to have the gift of gab and, after all, darling, it was your idea before it was mine."

She gave him a dirty look, and neither Sandy nor Johnny had any idea what they were talking about.

Everyone waited for someone to say something and finally, Sophie asked, "more coffee anyone?"

A corporate grown went up, and Sophie added, "So, Johnny, what have you decided to do after you graduate in what, five or six weeks?"

"I'm not sure. First of all, Sandy and I need to take some time and see my parents. You know don't you that they don't know yet that we're married?"

"Ach, Sandy, is this right?"

"Sorry to say, it is. We've both been so busy finishing up our schooling that we haven't had time to run up and see them. If you remember, they live about an hour away, and this is something we don't want to tell them on the phone."

"We're thinking of telling them when we go up for Thanksgiving," said Johnny. "I'm not sure when or how to tell them, but it's got to be done. Come to think of it; I don't think they know that I'm graduating early either."

"Tsk, tsk," said Sophie while shaking her head, "young people today. Tell you what, why don't we wait until you've seen your parents before we continue this conversation? It's not all that important anyway."

No one noticed the surprised look on Phil's face.

"You will never guess what Miss Lee and I were talking about today," Scott brought up casually.

"It's hard to say," said Leroy. "I would guess it wasn't about the hothouse you live in was it?"

"It's not all that hot," Elliot said revealing the slight chip he had on his shoulder about his finished shed. "As soon as we find another window and put it in, we'll be fine."

"A-huh, so while you wait to find another window, we have to sit out here and freeze." Leroy grinned.

"Aw, come on," said Scott, "it's not that cold, and we've got lots of wood to burn now that we won't need it to heat the shed. Besides, I wanted to tell you what Miss Lee and I were talking about."

"Henry?" Elliot said with guarded enthusiasm.

"No. actually, we were talking about the Chinese New Year."

"And was there a reason you and Miss Lee was discussing a holiday that's still three months away?"

"I don't remember how we got on the subject, but Henry was out of the store all day, and we just kind of took it easy. I didn't have any stock to check in, and the town was pretty quiet, so we talked most of the morning. I think we started with the party for Ming Toy because it will be held right after Thanksgiving and how Henry's auntie was getting frantic with last-minute party plans. I guess we were talking about how the Chinese celebrate various holidays and Miss Lee brought up the Chinese New Year."

"So, was it interesting?"

"What?"

"Chinese New Year? My gracious Scott, you don't seem to pay attention for very long, do you?"

"I guess I'm jumpy because of what you told me about the vases. I can't stop thinking about what I might be getting myself into."

"Speaking of vases," asked Leroy, "has he gotten any more in lately? You know if he ever has any extra ones, my Ruby could put them in the shop; I'd bet they would sell fast. Just like that electric palm tree. Right, Elliot?" Leroy punched Elliot in the arm,

"Anyway," Scott started cautiously, "Miss Lee said that the Chinese New Year is a huge thing and she hoped I would still be around it see it."

"What does she mean by, still being around?"

"That's what I wondered. I mean, we're friends and all, but there are days I don't know who to trust. Either way, she explained that the Chinese use the lunar calendar, not the one based on the sun that we use."

"I didn't know that," said Leroy. "Why is that and isn't it the Jewish people who use a lunar calendar too? I seem to remember that some years the lunar calendar has an extra month or something. I must be tough to follow, I mean, just think, birthdays could be a mess."

Scott left Leroy to work things out for himself while he continued. "I don't know about the Jews of the Chinese either, but Miss Lee said Asians based their New Year on the first day of the first moon. That's the reason their new year usually falls during the first part of February. She also said that the long paper dragon that dances down the street is the Chinese mythical symbol of life. Actually what I think she said was that the dragon symbolized water, which is the symbol of life as it 'flowed' down the street."

Leroy sighed, thinking that Ruby would never get one of those vases and completely missing Scott's narrative.

"And just ahead of the dragon," Scott continued ignoring the look on Leroy's face."

"A man is waving a gold paper orb in front of the dragon which symbolizes the sun, which also meant something. Wait, I remember. The sun is a symbol of new crops in the new year, I think, anyway, before the parade starts, the people have to clean their houses thoroughly, which removes the evil spirits. They also put up red and gold papers on their doors, which have lucky messages on them. I guess they are to welcome the good- fortune spirits. It's hard to remember everything she said; we talked for a long time."

"Is that all you talked about?" asked Elliot eager to learn more about Henry's activities.

"No, we talked about a lot of things."

"Great," Leroy said while looking at Elliot. "You'd better put more wood on this fire if we're staying for the long version."

"Well, now that you don't want to hear anymore, I'll make sure I tell you everything we talked about."

"That figures, go ahead." Leroy had to smile at Scott, proud of his young friend and the progress he was making at becoming a man.

"If you've ever been to Chinatown, you would have noticed those little shrines set up at all the businesses. They're usually right by the front door, and the regular food that's inside of them changes for the New Year celebrations because the families take the three main types of meat, pork, chicken, and fish."

"Fish is now meat?"

"If you don't keep interrupting the boy," said Elliot, "this story might go faster."

"Sorry," Leroy responded. "it's just that fish. . ."

"Okay," said Scott, "I know what you mean, and for some odd reason, they consider fish as one of the meats. Anyway," he started again. "They take the three types of meat and put them on a kitchen table in their home. They also put out some oranges for good luck, and rice cakes, and lucky money, and candles, and incense, all for the gods to eat."

Before Leroy could interrupt to comment about the gods eating the money and incense, Scott began again.

"Obviously the gods don't eat everything, especially the incense and the lucky money," Scott added looking at Leroy. "But they take it as a sign that when the burning incense is half gone, they believe the gods have both come and gone, and the food is now available for the family to eat. Later they burn the lucky money."

"Is there any more?" Leroy asked quietly.

"Only if you want to hear it."

Before Leroy could say anything, Elliot said, "For pity sake, Leroy. I don't know what you have to do that's so pressing; I find it fascinating and who knows if any of us will be here to see it."

Scott wondered why Elliot had said they might not be around come February, but he continued with his story, fully intending to ask Elliot what his reasoning was later.

"The lucky money," he continued," is special paper money that they buy, I think Miss Lee called it spirit money. I think she said that as they threw it on the community fire, it's supposed to take their prayers skyward as they ask for more. More, more, and even more in the coming year."

"More what?" asked Leroy.

"More of everything, More money, more good luck, more success."

"Auntie Change must be going through a lot of fortune money this year," commented Elliot. "She's going to need all the good luck she can get to pull off this party and the engagement."

Scott realized that he was losing his audience after hearing Elliot's comments. The New Year celebration would be after the party, way after.

"Is there any more?" Elliot wanted to know.

"Just that they buy papers with block prints of individual gods on them. Miss Lee said they are quite elaborate prints, full of colors, and they are available in all the shops. She said that she didn't think that Henry would carry them this year with his new clientele. Either way, these prints are hung up to invite the deities to come over to their house. She said they don't actually buy a god; they only pay the shopkeeper for issuing the invitation for the gods to come to your home."

"How very strange," commented Elliot, hoping this conversation was going to include information about Henry.

"They've got kitchen gods too."

Leroy tried to hide his yawn.

"As a business person, you should know these things, Leroy. They might come in handy someday."

"I highly doubt that. Is there much more?"

"I'll make it brief."

"Right," Leroy answered skeptically.

"The kitchen gods I was telling you about are all male, at least the ones in the commercial kitchens. The home versions could be either male or female gods. These are the little ones that are in those little shrines. They act like our version of Santa Claus. They watch the family during the year to see who's naughty and who's nice and they report all of their information to the Jade Emperor in the other world somewhere."

"The Jade Emperor?" Elliot found this interesting.'

"That's what she said. She also said the family rubs their god's mouth with honey to ensure they only tell the emperor the nice things."

Scott moved closer to the fire and held out his hands as well as putting his feet closer to the flames. "Anybody want to hear about why everything they eat is round?"

"No!" the other men said in unison.

"That's what I thought. I knew you wanted to hear more. As I was saying, they have special pancakes and omelets that are cooked to be a round shape, and they've got all sorts of dumplings and stuff that are traditional foods, but everything is round. They eat whole ducks to indicate prosperity in the coming year, you know, they want to be rich enough to afford a whole duck. Greens for some reason and lotus seeds and pomegranate seeds and peanuts are eaten in the hope for more children during the coming year. Even grapefruits and oranges and tangerines are good luck to eat."

Scott knew he had lost his audience but continued. "Oh, and they eat only half of a fish on New Year's Eve and the other half on New Year's Day so that the luck of the fish transfers from one year to another."

"Not fish again," moaned Leroy.

"Yes, fish. Remember this is what Miss Lee told me. Wait a minute, how did we get on this conversation anyway? I remember," Scott added before the other men could get in a word. "I asked Miss Lee if she knew how the hall would be decorated for Ming Toy's coming out party; was there a tradition for that?"

"Go ahead, is there?"

"Thanks for asking Elliot, there is. After the announcement of the wedding, everyone would be going outside for the lighting of the traditional paper lanterns, just like the ones they use on New Year's. Now I remember how I got off the subject. Anyway, many people make their own lanterns and others buy theirs. Either way, they light them and send them skyward." "Talk about your fire hazard!" Leroy was picturing Chinatown going up in flames.

"Tell me about it. That's why no one uses real firecrackers anymore."

"Firecrackers? What for?" Leroy was too curious not to know, even though he knew the answer would continue an already overly long conversation.

"Well, remember I gave you the reason why the celebration is held in February? That moon thing? Well, after the town sets up the viewing stand on the main corner, Mayor Daley and lots of Chinese dignitaries stand up these, freezing their feet off as the parade goes by. Part of the ceremony used to include speeches by everybody and then the audience would watch and listen as the firecrackers began shooting off that were strung back and forth across the streets for as far as you could see. Evidently, the Chicago Fire Department decided that was no longer a good idea seeing the buildings are so old. Now they just play a recording of thousands of firecrackers going off. Funny huh?"

"I think the funny part would be the number of tourists who show up for the celebration, never realizing the firecracker explosions aren't real."

Leroy rose to go home. "So, we're caught up on stuff for a while? My Ruby has a few things for me to do before Thanksgiving comes. She's got the whole family coming over and half the church. I think what she needs to have done could end up being a major task."

"Let me know if there's anything I can do; we want to keep your little woman happy."

"That goes for me too; I don't know whats going on from day to day and I just might have it off. Everything depends on Henry."

Leroy started his truck filling the alley with noise.

"He'll never change and fix that truck," shouted Elliot to Scott over the din.

"But would you really want him too?" Asked Scott, growing wise beyond his years.

CHAPTER 19

Henry's arrogance was reflected in his recently acquired sneer which Scott noticed for the first time that morning when he addressed Scott in his new, plush office.

"How could you have possibly gotten lost last night? I not only wrote the directions down, but I gave you a Chicago street map."

That's odd, thought Scott. I never told Henry that I'd gotten lost. He must be having me followed. Wait until I tell Clancy that. I just hope whoever was following me thought I was busy studying the map when I was taking the pictures. Good thing I left the opened map on the dashboard.

"Sadly, I get lost pretty easy. We only had one car when I was growing up, and my father took it to work. I grew up taking public transportation."

Quickly turning the conversation around, Scott commented, "You certainly do look especially cool today. Going somewhere important?"

"Not hardly," was Henry's curt answer. "I've been summoned by my dear, sweet auntie to make an appearance. I think she wants me to promise on my life that I'll be at this party she's giving for some girl from the old country. I still have no idea why I have to be there," he said distractedly while staring at himself in his new full-length mirror. "But I guess for some unknown reason it's highly important to her that I show up. I have an idea that she wants to show me off." He smoothed his hair while adding, "She's quite proud of me and my success you know."

"I would imagine, you've done wonders with her, I mean with your business."

"Yes, I have." He slipped on his coat. "So everything went well last night?

"Except for that getting lost part, yes. Some people came out of the building, took possession of the vase and gave me an envelope and signed the papers you sent. I didn't open the sealed envelope because it wasn't part of your instructions. Here it is."

"Right you are, and a little thank you for a job well done." Henry walked over to his desk and pulled out some bills and continued. "This is a little something for you to spend over the holidays, You're dad died recently, didn't he?" Without waiting for an answer, he reached back into the drawer and drew out a few more large bills and placed them in Scott's hands. "Maybe this can help with some of the funeral expenses."

"Thank you." Scott tried to look humble as he stuffed the money into his pocket working hard not to add any resentment to his face seeing his father had died more than a month ago.

"And since we will not need another delivery of any sort for the rest of this week, I think Miss Lee can run the place without us, don't you agree?"

Scott found it creepy when Henry started using words like we. He wanted no part of anything Henry was doing, so he just said, "Yeah, sure. When do you want me back?

"How about the Monday after Thanksgiving? That is if my aunt doesn't need you. I'll ask when I see her later."

"Sounds good to me," Scott said, but thought to himself, so if his aunt needs me, how does he figure he'll get in touch? Hopefully, he knows nothing about my personal life.

Miss Lee was busy watching over a large group of shoppers and did not even see him leave.

Later that afternoon, when he was telling Clancy and Elliot about the last night's delivery while getting out the photos he had developed at one of those new one-hour places, he suddenly remembered something. "Now I remember," he said out loud.

Both men looked at him as he continued, "I just figured it out. The symbol that was chalked on the door where I dropped the vases off is the same one that's on Henry's cufflinks. I knew I had seen it somewhere before."

"Could you remember it well enough that you could sketch it out for me?" Clancy was reaching for his pen.

"Sorry, I'm out of my league there. All I know is that it was the same one. It kind of looked like a little house with an extra roof. Oh yeah," Scott reached into his pocket. "Henry gave me this too., told me to use them towards my father's funeral costs."

Elliot counted out the bills. "Did you know that you had eight hundred dollars in one hundred dollar bills stuffed in your pocket?"

"Nope. I knew they weren't mine anyway, so what's the difference?"

"That's one way of looking at it," Clancy said as he smoothed the bills and placed them in a notebook.

"So what now? Wait until another delivery? He doesn't want me back at work until after Thanksgiving."

"Let's just wait and see what happens next." Clancy rose to leave but added, "When did you say this big shindig was going to take place that auntie was putting on?"

"Only a few days from now I think. There's been problem after problem with it according to Miss Lee. She said that so many people do not like auntie they are making it hard for her to do anything."

"Like what kind of problems?"

"Like the caterer who told her they couldn't get all the foods she wanted when she wanted them, so that delayed the party. Someone else, oh yeah, the town hall where she's having it said they were having trouble with the electrical wiring or something. Anyway, they've all finally run out of excuses so the party of the year should be soon."

Elliot queried, "From what you've said, it will be more like a surprise party for Henry. Didn't you say she planned to introduce Ming Toy to the community and then announce their engagement?"

"That's still the plan as far as I know."

"Well, let Clancy or me know as soon as you know what's going on for sure."

"No problem."

"So, asked Sophie the day after Thanksgiving when Sandy and Johnny came down for supper. "How was the visit to your parents, Johnny. Get everything ironed out?"

"You might say so, and then again you might say no we didn't. They were pleased that I'll be graduating early and at the top of my class. My father did take me aside after dinner and ask what I was planning to do with my new degree. I told him I had a few ideas and we talked a little bit before we left."

"And the marriage?"

"We didn't bring that up until just before we left."

"And?"

Sandy was surprised when Phil did not interrupt Sophie and chiding her for asking so many questions.

"And," answered Johnny knowing Sophie wanted all the gruesome details. "And it was quite a shock for them." He reached for Sandy's hand and continued knowing Sophie wanted to hear it all.

"Obviously mom acted pleased, but I don't know how she feels, probably disappointed and maybe hurt that we didn't include them in any of our plans. But," he went on defensively, "if we had gone to them, they would have done everything in their power to stop the wedding. Or at least deliberately delayed it," he added.

While Sophie cut into the lasagna that Sandy had made for supper, she thought carefully about her next question.

"When you said delay the wedding, do you mean delay it long enough to talk you out of it, maybe your dad offering you a spot in one of his offices to keep you so busy you too might have drifted apart?"

"I wondered about that too. I've got the kind of parents who say they stay out of my life and my decisions, but they don't. They had a fit when I quit college to make a living playing my guitar. I mean, I was good and thought I could make it. Obviously, I wasn't good enough. I ended up playing a lot of dives which didn't pay much, and I hooked up with a mediocre band for a while, and I ended up sleeping on a lot of other musician's sofas. But I wasn't going to go home and do what they wanted, no sir. As it was, that attitude ended with me sleeping in a cardboard refrigerator box next to an apartment building for a while, and eventually someone stole my guitar, and it rained heavily one night, and I lost my home, and then I met Pete who turned out to be a really great guy who ended up making a huge difference in my life." He took a deep breath.

Sophie hated situations like this. On the one hand, she so wanted to find out about the visit to Johnny's parents, but now that he had brought up Pete, she was also anxious to find out how things were going between Pete and Sarah. Sandy hadn't said anything for a while about her sister and Sophie wasn't sure if Sarah was still in Europe with her mother. With restraint, while passing a basket of garlic bread, Sophie asked, "And now that you've gone back to school and are graduating in a few weeks, were they happy?"

"Oh sure. My parents are taking all the credit for that decision, seeing they were the ones who plucked me off the street, dusted me off and made sure I finished my schooling. I'm sure when I got involved with the Five, my mother wasn't happy. I mean, my dad doesn't mind me being on the Five's board, but actually living with 'those people' as my mother calls them doesn't go over well with either one of them."

"And now that he's stopped so low and even married one of 'those people', I think they're secretly embarrassed to have me in the family."

"Now honey," he squeezed her hand, "they'll just have to get used to you."

"What?"

"I mean, they'll learn to love you as much as I do, really."

"Well they'd just better is all I have to say. I'm not letting you go, whether your folks like me or not."

"That's the way to think," said Sophie. "Believe me, when you take that first grandchild to see them, they'll melt like candy."

"Well," Sandy was unusually defiant, "they'll just have to stay hard as a rock for now because children are the last thing we're thinking about now. I've got to get a job, did I tell you my school has three interviews set up for me? Anyway, I need to get a job and so does my husband. Honey, tell them what your dad originally offered you."

"He told me before that if I would go back to school and finish, he would set me up in a junior position in the business. I knew he always wanted that, planned for that, and he intimated that I would be on the fast track to partner. That was pretty heavy stuff."

"And after you told them about your being married?"

"They were polite," Johnny said while folding and refolding his napkin, "but somehow I don't think the offer still stands. Nothing was said before we left and we thought we'd give them all the time they needed to decide what to do next if anything."

Sophie reached over and put her hand on his. "That was very wise of you; parents need time to absorb things. You know, the minute a child is born, parents only want the best for them, but a parents' version of the best often differs widely from what a child sees as best. You're right to give them time. They'll come around, you'll see."

"But in the meantime," Phil said, "we need to confuse the issue just a bit more."

Sandy and Johnny looked at Phil and then at Sophie, who was sitting entirely mute for the first time. Immediately Sandy knew that one of them had a severe medical condition and she was sure the news wouldn't be good. Sandy grabbed her husband's hand and squeezed it tightly. Johnny was surprised by her gesture and the look on her face cautiously asked, "Is there something we need to know?"

"Yes, it's about Sophie and me."

Sandy interrupted before he could finish. "I knew it, which one of you is sick and what does the doctor say?"

"Sick, who's sick?" Sophie looked at Phil and then smiled at Sandy. "No darling, we're not sick, we're moving."

"Did you just say you're moving?" The news hit Sandy hard, and she now felt like she was sitting a dense fog, unable to see anything clearly. "So, you're not sick; you're moving?" She asked again.

"That's what they said, sweetheart. Let them explain, and we'll all understand."

Now it was Sophie's turn to take a deep breath. She moved the empty bread basket aside and began. "You know how we kept extending our honeymoon in Florida?"

The young couple nodded their heads yes.

"Well," she looked at Phil and continued. "We found out two things about ourselves. One, we liked Florida a lot and two, we realized we liked the kind of people we met down there."

"What do you mean, the kind of people down there? What makes them so different?" Sandy was curious.

"Different like open and friendly, like they didn't have a care in the world. And time seemed to stand still there, and that was okay with us. The only things we had to concern ourselves with was which of the relatives we were having supper with which night and where and when was the next shuffleboard game was going to be."

"Not only did Sophie come to every one of my games," Phil beamed at the memory, "but she bought one of those Florida sundresses to wear to the games along with that big purse with the scarf on it."

"Phil, you silly old man, that was your idea."

"And I noticed you didn't object."

"Well, not so much, I guess. Anyway, we've talked about it and talked about it, and we've decided to take advantage of a senior village down there and move in right after Christmas."

Phil continued, "They only had one unit left, and somebody else was looking at it too, so we signed the papers before we lost it." He looked pleased with himself.

Sandy and Johnny looked at each other, but neither one knew what to say, or where to begin to ask questions.

"We realize this is a sudden announcement. And you've already got a lot on your plate to consider, but we wanted to put our offer to you on the table."

There were blank stares from the young couple.

"So are you saying we'll be homeless in a little more than a month?"

"Now Johnny," Sandy teased, "we could always move in with your parents."

"That's not even funny. I suppose we could get a place as the Five, but the rooms are made for singles, and we'd probably need to build a new double room somewhere if there's room."

"Ahem," Phil semi-coughed to get their attention. "I think Sophie has more to say on the subject and I think it will give you an interesting alternative to think about. Sophie, darling, say your piece."

She began again. "As I said, Phil and I have been talking about this decision both for here and in Florida, and we want to include you two in our plans."

Neither Sandy nor Johnny said a word, so she continued. "If it works out for the both of you, we would like to offer you this house at a deep discount so you can do whatever you want with it. It's going to need some work, and that's another reason we decided we would rather have you two have it. We're too old to do what needs to be done, and neither of us is in the best of health anymore." Seeing the look on Sandy's face, she added quickly, "No, neither one of us is ill, at least not to our knowledge, we just want to have a little time to ourselves to rest and enjoy doing nothing after working hard all our lives."

The young couple looked at each other, but neither one knew what to say or where to begin to ask questions. They waited.

"We realize this is a sudden announcement and you've already got a lot on your plate to consider, but we wanted to put our offer on the table too. We realize that the next step will be to sit down with you two and go over finances, but if this is something you'd be interested in, Sophie and I will make the deal good and sweet. And," he added, "we do not want you to feel that you are obligated in any way to take our offer. We've already spoken to a real estate agent, and he thought it would be a wonderful building for some corporation to buy. They said being on Foster Avenue would be a huge advantage for selling it."

"Well," said Sandy, "there would be plenty of parking in the back for cars. And there's also a bus stop right across the street and according to my sister, a great little diner." She had a hard time holding back tears.

"I definitely would not mention the diner," Sophie said, tearing up herself.

"Listen, kids," said Phil while sneaking another small piece of the now cold lasagna, "we want you to take your time and think this through. Don't feel you have to take our offer. We're fine either way."

"Phil Rosen," Sophie said while slapping her husband's hand. "If you are expecting to live a long life in the sunshine state which will include lots of shuffleboards, I would advise you to lay off the extra calories. We've both got to trim down so we can live our new lives with the jet-setters down south."

Phil placed his fork down on his plate, and Sophie put her hand on his arm and lovingly said, "Okay, we'll start tomorrow, for tonight eat, eat and enjoy."

Claire called another meeting of the minds and this time not only were Clay and the Duffer in attendance, so were Johnny and the long-absent and now famous restaurateur, Tony.

"Now that Thanksgiving is over," Claire said sounding more and more like the president of a major corporation than the accountant for a homeless shelter, "we have called this meeting to discuss the future of the Five." She sat down at that point to the surprise of all.

When Johnny rose to speak both Clay and the Duffer were worried about their futures. Both men had found a home at the Five and now that Claire had practically taken over, and Duff had gotten his new van, they were worried what the results of this meeting would be.

"As you know," Johnny started with a formal tone, "this non-profit organization began several years ago almost by accident. Tony, Steve and I, Steve, for your information Claire was the third partner that started the Five and is now in the Air Force stationed somewhere overseas, and Tony and I came into this venture a bit sideways with help from my father and his rich friends. They are still the ones who fund us, and so far we have done pretty well. We could do better, but now that Steve is gone and Tony has become a big shot, and as for me. . ." Johnny twisted his new wedding ring, "As for me, Sandy and I got married, and I'm not sure where my future is just now."

The room went silent for just a second, and then Clay said, "Congratulations son, may you have many, many happy years!" His voice was full of cheer, but his heart was full of dread.

"Here, here." Added Duff with his eyes on Claire while he banged his empty coffee cup on the table.

"You old dog," was Tony's comment as he stood to shake his friend's hand. Why all the time I thought it was Claire you were going to marry."

Johnny quickly recovered and said to the group, "Thank you everyone, but it's always been, Sandy. On the plus side, Claire is now employed here full time, and she's the greatest bookkeeper we've ever had."

More cup banging from Duff.

"More like a master sergeant," Clay muttered under his breath.

Johnny was still smiling when he added, "Anyway, the reason we're all here today is there needs to be a reorganization of the Five. Tony and I have already met as the last official representatives of the place along with a few of my father's friends who are board members and knowledgeable men as to where to go now. We have finally come to a satisfactory conclusion, and we hope you find the same."

The Duffer's stomach began to unknot, and Clay crossed his legs and sat back, visibly more relaxed now that it sounded like the place would not be closing.

"First of all," Johnny began. "Tony will continue to fund the organization through his generous contributions in hopes that his business will remain solvent. He has pledged a certain percent of his profits to the running of the Five so each month the figure will vary slightly.

"Secondly, we are interested in creating a few new official positions so this place can continue to run smoothly as it has been thereby allowing us to become a certified business with all its legal perks.

"We still believe there's a place for people like the ones who live here, the ones who just need a hand out of their circumstances and back into the mainstream of life. So, after discussing this with Claire," both Duff and Clay looked at each other in astonishment, "we have offered her the position of daily operations manager. This will give her the authority to present future programs to the board that will help us grow.

"She has already suggested that we use the back half of this massive building to build new rooms for women and possibly build larger quarters for small families. Looking at Claire, he continued.

"I believe you've talked about an eventual daycare center, not only for the children that will be living here but as a service for the neighborhood kids to produce income for the Five.

"Something else Claire will be discussing with you," he looked at Clay and Duff, "is the idea of offering ballet lessons in the same room as the daycare after the kids have gone home for the day. She would only need the addition of an entire wall of mirrors and a professional ballet barre."

Duffer caught Claire's eye and smiled a wicked smile saying without words, "You clever person you." She ignored him but had the smallest smile on her lips.

"Even though she will have a new position," Johnny continued, "she has agreed to keep her original accounting position guaranteeing us that she will be the best accountant this side of Wall Street."

Everyone clapped as Claire smiled graciously at the group.

Great, thought Clay. That's all she needs, more authority. Maybe it's time to leave and find someplace else. He managed to smile along with the rest of the group and to clap only halfheartedly wondering where he could find a place as wonderful as this.

"Now for our second choice concerning our new positions.".

Clay wished the meeting was over, not wanting to hear what was going to be said next, but Johnny continued.

"Clay, would you consider being in charge of all the inner and outer workings of the Five? You know, like a building superintendent? It's pretty much what you're already doing, but we see that you are very good at what you do and we're offering the job to you, meaning there will be a salary attached. If you need to, take some time and think it over but let us know as soon as possible."

Clay was dumbfounded. "Building superintendent you say? My, my."

"And Duffer." He tensed when Johnny called his name.

"Yes," he squeaked out his response.

Since Claire thinks the world of you," she smiled at him sweetly, "she suggested that you attend the Dewitt Industrial School on the Five's dime and pick up some cooking pointers. Before you say anything, I mean learn to cook like the professionals, and maybe you would be interested in holding cooking classes here because you had your certificate."

"If Duff wants to learn to cook," interjected Tony, "I could have him come to work for me in my kitchens. Do him good to learn some authentic Italian dishes. And I wouldn't charge him a dime."

Duff stood up ready to defend his cooking skills and position and Johnny intervened. "We're just messing with you Duff. We all think you're doing a fantastic job here, saving us so much money setting up accounts all over the city to harvest out-of-date foodstuff. So," before Duff could respond Johnny added, "We all want you to keep up the good work and from now on yours will also be a paid position."

"I hardly know what to say." Clay groaned out loud. "Except thank you. Thank you not only for the official position, but telling me I was doing a good job. I haven't heard that too often in my life, and I appreciate it more than you could ever know."

Saying that he sat down with his head facing down to the floor embarrassed that he had shared a painful part of his past. Suddenly he looked up and asked, "But the logo on the van will still be up to me, right?

Johnny smiled. "Have at it, Duff. Now, where was I? Oh yes. Tony and I will stay on the board, but neither of us will be involved with the running of the place, physically" he added. "Tony already has a hard time pulling himself away from Annetties, but I think it has more to do with their account, an attractive woman named Pam." He glanced over at Tony.

"And now that I am a married man with a wife to support, I need to make some solid decisions. So, any questions? No? Well you know where to find me, and you all have my number on Foster Avenue, so don't hesitate to call anytime, I'm not far away."

It was Duff who broke the silence by asking, "Coffee anyone? I can quick make some. If I knew what this meeting was about beforehand, I would have baked a lemon cake. Now you're stuck with the packaged pastries."

Everyone declined his invitation, and the meeting broke up. Clay headed back to his room leaving only Claire and the Duff alone in the office. Duff asked Claire if maybe she would like some coffee and she said no, and he asked her if she'd like some pastries, and she said no, and then out of the blue he asked if she would want to run down to Superdawg in the new van and grab a Chicago dog and she said yes, she'd love to.

"I'll get the keys," he said smiling.

"I'll grab my coat," she added.

Clay placed his key in the lock on his room with a smile on his face. He loved coming into this place that meant so much to him. He was raised in a ramshackle apartment that was way too crowded for his large family, and he grew up sharing not only his bedroom but his bed as well with several brothers, and now he finally had a room all to himself.

Each time he opened the door it felt precisely like coming home and perhaps this was the happiest home he had ever had, especially now that he was a salaried part of the official organization. For the first time, he felt the weight of his personal worth and value and was pleased with the feeling.

Unknown to anyone at the Five, the guys from the thrift store helped him squeeze in an ancient recliner several weeks ago when the Five was empty. It was his pride and joy. It also was his secret. If anyone found out about it, they would be in his room at all hours asking to borrow it or maybe just sit in it for a while. But it was he, and only he, who lowered himself into his chair. From his vantage point, he could see his two rows of thrift store paperback books on his multi-purpose wall, one shelf bursting with westerns and the other of true adventure books like the one he had set aside to read during the coming winter, Kon-Tiki. He had heard about this book by Thor Heyerdahl which chronicled his almost five thousand mile expedition across the Pacific Ocean on a hand-made balsa raft and that it was such a good story it had been translated into 67 languages. He was anxious to start it, but first had to finish Catch 22, a book out only a few years and full of interesting commentary. Yes, he was finally a very happy man with a happy future in this room of his own.

Chapter 20

The weather that had been pretty chilly up to that point, but it had suddenly turned warm again during a surprise second Indian summer. Madam Chang had cornered Scott as he was leaving Chinatown and made him return with her to her office where she laid out the plans for the big night and insisted he be there.

Or what, you'll fire me? He thought to himself. Maybe it was time to leave, after all, his mom offered him part of the money that his father had hidden from his family all these years. Money that was now so welcome for things like college fees if he wanted to go, but the trouble was he still didn't know what he wanted to be, but he knew Chinatown was pretty much over for him.

After running what seemed a thousand errands for Madam Queen, he was finally dismissed and was made to promise that he would be at the party the following night and dressed as well as he could. She didn't say why she wanted him there, but she insinuated that he had no choice to refuse, especially since he hadn't gotten a paycheck from Henry for several weeks. Henry's extra cash bonuses should have been enough to see him through, but Scott never got to spend a dime of the money and still in the back of his mind he wondered if what Clancy and Elliot did with the cash was on the level. By this time he must have given them over fourteen hundred dollars or so and there were always rumors about the crooked Chicago cops and what did he know for sure about Elliot? That is besides the stuff he told his mom and him about being thrown over by the girl he was to marry, but that happened years ago and they really didn't know too much about the rest of his life. Scott thought about these nagging questions as he left Madam's office and headed to Elliot's alley.

And where did he get his money? That still bothered Scott. He always seemed to have enough for food; including steaks one night, and the beds and the sleeping bags and the electric heater they used to keep the shed warm, even the insulation must have cost him a bundle.

And where does Leroy fit into all of this? Are the three of them in some sort of scam together and why in the world would they want to involve him? They didn't even know him at; first, just picked him up off the street and now Elliot was sweet-talking his mother. Maybe he was really after the money his dad left in his will, money that his mom should have had all along; it would have made her life so much easier.

"Wow, you look like you have the weight of the world on your shoulders son."

Elliot had the shed door propped open and the new oddball window open as he was taking the sleeping bags off the line feeling if they were dry.

"It's so nice and warm I thought I'd spruce up the place before winter sets in. I even took our bags to the Laundromat and washed them. Can you believe this weather?"

When Scott did not respond Elliot added, "How did it go at work today?"

"Fine."

"Just fine?"

"Yeah, I guess." Scott knew he had resorted back to his junior high school attitude and right now he didn't care.

"Okay then, are you going to be here for supper? Leroy's coming over, and so is Clancy."

"And I suppose we're having steak on the grill again?"

"No, as a matter of fact, Clancy's bringing ribs. He didn't work today and wanted to bring the supper to say thanks for the food he's eaten here. There's a great place over on Cicero that serves a full rack of ribs and those thick potato wedges along with coleslaw and pickles, and that's where Clancy's getting them."

"Oh."

"Okay then," Elliot was getting upset. "Can we count you in for supper?"

"I don't know yet; I've got things to do to get ready for the big party tomorrow night."

"I thought you weren't going."

"I thought so too, but Madam Chang caught me and insisted I be there. I have to stay around to get paid someday because if you remember, you and Clancy took all my money."

So that's what this is all about, thought Elliot.

"You know, I never thought about that. Here," he opened his wallet, "would fifty bucks hold you until we get this all straightened out?"

Scott wasn't sure if he should take the money or not seeing he didn't know where Elliot got it.

"Here," Elliot held out the bill, "you deserve it."

Scott reluctantly took the money and said he had things to do and he still wasn't sure if he'd be back for supper or not.

As it was he stuffed the money into his pocket and walked the few blocks back to Chinatown so he could climb the stairs to the L platform to think. He watched the riders get on and off for an hour and each time the train pulled out he looked down at Chinatown trying to think of what to do. He thought about calling his mom, but in the end, decided not to, why worry her, especially seeing she was becoming so attached to Elliot.

The hall was decked out in unbelievable splendor. It must have cost Madam Chang a fortune to turn the Culture Center into a beautiful summer garden complete with real grass, fountains, small trees and real flowers. There were small lighted Chinese lanterns in all the trees, and after he checked carefully, Scott noticed there were lights at the bottom of each tree shining upwards illuminating each one. Not only did they illuminate each tree, but the beam of light traveled upwards to the ceiling and looked exactly like clouds in a night sky. There were beautiful gold lanterns on each table which sported red tablecloths for good luck. And in the very middle of each table was the traditional lazy-Susan on which food would be placed and then continuously turned to serve everyone around the round tables.

The front of the room had two elaborate gold chairs on a stage-like area. Scott thought they probably were the ones from her hallway because they looked the same. He could see it now, she would seat Henry on one chair and then introduce Ming Toy to him and the audience at the same time, placing her on the chair next to his like a King with his Queen.

As he was heading to the food area to see what was being served for the big dinner, Madam Chang found him and hissed into his ear, "What you doing here? You no supposed to be upstairs. Go downstairs, take coats."

She disappeared as quickly, and Scott realized his job was to stay on the bottom floor and work as a slave again. Oh well, he thought as he walked down the stairs, there's nothing keeping me here, and if I wanted to, I could continue walking until I got to the door and then open it and leave. But he didn't, and when the guests starting coming through the door he had all he could do to keep up with them; each one deciding that if the evening turned cold, they should at least wear a light wrap.

There was live music playing upstairs, but Scott barely heard it with the noise around him. He noticed that everyone was dressed in their most elegant clothes, many women in their traditional Kimonos or beautiful silk dresses and even some of the men sported their native outfits. The stairs looked like a bright river with its flowing stream of colors winding their way upwards to the beautiful garden of surprise waiting at the top of the stairs, and the air was filled with several languages, none of which Scott understood. He figured the room must be packed by now and when the guests began to thin out, he sneaked upstairs for a peak.

The room was jam-packed, and it was stunningly beautiful. It looked exactly like every picture of a Chinese garden that Scott had ever seen. Many women had even taken out their fans and were gossiping behind them to the other ladies nearby.

Noises downstairs drew his attention, and the caterers were back ready to climb the stairs with even more food, this time delicate pastries. He motioned for them to wait as he hurried down the stairs leaving them free for the men who carried the large trays upstairs who were speaking to each other as though they were arguing. As soon as the men were gone the door opened once again and Henry entered dressed resplendently in a new dark suit. He tossed his hat to Scott, straightened his already perfect tie and bounded up the stairs where his aunt was waiting. Even Scott had to admit; he was a handsome man, lithe and full of life, so Scott followed after him in time to hear Auntie Chang's voice say something in Mandarin.

For the first time, she sounded kind and loving and was naturally introducing her nephew to the crowd. Scott imagined he was eating up all their admiring glances. Scott edged over to the side of the room behind a small tree so he could move closer to the front but stay unseen by auntie. He didn't want to miss what would happen next for the world; he wanted to see the grand moment when Madam brought Ming Toy out of the back and dropped the bomb as to why she, and her unsuspecting nephew, was there.

But auntie decided to delay the introduction and was apparently going on and on about her nephew, and he sat there in the gold chair lapping it all in like a cat laps cream. She spoke in her native tongue, sometimes slipping in a few words in English, but when it was finally over, there still was no future bride introduced.

Instead Madam summoned all the servers to begin taking the food to the tables and then gestured for everyone to eat. Scott was wondering why the change in plans, but kept out of sight so no one would see him, especially auntie as she moved around the room like a queen entertaining the peasants.

After everyone had eaten and the music had quieted, Madam Chang, also decked out in a fabulous red kimono with Chinese scenes embroidered with gold thread, stood and made a toast. Everyone complied and stood up, and while standing, raised their glasses, and she said something and the crowd laughed and then she said something else while looking and Henry and the crowd cheered. Whatever she said next must have been the end of the toast because everyone brought their glasses to their lips and drank. Then they put their glasses on the tables and clapped their hands enthusiastically. Scott wasn't sure who they were clapping for or why, but everyone seemed happy, and the waiters kept busy refilling glasses. Auntie then motioned for them to take their seats and a hush fell over the room. Henry looked like a lamb led to the slaughter and Scott thought he deserved every nasty thing his aunt had planned for him. Yes sir, he would marry this girl whether he liked it or not. And she would marry him whether she wanted to or not.

Ming Toy was a petite woman whose skin looked exactly like one of Henry's luminescent vases and her tiny hands looked indeed like fine porcelain. When auntie brought her out onto the floor from a door on one side of the stage, she walked with her head slightly down and took very tiny steps. She too was dressed in a beautiful kimono of soft blue and her face was made up traditionally with white rice powder covering her face, and then her makeup very skillfully applied.

Madam Chang led her across the front of the room and finally stopped in front of Henry and said something. Henry had not yet caught on, and he stood ready to shake her hand or bow or something. Madam must have given him a dirty look because he withdrew his hand mid-bow and straightened up. Madam then led Ming Toy to the chair next to the one Henry had been sitting on and motioned for her to sit and then she turned to Henry and motioned for him to sit next to her. She then turned to the crowd and made an announcement.

Scott was pretty sure by the look on Henry's face what the announcement was. Evidently Madam had planned on Henry's proper upbringing not to make a fuss and save face, but this was not the Henry she thought she knew, this one was cocky and arrogant and wealthy, and this was the Henry who would not play the game and the one who deliberately walked away from his bride to be and his great and mighty aunt and headed for the stairs.

At the same time, hundreds of real fireworks went off in the street and immediately Scott hoped there weren't any police around or that the guys in the fire station just a few doors down didn't hear them or someone was going to jail for attempted arson. Sirens followed the firecrackers, and then things became a blur. As Henry pushed him out of the way to get down the stairs, there were more guest coming up the stairs and if one of the groups didn't move there would be a collision mid-staircase.

Suddenly Henry turned on his heal and headed back up the stairs. He grabbed Scott from behind a tree at the top of the stairs and held him in front of himself while pushing a small gun into the side of his neck. Ming Toy was crying, her dark eye makeup running in little streams down her white cheeks.

Henry maneuvered Scott to the front of the room watching the stairway, and soon the place was filled with cops, and Madam gasped when she saw the gun, and she could hardly believe Henry was saying in perfect B movie English, "Take one more step, and I swear I'll shoot him."

It was like a dream in slow motion. Unknown to either Henry or Scott, a single cop had entered the room by the same door as Ming Toy had and was inching up behind them. Out of the corner of Henry's eye, he saw the officer and turned and shot the cop dead. As Henry watched the cop slide to the floor, there were several law officers who dove for Henry and wrestled him to the floor and took away his weapon. Scott was shaking uncontrollably.

They cuffed Henry and drug him away while the guests were still sitting at their tables with confusion written all over their faces. It was only much later that Scott remembered seeing Auntie standing there with her tiny red mouth forming a perfect O and that Ming Toy had fainted dead away on the floor.

In all the commotion it wasn't only Henry who was arrested, it was Queen Auntie and much to his surprise, him too, and he strongly objected as they pushed him down the stairs in front of them. When they got to the bottom they put each of them in separate squads, an act for which Scott would be forever grateful, he would have been grilled mercilessly by Auntie if they had ridden together. Oddly enough he was disappointed to not go in Paddy's wagon, now that he knew what it meant, but then again, it would mean quite a tongue-lashing from Auntie for as long as the ride lasted because she, no doubt, would blame him for everything. What he didn't understand was why Auntie arrested? Was this Ming Toy person illegal after all, and why did they arrest him? Maybe this had to be something to do with the vases, and Auntie in on it too? Who else, Miss Lee? Would they find and arrest her also? Probably not Ming Toy, but the last time he saw her she was out cold on the floor and not outside being put into a squad.

Scott had never had a reason to go to the local precinct's police department, but it was as gray and cold as he thought it would be. Everything was old; the paintwork on both the walls and the doors, and the cop's desk had also seen better days, much better days. He and Auntie were taken into the booking room where they were told to empty their pockets and then they were fingerprinted along with a full-face and a side-view mug shot. Auntie was furious that her hair was all messed up for the photos and all through the process her objection, in both her native tongue and English, could be heard all throughout the building and Scott pretended not to know her.

While he was wiping the ink from his fingers he felt like he had been dropped into an old movie and that none of this was real, not the cops, or the party or even Henry being led away in all his finery, and with the performance his aunt was giving, he hoped they'd be separated soon before she started in on him. But he had nothing to hide, so he wasn't worried. Well, he had delivered the vases so maybe he could be charged as an accessory to a crime. Great, just when I was about to start my life, it seems to be ending.

Ending, that made him think. Wasn't the Chinatown area Clancy's beat and didn't Clancy work nights and shouldn't he have been involved, seeing this was the ending of their sting operation?

I've been set up. Scott thought as he sat on a hard chair waiting to go somewhere else. Evidently not only were Henry and his stooges involved but Auntie and Clancy and Elliot and Leroy and sideways, himself. Suddenly nothing mattered anymore. It had been a long process and a false friendship just to win his confidence so they could get him involved, and now it looked as though he was the only one being arrested, well he and Madam Chang and naturally Henry. It was getting hard to think anymore, and by the time a cop came to get him he had given up trying to make sense of any of it. Evidently, he was headed for a cell so he'd just have to wait until tomorrow to see if anything made more sense, and he'd also wait until tomorrow to call his mother, to add even more bad news to her life.

But his mother already knew about his arrest. Elliot had taken her for lunch right after Thanksgiving and explained in detail what was going to happen. She showed up at the jail first thing in the morning and was permitted to see her son and to find out how much bail was.

"Mom, I didn't want you to know about this, you've already got enough to worry about."

"I have nothing to worry about dear. Do you remember Elliot's question from a long time ago, you know believers, non-believers, and unbelievers? Well, I have become better than a believer, I'm trusting God for absolutely everything, and everybody in my life and that includes you."

"So you weren't worried?"

"I was concerned, and I'll be concerned until I know for sure that you are in the believer category. But for now, I have to trust God that He will work in your life no matter how He has to do it until you get to the place you need to be so you'll be ready to listen to Him."

"Great, I've been arrested, and all you can talk about is God."

"I know you mean that sarcastically, but once you understand the depth of what I just said, you'll look at life completely differently, trust me."

"Speaking of trust," Scott started to say, not sure where to start. "Speaking of trust," he began again, "do you trust Elliot?"

"Yes, I'd trust him with my life."

"But you don't know who he is."

"And what would that be?"

"I'm not sure. I mean I'm not sure of anybody anymore. Is Clancy really a Chicago cop and if so, is he a good cop or just another one on the take? And Elliot, is he really a homeless drifter and what about Leroy and Madam Chang and Henry? I'm so confused."

"I'll bet you are and we're going to clear some of that up this afternoon; that is if we can."

"Clear up what?"

"Most of your questions I hope, but first I'll have to make a phone call, but now," she turned to leave, "I've got to see about your bail."

They took the red line south to Holy Cross hospital where mother and son rode the elevator to the sixth floor. Ellen hadn't told Scott why they were there nor whom they were seeing. He questioned her relentlessly, as he had done when he was four years old, but she remained silent to his barrage. He just hoped it wasn't a family member, especially one of his four nieces.

The room number was 617, and the last thing Scott whispered to his mother just before the entered the room was, "Do I know whoever it is here?"

"Oh yes."

She pushed the door open and went directly to the bed next to the window. The curtain had been pulled around the bed, and she motioned for Scott to stay where he was while she peeked around to see the patient. Meanwhile, Scott felt stupid standing between the first patient by the door and the TV on the wall.

"Hello," he said trying to look casual.

"What?" the patient yelled, "speak up sonny, what did you say?"

Scott shook his head and waved his hand as if to say, 'it's not important.'

Ellen came out from around the curtain and asked, "Annoying the patients are we?"

Before he could answer, she motioned for him to come on the other side of the curtain where a man was laying hooked up to an IV and very pale. Scott looked at his mother as to say, so, who is it?

The middle-aged man in the bed smiled weakly at Scott and said in a voice that was hoarse, "It was quite a night wasn't it boy?"

Scott moved closer and said "Elliot?" he asked as though he didn't believe it.

"That would be me all right."

"What in the world happened to you?"

"Maybe you'd better grab that other chair and sit down next to me so I can fill you in."

"You fill me in? What do you know about last night?"

Elliot snaked his arm out from under covers with a grimace on his face, held Ellen's hand and whispered, "I told your mother everything, I figured she deserved to know seeing it was her boy that was involved."

"That's what I want to know, exactly what was I involved in?"

Scott looked at his mother to see if she thought this was all on the level and she nodded her head yes. "You can believe every word this man says son; it's all the honest truth."

Chapter 21

Elliot pushed the button on the side of his bed so he could sit up, although badly wincing as he did. "It's hard to know where to start, but I'll talk as long as I can. Ellen, would you go to the nurses' station and get me some more ice water. I'd like to tell Scott everything, and it might be a long story."

"Certainly dear." Ellen left the room, and Scott was surprised that she called this man, who was a virtual stranger, dear.

"Okay," he whispered, "let me see how far I can get. It all started when I saw you in Chinatown standing against the building. Remember I was so bad-tempered?"

"Oh yeah, Jolly Ollie you weren't."

"And that was for a reason. We had to see if you were the persistent type because we weren't looking for a quitter."

"Looking for someone to do what?"

"Someone qualified to help with the operation of course."

"Operation, what do you mean by that, what kind of an operation?"

Ellen returned to the room and helped Elliot with the water. Scott noticed he wasn't using his left arm but holding his straw with his right as Ellen held onto the cup.

"Ah, that's better," he said his voice sounding stronger. "As I was saying after we picked you…"

"Wait a minute; you keep using the word we, does that mean you and someone else or is it what my mother always referred to as the royal we?"

"No, it was me," he lowered his voice, "and the other members of the Asian Task Force."

Now Scott knew he was being put on, that is until he glanced at his mother and saw how serious her face was.

"You're not kidding are you?"

"There are days I wish I was, but not this time."

Elliot's roommate turned up his television so he could hear his game show better.

"Wow, I can't wait to hear this," Scott said in a lower voice and moved closer to Elliot.

"Let's go back a long way to when I graduated from Ag. Collage. You know the beginning of this already. After my fiancé walked away and married my brother, I just drifted for a while. Conventional thought is that men get over things faster than women, but it took me a long time to not hate the world and everyone in it. I had been hurt so I hurt everybody that came into my way and part of that hatred included drinking.

"I'd never been a drinker, but it seemed like everyone else was using alcohol to drown their sorrows, so I thought I'd try it too. I only spent time in the bars that played the country songs; you know the ones where the 'she done him wrong' songs were played endlessly. I'd listen, cry and drink.

"Then one night I saw one of my friends from college on the street. I didn't feel like getting reacquainted, so I ducked into my old haunt but he came in after me and sat down next to me at the bar, and we started talking. I noticed he refused when I offered to buy him a drink, and I ask what he was doing here alone if he didn't drink.

"I came here to see you," he said.

"What do you mean, see me?" I was instantly curious about his opening comment.

"I mean last year I was just like you are now, I'd sit here night after night downing drink after drink justifying my actions because I'd been hurt and drinking was a good escape and." Elliot paused for emphasis, "it was only a cop-out to avoid what I knew God wanted of me."

"Man you're crazy," I told him. "What's this got to do with God?"

"I thought the same thing," he said, "and I would argue with anyone who told me this was a God thing. But one day a guy at work cornered me and challenged me to think about a few things. One of them was that I could continue to waste my time and my money and my body and my mind by feeling sorry for myself. He also said that whether or not I realized it, I was blaming God for what happened. He said that we as humans expect a wonderful life from God. After all, He made us so it should be his responsibility to take care of us."

"Yeah, got you so far, I told him, but then he hit me with the hard stuff. He said to me that to become an actual child of God I had to see God for who He was. He said that God wasn't an old out-of-touch grandfather in the sky, but He was my creator and my living Redeemer. When I asked him what he meant by redeemer, he explained that according to the law of life, I would have to pay for my sins someday.

"Well that ticked me off, and before I could fire something back, he added, "Just think about it, if you jumped off a fifty story building you would not break the law of gravity, you would break your neck. And if you broke any other of the laws of nature, you'd pay for them too because it's just the way God set things up; certain rules can't be broken."

"He was starting to make sense, so I let him continue even though I didn't want to hear any more.

"He then told me about breaking God's law, you know the Ten Commandments? Well, he also included lots of others, like abusing my body like I was doing and hurting other people and the worst one, not trusting God. I asked him why I should believe in God, look what he did to me, broke up the perfect marriage and ruined my life.

"By this time I think we'd moved to a table because the bartender was giving us dirty looks talking about religious stuff. When we got to the table, he let me have it with both barrels. He said that God's plan all along was to have fellowship with Him. That's why he put us on this earth. But we see it all differently. He said that most people treated God like a rabbit's foot that they rub when they need Him and He'll come and grant them their wishes. Even in my foggy state of mind, it seemed like that was a pretty accurate picture of how it was supposed to work as I knew it.

"But then he tells me, we've got it backward. We are to live for Him, not the other way around as we all think. When you start looking at our lives as God does, you see another side, and it's not a pretty sight. We're always running scared to Him so He can get us out of a jam, foxhole conversions they're called after the men who were in foxholes during the war. They would promise God all sorts of things if He would just keep them safe. Naturally when the crisis was over the promise was too. I'll bet none of those people ever thought that God knew their hearts and that He knew full well they wouldn't keep their promise, yet He kept them safe anyway.

"And that's why God sent his Son Jesus. His plan from the very beginning, even before man was made was to provide a savior because He knew we would screw up immediately and get worse and worse as time went by. By this time I was getting sleepy because the room was warm and I had been drinking a long time. He noticed this and asked if I had time to meet the following day, to go for lunch.

"Obviously I wasn't planning on going anywhere to see him ever again, but noon came, and something drew me to the restaurant. He didn't even wait until the waitress came to take our order, he started right in on me by asking if I had ever heard John 3:16 from the Bible and I said of course, who hadn't. I think he asked me to tell him what it said and I said I was a little fuzzy on the details, so he quoted it, and was quoting it when the waitress came. "For God so loved the world," he said, "that He gave His only son so whoever believes in Him will not perish but have everlasting life."

"The waitress gave him a look like she'd like to throw him out talking about the Bible and all and she deliberately interrupted us to get our order. He didn't let up though, he said from the very beginning God knew His Son had to die and die for stupid, willful people who didn't give a rip about Him, but He died anyway. He also told me that God took the punishment for my sins. I asked him exactly what that meant, and he said, the penalty for my sins was going to hell. Then he said something I'd never heard of before. He told me that if I didn't believe in hell, then I couldn't believe in heaven either. They were both first mentioned in the Bible, and if I chose not to believe the Bible, then I could forget everything and find something else to believe in after death, or I could feel the weight of my sin and know that Jesus death was for me, to take my sins and make me holy because He was and still is the only God who loves us.

"He said if I thought about it, all the other god's people worship didn't love them but were demanding of their time, and their money and their service and none of them had ever risen from the dead and was now living and passionately loving humanity still. He said that God just wanted to love us, and we won't let him, I mean, how stupid is that, to turn away from the creator of the universe just because He loves us?"

"Well that blew me away, and when our meal came, he was silent letting me think about what he had said and letting the Spirit of God work on me while I ate. By the time the meal was finished, I knew he was right and just before the same waitress came with the check I said, "So what do I do about being with God?"

"The waitress had overheard my question and looked ill, I think she said something like, "Not you too," then she turned on her heal and left. My friend said to pay no attention to her because God was working on her too because each time he ate at that restaurant he would pick her table and tell her how much God loved her. I remember he smiled and that's when I knew I wanted what he had. He suggested that if I was ready to be saved, we should talk to God and tell him that I was tired of going it alone and needed him as my Savior and my Lord and tell Him I understood why He died. When I raised my head after making my request to God, I knew I was different, I felt, I felt wonderful, clean and light. I shook his hands and noticed he had tears in his eyes. He invited me to a Bible study and not only did I go, I told them all what I had just done and when we left the restaurant I hugged the waitress and left her a big tip. I told her God loved her too and that I'd be praying for her, and if looks could kill…"

"Okay," he said taking another drink of water. "That's the biggest and best decision I made and from there on out the rest were relatively easy. By laying aside my anger it was a lot easier to get on with going forward.

"Well, at one of the Bible studies I met this guy who was just starting as an FBI agent. As soon as he shared that I knew that's what I wanted to be too. I grilled him with tons of questions and found out that even though I had a four-year degree, I need to take more classes, other classes, so I went back to school, graduated, and then applied to the bureau. They did an extensive background check, I mean they even talked to my kindergarten teacher; I was hired and trained as an agent. I've worked for the FBI ever since and served all around the world. This Chinatown case was my last one, so after all the years I served, they let me set up the sting anyway I wanted to. That's where Clancy comes in."

"So is he, or isn't he a real cop?"

"You bet he is one of Chicago's truly finest officers and a member of the Asian Task Force along with me and a few others."

"So when you say task force, what do you mean?"

Elliot laid his head back on his pillow and held up a finger as if to say, just a minute. After another sip of water, he began again with a weaker voice.

"The Asian Task Force is the cooperation between the local cops and the FBI for a particular reason; this was created to address the rising drug traffic by Asian gangs in Chicago."

"You said drugs, not stolen vases?"

"Ah yes." He paused again to catch his breath. "The vases, this is where I need to apologize to you. You were so young and so sincere and so innocent I didn't want you to let slip any information, so you had to be kept completely ignorant of what was happening. I made up the vase part because they were partly involved with the case."

Scott's feelings were hurt when Elliot called him innocent. Sure he wasn't aware of the drug trouble, but he considered himself pretty street smart, that is until now.

"I know you might not believe it, but you were an important part of the operation, and we couldn't have pulled it off without you."

"So I was the sacrificial lamb tied out to a tree so you could catch a lion."

"Sort of, yes, but when I got to know you and your mother," he squeezed her hand, "I considered not using you because I didn't want to hurt either one of you."

"I see," Scott was not convinced. "And the shed, did you really build that? And come to think about it, were there any people in the front house that you said was some sort of half-way house?"

"Yeah, there were. But would you use the back door if you lived there? I think they thought the front door was way safer and closer to the street and public transportation and yes, I did build the shed and I had to dress like a homeless person, smell like a homeless person and scavenge the materials for a shed like a homeless person. I think I did a pretty good job working with the pittance of money the bureau gave me. Hey, that reminds me, like my clean face? Those whiskers were driving me crazy, and I almost shaved for your dad's funeral, but I had to stay in character, but not anymore."

"Yeah, you look okay," Scott said slipping in sullenness. "So for some reason, you picked me to be your guinea pig and landed me right in the middle of everything."

"But you were always safe. We never let you out of our site. Remember that old geezer, the one who liked to cause automobile accidents on busy days?"

"Yeah."

"Well, he's one of us."

"That old guy?"

"He's a true Chinese guy but only thirty or so, he's also a master with makeup."

"So all that 'poweese' stuff was fake?"

"Yep, it was done for you and to give him credibility as he worked undercover."

"Was there anybody else that was undercover keeping an eye on my every move?"

"None, really, we just wanted to make sure you were one hundred percent covered at all times."

"And Miss Lee?"

"She had absolutely nothing to do with it, and she was, and still is, as much in the dark as you were."

"So what you're saying is that she and I both thought it was about the vases."

"Well yes, it was about the vases."

"I thought it was about drugs."

"Yes, it's about the drugs he sold that were in the vases."

"Wait a minute, what do you mean the drugs were in the vases? When I delivered them there was nothing inside."

"Well, you're half right. One of the reasons we knew the Henry was our guy was based not only the large amounts of money he was giving you, but when you mentioned that even though Henry didn't drink coffee, there was powdered cream and sugar in his office, we knew for sure that he was importing the drugs. China White to be exact, a dangerous drug that can be snorted, smoked or injected and is highly addictive. As a person's system gets used to the drug it takes more and more to get the same high. The pure stuff is also cut with things like sugar and creamer or starch, so that's what he had been doing when you saw the sugar on his jacket, he was cutting the stuff he got from the homeland in the vases and then putting it back in the vases to be sold on the street garnering everyone in the chain huge amounts of cash."

"But I told you there wasn't anything in the vases."

"No, you're right. The vases themselves looked empty; the drugs were sealed in that porcelain rope piece that held the top and bottom together. Henry would first crack open the extra part and remove the drugs. When he had finished cutting the stuff, he'd package it in small bags and stuff them back into the rope where the drugs were when they got to the U.S.

He'd seal the vase together again with special glue. That's why he didn't want you unpacking them or touching them in any way."

"So all that stuff he told me about the vases, you know how valuable they were and how hard it was to make them?"

"You said once that he sounded like he was talking like he had just researched the subject and was just repeating everything he had read, well he had. He had to make you believe that it was the vases that were so valuable to him so you would take extra care when you delivered them. If one had broken, you probably would have figured out right away where the powder was packed. Another thing that tipped us off was when you said he had three dots on one hand and when you drew the symbol of the house-like picture, and it matched Henry's cuff links we had our proof, he was working hand in glove you might say with the members of the Hung Mun Tong, a very dangerous group of people. Evidently, Henry had used his ability to import articles directly from China and when the gang found that out, and easily guessed that Henry had a big head and liked flattery; so it was probably easy to con him into the drug trafficking, especially when they mentioned how much he could make on the sweet deals. We don't know for sure yet, but we're talking street values of the drugs in astronomical figures, not to mention all the lives that are ruined because of China White."

Ellen saw that Elliot was losing his voice again so she continued.

"Elliot told me the reason they arrested Madam Change wasn't that she had anything to do with drugs, she was operating as the 'snakes head' for years."

"Snakes head?" Scott didn't want to hear anymore, but his mother continued.

"It's obviously slang, but it refers to anyone who deals in human cargo. They will often get as much as a fifteen thousand dollar commission for smuggling an illegal alien into the U.S, using the vague promise of employment at the end of their journey. What these Chinese women don't realize is they end up in the sex slave business once they get to the United States, but more come every week, thanks to a very evil, selfish, and very greedy woman. Once some of them are here they turn to a life of crime, joining the local gangs, to have any money at all. That's why this gang in particular is very dangerous."

"Elliot, do you think Ming Toy was human cargo?" asked Ellen with concern.

He opened his eyes and said drowsily, "That's up to the courts to decide. Madam Chang has brought in many people from China, and now each case will have to be documented. If she was trafficking in illegal's, she'll be spending the rest of her life in prison."

"Wow."

"Yes wow. This was a huge case we've been working on for some time."

"What do you think Henry will get?" It was still hard for Scott to absorb all the information.

"It's hard to say. We've got him on drug charges already, and you'll be asked to testify at the trial. We've already arrested the men at the warehouse, thanks to your directions and descriptions. One of the gang was shot on the street just before we arrested Henry."

So it wasn't firecrackers I heard outside.

"I'm very proud of you, son," his mom said. "Wait until your sister's find out about it, they'll flip."

Scott sat silently and then rose from his chair, "I think I'll go downstairs to the cafeteria, I've got a lot to think about."

"Take all the time you need," said Elliot with closed eyes and a haggard face.

"Excuse me," Scott asked one of the nurses at the desk, "could you tell me what's wrong with the man in room 617, the one by the window, name of Elliot Nussbaum?"

She thumbed through her chart and said, "He was shot last night and lost a lot of blood, it's amazing he's alive at all, the bullet just missed his heart."

CHAPTER 22

It was only a few minutes until his mom joined him in the cafeteria, carrying a cup of coffee over to where he was sitting by a window. As she sat, she asked, "How are you doing?"

Scott took a deep breath and continued to stare at the heavy traffic that snaked through Chicago's south side.

"Would you like to talk about it or wait until you've had some time to think it over?"

"I don't know," he said staring at the floor. "I don't know what I think or how I feel."

She wisely kept quiet knowing that he would begin talking when he was ready. Scott had never been one to fret about something for long, and she always admired him for that, unlike his sisters, he never let anything fester and grow worse.

"It's just that," he said, "well it's just that I feel so, so, I don't know, used? I mean, here I was thinking that this cranky old homeless guy was a genuine guy and a nice guy to boot and come to find out it was just some impersonal FBI hot shot that was just solving a case and using me to do it."

They both sat silently, both thinking, well Scott was thinking, Ellen was asking her Father to give her the words her boy needed to hear.

"Do you know why Elliot's here?"

"Yeah, I talked to the nurse after I left the room and she said he'd been shot."

"And do you know where he was in the building when he got shot?"

"I thought he got shot outside because I heard what I thought were

242

firecrackers outside and now I realize they weren't, Elliot just said it was a gang member."

"You're right, but he was not shot outside the building; he was shot inside by Henry. He was the cop that came through the side door. He knew Henry was a desperate man whose life exploded in front of him when the cops came, and I would imagine that Henry felt trapped by his aunt too when she announced his engagement to his complete surprise. Henry would have killed you in a second to protect himself, and even if he could have gotten outside with you as a shield, he probably would have killed you then, before he could run so you could never testify against him. Elliot thinks that was his plan from the very beginning; to hire you, the only white boy in Chinatown, that way if anything ever went wrong he could blame you and not one of his of race and say it was your fault or your idea and get away Scott free. After all, you were the only one making the drug deliveries, and he took great pains to keep himself out of the action. If you ever asked any questions or wanted to quit he would have told you that you could never leave or he would turn you in as running the whole thing."

Scott sipped his Coke and realized that what his mother said might be right.

"And yes, Elliot did use you in a way. But he wouldn't have done that if he thought you wouldn't be good at what they needed to be done."

"But I didn't know what was happening."

"And now that you think about it aren't you glad you didn't? You would never have been able to get as far as you did if he thought you were on to him."

"So when did you learn all this stuff?"

Ellen smoothed her skirt and looked a bit shaken. "I, um, well the truth is, Elliot have been seeing each other."

"You're kidding, when, why?"

"During the day when you were working."

"Wow, this is like role reversal, isn't it? Here my mom is sneaking out with her boyfriend behind my back."

"Now Scott, it wasn't quite like that."

"And how is it different?"

She looked at her son and ran her hand down his face while smiling,

"It isn't. But we are just drawn to each other and believe me I've thought and thought about it, but it's just the way it is. I think I love him, especially because he loves the Lord. And," she added before he could say a word, "I admire him greatly, not only for what he does but for what he did for you. Scott, do you realize he was prepared to die for you?"

"I suppose."

"You suppose nothing. He likes you so much he would have given his life for you," she said again for emphasis. "Maybe that makes what I've been telling you all your life a little clearer too; God did give His life for you. Elliot took the bullet that was meant for you."

Scott turned back to the traffic and Ellen walked to the counter to refill her cup.

"So, what do you think?" she asked.

"About what?"

She hated when her kids did that to her. "About what both Elliot and God did for you? You know, you've been sitting on this spiritual fence so long I wouldn't be surprised if you were getting splinters."

"Give me some time mom; I need to think. It's been a wild twenty-four hours, and I haven't had time to think yet."

"Are you going back to the duplex?"

"No, I think I'll go back to Elliot's. It looks like our warm spell is over already, so I just want to check on things and make sure they're okay, I'll turn up the heater and go to bed early. I don't know why though, I certainly don't have a job tomorrow, both my bosses are sitting in jail, and I don't think anyone is even thinking of bailing Madam Chang out, and if she's in jail she can't bail her nephew out, there's just something strangely satisfying about that."

"You know I'll be praying for you tonight, don't you?"

"I know, I know, and mom, thanks, thanks for everything."

"You're welcome."

"Hey, do you want me to wait for you and leave together?"

"Thanks but I think I'll go back upstairs for a while."

"Okay, see you tomorrow, I take it you'll be here?"

"Yes, until he's released."

Ellen had always wanted to learn to knit, and she found sitting by Elliot's bed every day as he slept was the perfect time to prop her instruction book on the bed and struggle with the stitches, but it passed the time.

Elliot drifted from asleep to awake during the day and when his fever started to raise the doctor's determined something was wrong and whisked him away. When the staff finally returned him several hours later, they said the temperature spike was due to an infection in the wound and added that his hospital stay would be extended a good ten days. Ellen bought more yarn.

Scott wandered the streets and often caught a bus to get off downtown on one of the Michigan Avenue's stops and then he walked the loop, visiting some of his favorite places. There was Morrow's Nut House which was always nice and warm, and now that Thanksgiving was over he viewed the Christmas windows at Marshall Field's along with thousands of others. Scott window- shopped up and down busy State Street and Michigan Avenue, but due to a decided lack of funds, he bought nothing. He did have time to think as he wandered the streets and people watched. When he got cold, he'd slip into one of the downtown stores to get warm and then out on the street again to walk some more.

He'd stopped in to see Elliot occasionally and finally came to terms with his mother's vigil at his bedside. He supposed that if anyone deserved a nice guy, it was his mom. But his jury of one was still out on whether Elliot was a nice guy or not.

One afternoon he found himself back at the Five talking to Clay because the Duffer was out again with their new boss Claire. There was a Christmas tree in the lobby, and there was another one in the dining room. Clay caught him up on all the changes and said there was still a room for him there if he wanted one, and with Claire's plans for change, he'd better get one quick while there was still some room left before all those mothers and children moved in and the place became a day-care and dance studio.

After talking for a while, Clay asked, "So, what have you been up to? It's been a bit since we've seen you."

It took almost twenty minutes to share everything that had happened since he had seen him last.

Clay was so intrigued by the story that he forgot to put sugar in his coffee and drank two cups of it black without realizing it.

"You're kidding," he'd say over and over. "This bum was FBI? Did you get to see his badge?"

"I don't know if they have badges."

"Everybody in law enforcement has a badge, don't they?"

"How should I know, I never knew a cop much less someone in the bureau. And I've never been out on bail before either."

"So exactly what does that mean, out on bail?"

"I guess it means that my mom gave them money and I get to go free until the trial."

"And when's the trial?"

"I don't know. All I know is that I have to keep in touch with the department."

"And this guy, this Elliot guy, what's his part in all this?"

"I guess he's one of the main players, but he's still in the hospital. For a while it was touch and go for him."

"And you said he got shot trying to get you free?"

"I guess."

"You don't sound very grateful."

"It's not that I'm not grateful, it's just that, oh, I don't know, I guess I'm still bummed out that he just used me to get his job done."

"Now wait a minute, you said that he saved your life and you're grousing about him using you to get his job done?"

"Yeah, more or less."

"And how old are you?"

"I'll be twenty soon."

"Don't you think you're a little old to be acting like a second grader? Good night boy, this man put his life on the line for you; I'd say that means something."

"I know, I know and don't think I haven't been thinking about it for the past few days, it's all I think about."

"And you haven't figured it out yet?"

"No."

"I beg to differ; I think you've thought it out and don't like the conclusion, am I right?"

"I guess maybe."

"And you're still sulking like a little kid. You should be on your knees thanking this guy for saving your life."

"But if it weren't for him, I would have never been in that circumstance."

"Now wait a minute. He had nothing to do with you working in Chinatown, did he, and he didn't arrange to get you a job down there with this wacko Chinese woman and her nephew either, did he?"

"Well, no."

"And he didn't arrange for Henry to get you involved with this drug stuff did he?" Clay was not letting up, "So what you're saying is that you did that all on your own and would have ended up at the same party whether he was involved with the case or not, right?"

Scott saw what he was driving at and had to admit Clay was right, none of what happened to him was Elliot's fault, he fell into trouble all by himself, and it was Elliot who came to his rescue.

Scott surprised Clay by suddenly standing up and saying "Hey, thanks for the coffee." He pumped the older man's hand and was out the door and down at the corner in time to catch the bus going back towards the hospital leaving Clay to wonder what just happened.

******

When Scott walked into Elliot's new room on the third floor, he was grateful that his mom was there and that Elliot was looking considerably better.

"Well, look who's here," his mom said when he rounded the curtain. "We were wondering if we'd ever see you again."

Scott was prepared to make up this big story about how he had been busy watching the shed and taking care of things because it had been snowing, but instead, he pulled up a chair close to his mother.

"I've come to apologize."

His mother started to say something like 'Oh honey,' and he kindly cut her off and said, "What I mean by apologizing is more like asking your forgiveness, Elliot. I was acting like a little kid about all this, but I talked to a guy a little while ago that made me realize that you didn't cause any of the stuff that happened to me, but you were there to help me when I needed it most. Will you accept my apology?"

"I would be honored to," he put out his left hand and weakly shook Scott's hand.

"And mom, I know this is going to make you pretty happy, and probably you too," he said as he looked at Elliot. "On the bus when I left that place they call the Five, after talking to this guy there, I realized what you've been talking about, you know, that we were all in a mess of our own making, and we should rightfully take the punishment for the things we've done wrong. In my case, Jesus, like Elliot, stepped up and died for me, well like Elliot almost did, to take the punishment for what I had caused myself. So, I decided that now was the time to ask Jesus into my heart, I ask His forgiveness for my sins and then gave my life to Him mom."

Just as he knew she would, Ellen started crying with a smile on her face. "Thank you, Father," she said as she looked with love at her son.

"I'm proud of you," said Elliot. "Now you'll never have to worry where your life is going or what you're going to do, and you have someone who already knows the path you need to walk and will walk it with you."

There was a commotion in the hall, and suddenly Officer Clancy filled the room with his presence. He clapped a large paw on Scott's shoulder and said, "I'm mightily proud of you too. Someday I'll have to tell you my own story about how I met the Master. When this trial is over," Clancy added while dragging another chair to the bed, "and you are proven innocent," he said, "because Elliot and I are going to be witnesses for you, you will be Scott free from the law. That's man's law, and now you're also free from God's law of sin and death because of Christ, so you are Scott free all over again."

"Free," whispered Ellen.

Scott echoed his mother, "Scott free," and he smiled.

If you would like to begin a relationship with Jesus
Christ today, it's so amazingly simple.

Tell Him of your sins and admit you can't go on without Him.

Ask for His forgiveness and invite Him into your heart and life.

He promised that He would make you clean and new.

You will never be sorry.

For more help, no matter where you live, phone 1-888-NEED HIM
Or go online to needhim.org

And may God bless you and bless you and bless you.

Epilogue

Sarah knew it was time to make the call, she had talked to her sister for several hours on the phone after returning from her trip to Paris with her mother, and now she knew what her decision would be. Even though she had finally made up her mind on this most important issue, she was nervous and could hardly dial the phone; her fingers were shaking so badly.

When he picked up the phone on the third ring, and when she heard his familiar voice she said quietly, "Hello, Pete?"

About the Author

Diane Dryden held a position as a feature writer for the *Washburn County Register* for over fifteen years, and she's also been published in numerous newspapers and magazines and is currently writing human interest features for an online news source.

She was born and raised in Chicago, and the city still holds a special place in her heart.

Even though she and her family live in a small Wisconsin town, they often return for the best pizza, Italian beef and hot dogs ever, and of course, being a north-sider, they make sure they take in a few Cubs games and attend Moody Church when they visit.

"It's a fascinating town from the north-side down to Chinatown in the south, and my books tell stories of the people who live in this city whose tagline is, whatever you want, whenever you want it."

This is the third novel in her Chicago series, each one weaving in characters from the previous books, *The Accidental King of Clark Street and Double or Nothing on Foster Avenue.* Each novel ending with her signature twist.

She highly recommends you don't read the last chapter or the final page first.

You are invited to delve into an experience that's so compelling; you'll never want to stop reading.

Printed in the United States
By Bookmasters